Prais

THE BONES OF YOU

LAURA STONE

"By the time the book ended I was in love with the characters to the point I couldn't let them go."

—*USA Today*

"Stone's sensitive debut ... plays the relationship with restraint, letting it unfold slowly and organically."

—*Publishers Weekly*

"Their beautiful love story will bring plenty of laughter, and even a few tears, as these men grab hold of their rare second chance. "

—*RT Book Reviews*

"Laura Stone is an author to remember and follow."

—*Daily World*

Bitter Springs

Bitter Springs

LAURA STONE

interlude **press** • new york

To Loki, Doc, and Sweet Caroline.
I'll take care of her until y'all meet at the Rainbow Bridge.

One look before his eyes begun to blur
    And then—the blood that wouldn't let 'im speak!
And him so strong, and yet so quick he died,
    And after year on year
When we had always trailed it side by side,
    He went—and left me here!

We loved each other in the way men do
    And never spoke about it, Al and me,
But we both knowed, and knowin' it so true
    Was more than any woman's kiss could be…

.   .   .   .

The range is empty and the trails are blind,
    And I don't seem but half myself today.
I wait to hear him ridin' up behind
    And feel his knee rub mine the good old way.

—From Badger Clark's "The Lost Pardner,"
Sun and Saddle Leather

AUTHOR'S NOTE

A YEAR BEFORE I WROTE this book, I took a road trip through the American Southwest, which is a second home to me. Even though I've lived there for years, there were a few places I hadn't seen, so I made a point of stopping off in Tombstone, Arizona. And while, yes, it's touristy and all of that, there's a cemetery called Boothill Graveyard that's fascinating. There's the ornate (for the spot) final resting place of Quong Kee, who ran the Can Can and was listed as a "Friend to All," and scores of others.

But in Row 4, there's one grave—one single grave, mind you—that stuck with me.

Two men are buried in that one spot, Bobby Jackson and Frank Hart. There are plenty of graves here, plenty of men who died at the same time either by hanging or shootout, husbands and wives struck down with dysentery (1882 was a rough year in particular), and mothers and their children. Everyone has their own gravesite. What was it about these two "best friends" that led them to being buried together?

I fell into a wonderful research spiral of the West, aided by the meticulously organized research branch of LA's Autry Museum as well as intensely researched books such as *Gay Cowboys* and *Love Stories: Sex Between Men Before Homosexuality* and many, many more. My mother's people—both white and

Choctaw—are from Texas, my father's from Utah and Wyoming, so I know cowboys. I know the mythos: the ultimate image of masculinity they represent. At least I thought I did. Turns out that the straight, white cowboy whom Hollywood loves was pretty uncommon. About forty percent of cowboys were black, first of all. And straight? Sure. Sometimes. Sometimes not.

We in our modern way of thinking often fall victim to the idea that we're more advanced than our predecessors, that only now are LGBTQ citizens being welcomed with open arms, that we modern folks are the ones who are finally realizing how gender and sexuality don't always line up in a rigid black and white definition, that all of this is new, particularly in post-eighteenth century North America. That's not accurate. (And anyone who thinks queer lives were never accepted until now never looked in a history book, quite frankly. We're here, we're queer, we've been here and queer for many a year, m'dear.)

And if you think about it, what on earth *were* all those fellas getting up to for months, if not years, at a time without ladies around to "satisfy urges" out there on the prairie, or while building railroads or mining for gold? Why, they were satisfying themselves with each other, and no one looked sideways at them. Oh, sure, you weren't supposed to be blatant about it, but in the nineteenth century, *no one* was, straight or otherwise. I read a letter—and boy, I sure love museum curators who make research material available online—from a Civil War soldier who was writing home to his sweetheart about a dance the soldiers held to "keep up morale."

In this letter he detailed how "boys" and "girls" were chosen out of the all-male group, and how his captain fell in love with his "girl," and all the soldiers knew what they were getting up to in their private quarters. (Hint: sex.) This was 1864 in a letter to a proper young lady. To pretend that homosexuality (or bisexuality or transgenders) didn't exist or simply were incredibly rare cases diminishes those relationships that thrived. Where on earth do you think the term "Boston Wife" came from? Or "Oxford Rub"? Bunkhouses were often called "ram pastures," and the term for two fellas owning up to wanting to get off with each other for a while—typically in a romantic relationship—was called "mutual solace".

The commonality of those terms should underscore the fact that there were families who knew about their "confirmed bachelor" and his "best pal," or their "old maid" and her "roommate." There are wonderful photos and love letters of these couples, proof that they were able to have loving relationships, that their families knew about them, and as long as everyone— even the straight folks—kept any salaciousness under their hats, they could keep on keeping on.

Over half of all North American Native peoples believed in more than two genders, in "two-spirits," as the term is commonly referred to today. And in some tribes, there were four and five. We'Wha, a Zuni ambassador to the US Government in the nineteenth century, was one such person and was welcomed as a man or as a woman, to use the (incorrect) Western binary terms of the time, when visiting Washington DC. In the 1800s! *By Congress!*

These people existed, and more importantly, they were welcomed in certain societies. It's important to honor them and it's important to honor the people in their lives who supported them. Was it everywhere? No, of course not. There are always those controlling types, no matter where you go, right?

But they were there.

One thing that has always been important to me in writing LGBTQ stories is to honor the fact that there are families who love and accept one another, even if they can't understand everything about their family members. *They still love each other.* We families exist. It's important that people who may be questioning their sexuality—questioning whether or not to come out, perhaps feeling trapped by the fear that their families might turn their backs on them—know that there are families who will love and embrace them.

There always have been these families and there always will be. It's not always a sad story, and to honor my children, their partners and their loving relatives, I will always write those stories. They're important, they've always been possible and they always will be.

(And if you're in need, then you're welcomed into my ever-expanding rainbow family.) <3

—*Laura*

CHAPTER ONE

San Felipe Del Rio, Texas, late August, 1870

RENALDO RELAXED HIS LONG LEGS, putting only the barest pressure of his knees against his horse's sides. The balls of his feet were light in the stirrups as his mount drove forward, her powerful hindquarters digging her hooves into the softened dirt of the corral as they rode toward their target. With the barest flick of his forefinger on the half-breed rein to instruct her, she tucked her backside down, remaining light and loose up front, walked her front legs into a perfect sliding stop, then kept her head held low and eyes trained forward as she backed up a few paces. Renaldo pointed his toes, letting her feel the slight change in his body, which told her that he wanted her to approach the trembling calf slowly.

"Very good, Paloma," Renaldo crooned. "Gently, gently."

He didn't bother roping the calf—the point was to continue Paloma's lesson that she would be allowed to decide the best way to stop. They'd worked earlier on tracking and heading. Now, all Renaldo wanted was to reinforce that he and Paloma

1

worked together, that they were a team, and that he did not expect Paloma to simply do as he commanded. That was no way to forge a strong relationship with such a beautiful, such an intelligent creature as Paloma.

"*Muy bien, mijo*," his father, Estebán Valle, called out. "You are truly a natural at this. You understand that all good horses, like children, need instruction. But it should never be harsh, never be cruel."

Renaldo laughed, leaning forward to stroke Paloma's high, dapple-gray neck. "Then how do you explain my sore backside from all the spankings Mama gave me when I was a child?"

"In two words: your sister."

With a snort, Renaldo slid off Paloma's saddle, kissed her cheek and smiled as he tossed the reins over her neck to give her freedom. He wrapped his reata, its leather well-worn and supple, around and around his forearm and palm as he left the open corral.

"*Por favor*, bring me a dipperful, *mijo*," his father called, rubbing his hand down the side of the horse he had been training all day.

With a nod, Renaldo tossed a hand up, grateful for the excuse to get out of the sun. Even though he'd lived here most of his life, the summers in the Rio Grande Valley were brutal and something of a shock every year when the hot, humid winds ripped through the river-bottomed canyons and out into the open vistas where his family's ranch sprawled.

He hung up the coiled reata, splashed his dusty face with water from the rain barrel he and his sister Calandaría were responsible for filling from the sweet-water creek that spilled across the north corner of the ranch, and took a sip, washing out the gritty sand from the corral trapped between his teeth with a mouthful spat on the dry grass before taking a much longer drink. He poured a little water over his kerchief and tied it around his neck, where it instantly cooled the hot, sunburned skin above his shirt's collar.

"Papa," he called, walking carefully with the dipper to where his father was wiping his forehead with a handkerchief.

"*Gracias*," Esteban said and drank it all. "Do you mind working without me here? I want to speak with your brother, give him a letter to send out before he leaves for Fort Clark."

"Of course not. Paloma will be a good girl for me, won't you?" Paloma whickered in response.

"Such a spoiled beauty," Esteban said, shaking his head at her. "Well, it's good to spoil who you love, eh, *papito*?"

Renaldo smiled at the clap to his shoulder and laughed when his father slung an arm around his neck and smacked a noisy kiss on Renaldo's forehead.

"You're getting too big for me to do that." Esteban sighed and hitched up his pants in the back. "You're almost twenty-one. But until Eduardo and Hortencia give me a grandbaby, you and your sister will have to be my babies to kiss and spoil."

Renaldo didn't mind. He watched as his father—gray-haired and bow-legged, with a chest deep and tanned and arms still strong even though his advanced age had caused his shoulders to stoop—walked back to their simple ranch house. He flashed back to their family's grand hacienda south of San Antonio where he was born: the wide courtyard, the stone floors, in the great room a large painting of his ornately gowned grandmother, which had been carried all the way from his mother's family estate in Mexico City as a reminder of their storied lineage.

3

Now, they lived in a more modestly sized home with a central great room connected to the kitchen where the family gathered: small bedrooms branched off on either side for Calandaría— the only daughter and Renaldo's twin—and their parents, and the bathhouse was a short walk from the kitchen door. The house was built from locally quarried limestone decked with stucco and had only hardpan for the floor that was Calandaría's responsibility to sweep every day. Still, they were doing far better than many of the Anglos who were moving to the region; their sod-roof shacks were an eyesore on what was once an empty prairie, bordered by the river and, to the east, by the Balcones Escarpment in the far distance.

The family of Esteban Valle, of which Renaldo was the youngest of five children, had moved west from San Antonio to the border of Texas and Mexico on a land grant when Renaldo was five. Esteban hadn't been able to resist all the acreage being handed to them. It was perfect grazing land for their sheep and longhorn cattle, not to mention near the wild herds of mustangs with which Esteban was obsessed. He was ready to train his sons to become rancheros or *mesteñeros,* men who roamed the plains to catch and train wild horses.

Renaldo sat on the top rail of the corral, watching Paloma snort and hop around, so light of foot that she seemed to fly into the sky, kicking her back heels in the air every third hop or so—her feisty little kicks and hops were something she did when in a good mood and which gave her her name. She was the first wild horse that was solely Renaldo's responsibility to train and, at five, she was ready to graduate to a spade bit and become one of the finest cattle horses Vista Valle had produced. He was extremely proud of her and couldn't bear the thought of selling his feisty gray-dappled dove, but that was for his father to decide. Until Renaldo came of age, everything was in his father's control.

Renaldo whistled one long low note and ended it on a sharp high sound. Paloma snorted heavily and calmed down, nodding her head and pawing at the ground playfully with a loud whicker. Renaldo sat still, calling her name under his breath over and over.

"That's it, there you go," he muttered when Paloma finally nodded closer, blowing her breath hot and humid over Renaldo's cheek. He sat still as she lipped at his ear and dark hair, nickering and chattering in her way as she reacquainted herself with his smell.

Apparently deciding he smelled just as he had ten minutes before, she stretched out her neck, bumping his hands with her muzzle. He scratched under her chin, and she went still, with her big eyes heavy-lidded and ears up high, focused on him. Grinning, he said, "You are shameless," then moved his hands to rub her jaw and cheek the way she liked.

"Nice ladies get affection," he said, his voice low and calm, his hands never ceasing to rub and soothe her. She was a sweet girl, for all that she liked to put on a show for his father. He hopped into the corral, hands in his pockets, and walked away, laughing softly when she followed and snorted over his neck before pushing her muzzle under his arm.

He walked the perimeter as she followed him. "You *are* getting spoiled. Who will want to buy such a pampered *caballo*? Better watch it." He ran his hand across her flank and down her thigh, feeling the solidness of her cannon bone down to the pastern and ending at her hoof, which she lifted for him to inspect.

"Or you'll end up a present for some stuffy city girl back east, walking over cobblestones to drag her carriage to shops instead of riding out in the open like you want."

"Maybe the city girl will run away to join rebel forces in the south," Calandaría said, hitching up her skirts and petticoats to climb onto the fence and watch. If their mother caught her, she'd chew her ear off. "Maybe this girl won't want to do what you and Eduardo and Papa expect all women to do: Make babies and keep house."

Renaldo held Paloma's muzzle and looked into her eyes. "It sounds like Mama has another young man for my sister to meet, doesn't it?"

"Ugh, he's disgusting," Calandaría scoffed, dusting off her skirt. "He's older than Eduardo."

At Renaldo's raised eyebrow, she said, "Thirty-two!"

"Oh, ancient, yes." Renaldo ducked away and laughed when she kicked at him playfully.

"He's been writing to Mama for months, asking about me. He sent Papa some ridiculous spurs as a gift. I hate him."

"Have you seen him?" Renaldo asked, whispering praise to Paloma as he stroked her head, checking the spade bit in her mouth. It sat perfectly. He would be able to stop using a bosal, the special noseband that fitted around her nose and jaw, only needing the reins and his usual gentle hand.

"Of course not, but I don't need to in order to know that I won't have him. Mama is getting nervous because I'm getting 'too old.'"

Renaldo looked up to see his sister rolling her eyes.

"Just because *she* was married at twenty," she said, "doesn't mean I'm too old because I'm *not*. We're not even twenty-one

6

for another week! You boys are so lucky not to have expectations on you until you've made a name for yourself."

Renaldo laughed. "Don't let Silvestre hear you say that. If Papa would allow it, he'd marry that girl from town he's been courting this very minute."

"I don't like her. No schooling, no form. She just makes cow eyes at all the unmarried men; she never has anything interesting to say."

"Better the unmarried men than the married ones, though."

She made a very unladylike snort. Renaldo tossed his dirty hat at her to hear her squawk, and then led Paloma out of the corral to be rubbed down. He loved his sister. Calandaría was smart, thoughtful and, as his twin—ten minutes older, she never let him forget—she had been Renaldo's childhood playmate and best friend. Their older brothers were too invested in becoming upstanding men and working their livestock to spend much time with them, so they'd always relied on each other's company.

As he led Paloma into her stall, he glanced back to see his sister frowning, the negative emotion unfamiliar on her usually cheerful, lovely face. They had the same nose, a slight downturn at the rounded tip, and wide-set, deep brown eyes. Calandaría had often teased Renaldo for having lashes as thick as she did. They both had high cheekbones and full bottom lips, but Calandaría had a point to her chin, whereas Renaldo's was square like their father's. Calandaría's hair was jet-black and long like their mother's; Renaldo's was shot through with shades of brown from working outdoors. He also had over half a foot in height on his diminutive sister, but there was no question they were twins. They had the same easy smile, the same dimples, the same way of standing with their weight on their left legs. They also both unconsciously sought one another out for comfort in times of trouble.

Calandaría and he had been sent back to San Antonio together for what their mother considered "proper schooling" as teenagers and had clung to one another among the strange, stuffy people who surrounded them. The busyness of the city and the haughty demeanor the old families put on to impress each other left him aching to get home to open land, to his brothers and parents and to the ringing silence of the prairie and canyonlands where the only creatures he needed to impress were the animals his family raised.

The thought of his sister marrying and leaving their family's estate made him sad; the thought of being pressured himself to marry to some unknowable woman was almost impossible to believe and left him feeling anxious and restless. He wanted to stay where the world around him was quiet enough for him to live happily. The ranch would go to their oldest brother, Eduardo, and Renaldo and his other brothers could continue working there or set up their own establishments on the outskirts of the family's generous land grant. Unless he wanted to, he didn't have to leave.

As he led Paloma into the barn, Calandaría caught up and, groaning, unraveled her ornate, heavy braid. She held an extra coil of black, glossy braid, false hair made from a horse's tail their mother had made Renaldo collect. "Mother makes me wear this every day, now. It gives me a headache."

She was braiding Paloma's mane, weaving her hairpiece into it, when they heard a screech outside. Paloma snorted and kicked a bucket, sending Calandaría scurrying out of harm's way.

"A lady doesn't let her hair down in public!" their mother shouted, snatching the hairpiece from the ground before Paloma could stomp on it as his sister muttered under her breath.

"A lady doesn't come shouting around skittish horses," Renaldo said, soothing Paloma and glaring at his mother.

"Watch your mouth, *mijo*," Juana Maria said, pointing ominously at him. "You are not so big that I can't still turn you over my knee." She turned to Calandaría, grabbed her upper arm and pulled her toward the barn door. "You are going to ruin your complexion out in the sun without a hat! And taking your hair down? *Mija*, you will be the death of me. It took us two hours to do your hair this morning!"

"Ay, Mami!" his sister wailed. "Let me save you the trouble then. Let me wear my hair Mescalero-style!"

Renaldo caught his sister's wink before the two women turned the corner. There was no way their traditional mother—who still wore petticoats, a corset and whatever other befrilled clothing the women of her youth dressed in—would ever consider letting her only daughter wear her hair down in a far more simple style like an Apache woman.

He lost himself in the routine of grooming Paloma and getting her and the other horses fed and watered. His brothers would tend to the needs of the other livestock not grazing out on the range before dinner, so it was a shock to see Silvestre, the middle child and six years Renaldo's senior, nervously creeping about the barn in the growing twilight as Renaldo was closing it up for the night.

"What are you doing?" Renaldo asked, leaning against the shut barn door.

Silvestre wouldn't look him in the eye. "Nothing," he said, smoothing his hand over his glossy black hair. Silvestre was what the girls in town called dashing, and he knew it. Renaldo thought their mother would have been better off having Silvestre for a daughter instead of Calandaría—at least their mother wouldn't have to nag Silvestre to have better grooming habits. He was always impeccably dressed and styled.

"Just getting a moment's peace," Silvestre continued, rocking back on his boot heels.

"Hmmm," Renaldo said, eying him suspiciously, but unable to figure out what his brother was really up to. "See you at dinner."

Silvestre nodded in an irritated way. Restless, eager to prove himself a man to anyone who had the misfortune to cross his path when he was in one of his moods, Silvestre left broken hearts and bad feelings left and right and drove their older brothers Eduardo and Francisco crazy, which was why Silvestre was Renaldo's least favorite brother.

Until Eduardo took over the ranch and Francisco found a wife, Silvestre was trapped by custom and the proviso within the *empressario* grant to wait his turn, and the older he got, the more impatient he became. Renaldo shook off his own irritation as he came into the house to wash up.

"Papa and Eduardo won't be home for dinner, *cariño*, so would you say grace?" his mother asked, carrying a large platter of food to the large, rough-hewn dining table in the center of the great room.

He took the plate from her hands and kissed her cheek, then smiled at her pleased reaction. "Of course."

Calandaría swept past him with another plate of food, calling out so their mother could hear her, "I'm so grateful to be a woman, denied the task of having to bless everything for everyone all the time."

She grinned at Renaldo as their mother began muttering under her breath, crossing herself.

"I don't know *where* you got this wild spirit from, *china*," Juana Maria sighed. "This is why I didn't want to leave San Antonio to come to this godless place."

"I'm sorry, Mami," Calandaría replied, kissing her mother's cheek and wrapping her in a hug. "I'm a terrible, naughty girl."

"You are, you are." Juana Maria smoothed the stray hairs from Calandaría's forehead and kissed her over and over. "You must understand that you will never catch a husband being so bold!"

"Oh?" she said innocently. Renaldo quickly looked at the floor to keep from laughing.

"Maybe," Renaldo said, sitting and stretching his legs under the expansive table, "she needs to find a man who knows how to break horses. A man like that knows how to stop a wild thing's impulses and get them under control."

"My beautiful, smart boy," Juana Maria said, kissing the top of his head on her way back to the kitchen. "This is exactly why I want your sister to meet *Señor* Aguayo in September."

Calandaría turned away from her mother and made a face at her brother, then pantomimed strangling someone.

"And do not for one minute think I don't know what you two are doing," Juana Maria said, her back to her children as she swept onion peels into a bucket to be carried outside. "Disgraceful, the both of you."

"We love you, Mama," they said together, as they'd done since they were small and caught trying to ride on the backs of their sheep, filling Silvestre's new boots with mud, or flinging cow chips at one another.

"Such wicked babies," their mother said, almost able to hide her pleased smile.

IMMEDIATELY AFTER SUPPER, SILVESTRE BOLTED from the table and hurried out the door, calling out a thank-you for the food as the door swung shut. Renaldo and Francisco glanced at their mother, who was frowning.

"Let me help you, Mama," Francisco said, standing and gathering up dishes. His voice was as soft and as quiet as his demeanor,.

"No, no, leave it. You worked hard all day, but thank you, *cariño*." She reached over and cupped Francisco's face, rubbing her thumb tenderly over the birthmark high on his cheekbone as was her way of reminding him that she didn't see his face as being disfigured. "Calandaría will help me."

Calandaría cried out, "That's not fair! I did all the cooking!" At the sharp look her mother gave her, she grumbled, "They could at least take the scraps out."

"I'll do it," Renaldo said, squeezing his sister's arm genially before carrying the old copper pot outside.

The heat of the day had broken with nightfall, leaving the air much cooler; the harsh wind had dropped to a gentle and pleasant breeze, filling the night air with the scent of sagebrush and milkweed. Traces of light were still clinging to the horizon, but the stars overhead were scattered in their familiar, beautiful pattern. Renaldo stayed outside in the open, breathing deeply the scent of plant and animal, pleased and content with the sense of peace it gave him.

A noise—the sound of something knocking into a wall—startled him out of his reverie. He stood still, head cocked to listen again, and could hear someone making a low, pained sound. He took off running toward the barn and paused, waiting to hear it again. When he heard a deep, almost guttural noise, he slipped through the partially open door. His eyes immediately locked on a glowing lantern hung on the far wall. He distinctly remembered blowing out the flame before closing up for the night.

Again, a sound, this time high, soft and gasping; he turned in place until he saw Silvestre's back heave as he fought against someone. Renaldo walked swiftly to help his brother fend off whomever he was grunting and straining against and stopped in his tracks when he came to Silvestre's side.

Patricia, the young woman from town, the one whom Calandaría could not stand, had her skirts up around her waist and her hands held high above with one of Silvestre's hands pinning them in place against the barn wall. Her foot was hiked up on a saddle bench and her breasts hung over the top of her loosened shirt. She gasped his brother's name over and over as he thrust into her soft, pliant body. Both of them were completely oblivious to Renaldo's presence.

Renaldo hissed, and Patricia opened her eyes, moaning and smiling lewdly at him before catching Silvestre's mouth in a passionate kiss. It was obscene, all of it. Renaldo shoved at his brother's shoulder before turning away to keep Patricia's naked body out of view, shouting, "Silvestre!"

Silvestre looked up, eyes heavy-lidded until they met with Renaldo's, then they shot open. "God dammit," he muttered, dropping his hands.

"No, no!" Patricia cried, grabbing him to pull him flush against her exposed body. "Make him leave!"

Silvestre's face broke slowly into a wicked grin. He cupped Patricia's ample breast and turned to Renaldo, who had never seen… he didn't want to see this.

"What is wrong with you?" Renaldo cried. "Cover her! Cover yourself! Have you no shame?"

Silvestre continued to stroke over Patricia's dusky areola with the pad of his thumb, dipping down to kiss the fullness of it. "What's wrong with *me*? What's wrong with *you*? Can't you see this beautiful woman—" He caught Patricia's mouth in another kiss before dragging the tip of his nose down the length of her neck while thrusting his hips forward sharply and making her sigh and moan his name again. "—is enjoying herself? Don't you want to watch? See what it is to be with a woman? Finally become a man?"

Patricia laughed with her head flung back against the wall. "Oh! Have you never, little Renaldo? But you're so handsome! Almost as much as your brother." She buried her hands in Silvestre's black hair as he continued to grind and roll his hips against her. "I know someone who could help you. Maybe even me if—"

Silvestre shut her up with another kiss.

Turning away and stalking off with hands clenched at his sides, Renaldo's face burned with shame even though it shouldn't; *he* shouldn't be the one ashamed just because the sight of Patricia's body stirred nothing within him, that the thought of being with her or any of the other young women in their town left him with a churning gut and a need to isolate himself out on the prairie. It was his brother who should be ashamed for bringing such a creature to their home, ashamed of himself for treating a woman so scandalously. He kicked at a stone in the dirt path that led back to the house. Their *mother* was just yards away inside their family's home, and this was how Silvestre repaid their parents?

"What has you so angry?" Calandaría asked as she dumped the washing water out onto the dirt. "If you think carrying onion skins and—"

"Shhh. Come with me," he said, cutting her off and walking away from the house, away from the barn, away from everything that was wrong with their normally peaceful homestead. When he was sure they wouldn't be overheard, he turned and took his twin's hand. "I caught Silvestre and Patricia in the barn."

"Caught them?" Her eyebrows knit in confusion until it was clear. Then, she covered her mouth with both hands. "They were—!" At his sharp nod, she shook her head and made a disgusted noise. "I knew she was trouble." She dropped her temple onto her brother's chest as she'd done since childhood to find comfort. "Then again, I knew Silvestre was, as well. I shouldn't blame her, knowing what type of man he is."

He stared off into the night, the sound of the bullfrogs a mile off at the riverbank and the cicadas in the haas mesquite and pecan trees the only sound save their breathing. "This will kill Mama. That is, if we tell her."

"Renaldo, no! We cannot keep a scandal like this from her, or simply let Silvestre get away with it." She bit her lip and laced their fingers together, tugging gently. "Can we?"

They stared at each other until they heard a loud shriek from behind the house.

"*Ay, dios mio! Bruja!* Devil! You bring this shame onto my house? Onto your father's name?"

Their mother was screaming, and from the sound of it, hitting Silvestre—or possibly Patricia—with a wooden spoon. They raced to the barn to find Patricia grabbing her clothes around her body, attempting to slip out and away, and Silvestre, hands held out, trying to placate his mother. That wasn't all that was out.

"Shame! For *shame*, Silvestre," their mother gasped, breathless in her fury. "You stand there in front of me like this? Clothe yourself!"

Francisco took off after Patricia, who had managed to slip past the family, while their mother continued to beat Silvestre over the head with her heavy wooden spoon, cursing him. Silvestre couldn't seem to decide whether he should hold his hands up in defense or pull his pants closed until their mother turned away, crying, leaving him free to put himself to rights.

"How? How could you do something so vile to that poor girl?" Juana Maria asked of her son.

Renaldo and Calandaría glanced at each other but said nothing.

"Disgracing a good Catholic girl, disgracing yourself!"

They could hear hoofbeats coming close; Estebán had returned.

"What is happening? Is there a fire?" Estebán asked, quickly dismounting and tossing the reins to Renaldo. "Is someone ill?"

"Oh, Papa!" their mother cried, falling onto his strong chest and crying. Kissing her hair and rubbing her back, Estebán looked utterly baffled. Voice muffled against his linen shirt, she cried, "Your son—"

"*My* son?"

"He is not mine, not if he is a man who would treat a woman so poorly, dishonor her in such a way just inches from where I lay my head every night."

Silvestre rolled his eyes while trying to pull his clothes and hair together. "Mama, you don't sleep in the barn."

Juana Maria smacked the back of Silvestre's head. "Don't get a smart mouth with me, *tonto*."

Calandaría stepped forward, placing a hand on her father's forearm. "Ask Silvestre about Patricia," she said quietly.

Estebán's eyebrows shot up before his whole face fell. "Oh, son. Were you that desperate that your hand could not suffice?"

"Papa!" Juana Maria cried, pulling out of her husband's embrace, clearly scandalized.

"*Mi querida*, don't you think, given the current situation, that it would have been better that he had?" he said calmly. Juana Maria's response was to cry harder.

Silvestre had nothing to say, only stared off with a petulant, angry look into the dark where Patricia had vanished. Suddenly, he looked nervous, and the sound of people breaking through the scrub brush could be heard. Francisco appeared, gently holding Patricia's elbow, helping her across the bramble and ruts in the ground as they walked back. Renaldo could see that Patricia's face was tear-streaked—she dabbed at her cheeks with what Renaldo knew was Francisco's handkerchief—and that she'd managed to pull herself together, somewhat.

"Young lady," Esteban said, his voice stern and fatherly as he held out a hand. Francisco delivered the shivering creature to him, and then took off his light jacket and draped it over her shoulders. Patricia would look at no one but Silvestre, who refused to look back.

"I believe we adults need to speak privately," Estebán said, looking at Silvestre, Francisco and their mother. To the twins he said, "You two must go to Calandaría's room, please."

That was the room farthest from the great room, where they wouldn't be able to overhear.

"I am old enough to be counted as an adult!" Calandaría said.

"Calandaría!" their mother hissed. "Obey your father! What we have to discuss isn't meant for innocent young ladies such as yourself."

Renaldo nodded at his father, who looked as if he'd aged ten years since he saw him this afternoon. Francisco stood behind their mother, angled toward Silvestre as if he imagined their brother would make a break for it. Given their mother's hot temper, that didn't seem too far-fetched. He nodded at his brother and followed his sister into the house.

"SHHH!" CALANDARÍA HISSED, WAVING RENALDO off. "I'm trying to hear!"

"You're not making much of a case for yourself as an adult, you know."

She turned and glared at him. He wanted to know what everyone was saying, too, but he felt he owed it to his father to at least *try* to obey him.

"… It isn't the first time, is it?" Estebán asked gently. When there was no reply, Renaldo assumed it was Patricia who had been asked. "Oh, my dear, what a mess you have gotten yourself into. With help—don't think I don't know of what my son is capable."

"I suppose you'll make us marry," Silvestre said, barely hiding the triumph from of his voice. "And then I'll be second to Eduardo when it comes time for you to retire."

There was only silence. Her face grim and angry, Calandaría turned to Renaldo. Renaldo couldn't believe what he was hearing. That Silvestre would do such a thing to a young woman just to get a larger portion of land and holdings after their father had always been so generous?

"Oh, she will be married to my son," Juana Maria said, her voice rising in anger. "It will happen within a fortnight. As soon as we can manage so that any babies coming won't raise too much suspicion as to when they were conceived."

They heard Patricia gasp. "How did you know, *Señora?*"

The scraping of a wooden leg on the hard-packed floor meant their mother must have shifted on her chair. With a voice softer than they'd heard from her all night, she said, "I've given birth to seven and have buried two. I know very well the look of a woman who is expecting."

Silvestre chimed in, "Then that means I'll have a grandchild for you even faster than Eduardo, Papa. I've said for years that waiting for them to fulfill their duty to the family before I was allowed to marry is ridiculous, and—"

"You will not give me a grandchild." Estebán said sharply.

"*Estebán!*" their mother whispered.

"Juana Maria, I would never insist on what you think. And I have decided how we will handle this." Their father sighed deeply. "Patricia will marry Francisco—"

"What?!" both Silvestre and Patricia shouted.

"—and you, Silvestre," he continued, his voice filled with disgust, "you will be spending your life in the service of your God, whom you have so offended with your greed and lust."

"Mami," Silvestre said, his voice the beguiling tone he used to charm the women both young and old to get his way. "Mami, you won't let him take my child from me, would you?"

"Only your child you think of? Or is it truly only yourself you're worried about, *mijo*? What about this poor soul you've so shamelessly treated? Your father is right. To reward you with a family—with the no-doubt beautiful child that Patricia will have," Juana Maria said, her voice soft and kind, "would be to sin ourselves."

Patricia could be heard softly weeping.

"You," their father said, angry once more and clearly speaking directly to his middle child, "you will sleep in the barn tonight with the rest of the animals. I am disgusted by you and cannot bear to look at you for one minute more. Go! We will speak in the morning."

Calandaría and Renaldo backed away from the door in case anyone came storming down the small hallway. Silvestre slammed the front door as he exited.

"Patricia," their father said, voice far more gentle, "would you do us the honor of staying with us so that we can tend to your needs before you marry?"

Nothing but more crying from Patricia.

"Calandaría?" their mother cried out. "I know you've been listening. Come take your new sister to your room and help her get comfortable. We'll speak to her family in the morning."

The twins looked at each other. Renaldo pulled his sister to standing and joined the family in the main room. Patricia was on the floor at their mother's knee, weeping, as Juana Maria shushed her and stroked her wild hair back into order. Francisco was leaning against one of the main supports, flummoxed and breathing shallowly.

Renaldo was glad for him, glad that his kind, intelligent brother would have someone beautiful as a wife. Francisco had always kept to himself because of the large blemish on his face. Having been teased mercilessly back in San Antonio meant that Francisco had withdrawn, became very shy with anyone who wasn't family and had never attempted to court a woman, even though Renaldo knew he wanted nothing more than a family of his own to love, to attempt to recreate what their parents had.

He was just sorry his brother would be forced to marry such a wild, faithless woman, remembering her offer in the barn with distaste.

"We will wait for Eduardo to return from Fort Clark tomorrow before we speak to Patricia's family," their father said, sighing and rubbing his hand over his face.

Looking at her parents with unease, Calandaría held out her hand to Patricia. "Come now," she said, unclenching Patricia's hand from her mother's knee. "Let's go to my room, and I'll help you comb out your hair."

Patricia looked at Francisco and burst into fresh tears. Renaldo's hand clenched at his side at the look of shame that flashed over his brother's face. After the girls had left the room, Renaldo approached his father and said, "I think a little mescal would help us tonight."

His father laughed wearily and nodded. "Francisco? Come, let us toast your impending nuptials."

Juana Maria appeared with four tumblers and a bottle, quickly pouring generous drinks and passing them around. Their father looked at her in something akin to shock. She shrugged, saying, "Can't a mother celebrate? Or consider this me wiping away the memory of what I witnessed tonight," and waved her hand dismissively, then tossed back the entire contents of her glass in one swallow.

"How did you come to find them?" Renaldo asked.

"You were taking too long for something so simple as carrying out scraps, so I went to find you, *mijo*. Instead, I found … well." She poured herself another glass. "Something a mother never wants to witness."

"Francisco," their father said in his quiet way. "I am sorry not to have consulted you before making a decision like this. If you will not have her…" He glanced at Renaldo, who felt an icy shiver run down his spine and his lungs constrict.

"No, father," Francisco said, almost sounding eager. "It's what's best. I see why you've chosen as you've done."

With a deep sigh and a nod, Estebán said, "Thank you, *mijo*. You are a good man." To the group, he said, "*Salud*."

As they all clinked glasses, Renaldo watched Francisco, noting the shocked yet pleased expression blooming across his face. He could understand why Francisco could be so eager about this, even if he was acting as his younger brother's second.

And better Francisco than Renaldo, who shuddered at the thought of being in Francisco's place. The mescal burned the back of his throat, burning through the sick lump which was close to choking him at the memory of Patricia's offer, of his brother taunting him with finally "becoming a man."

Francisco smiled at something Juana Maria said, and Renaldo could see how excited his brother was by the prospect of having a wife, a family. Renaldo worried that something must be fundamentally wrong with him, something inside of him broken, for not even entertaining the thought of a woman he understood to be beautiful, but who inspired no passion in himself. Was he still a child, not yet a man, for dreaming only of living here on the ranch with his parents, his siblings, raising horses and living a quiet life? Shouldn't he long for a woman like Patricia? The thought had him reaching for the bottle of mescal once more, and as the harsh liquor burned its way through his belly, he gave silent thanks that this responsibility was passing him by, that he could remain just as he was for a while longer.

THE NEXT MORNING WAS SOLEMN, as if they were preparing for a funeral. Where normally there was laughter and teasing, no one spoke. Silvestre had come in to eat a quick breakfast with their father, and only when he'd left the house were the others—especially a still-shocked and trembling Patricia—allowed to sit and eat. Renaldo nodded at her, cutting his eyes to Calandaría, who sat with her mouth pressed into a tight line.

"Good morning, Patricia," Francisco said, his voice timid and unsure.

Tears rolling down her cheeks, Patricia dropped her gaze to her plate.

Calandaría's face grew stonier. "In this house," she said, her voice clipped, "we greet each other with politeness at the very least. Are you enjoying your breakfast, Patricia?" She looked at Patricia with a raised eyebrow, pointing at the delicious food their mother had made for them all, the spicy chorizo scenting the air. With more force than necessary, Calandaría spooned some of the persimmon preserves onto her plate next to her *torrejas*.

With a heavy sigh, Patricia squared her shoulders and looked at them with cool detachment. "Good morning, Francisco. Yes, the food looks delicious. *Muchas gracias, Señora* Santos de Valle."

Juana Maria smiled at being addressed properly, wiping her hands on her apron. "We must feed you well!" she said, adding more to Patricia's plate. "We want you healthy and strong, both in body and spirit."

Calandaría and Renaldo exchanged a glance. After their mother's temper was spent, she was sunny and playful, effusive with her affection and attention. Patricia could have done far, far worse.

After they ate, Renaldo and Francisco joined their father and brother at the barn. Silvestre looked terrible, like a cat dragged out of a fight he was losing. His normally perfect hair was in disarray, his clothes were stained and his face was twisted with anger. Eduardo rode in, dismounting at the sight of them all standing there as their father saddled his best horse.

"*¿Qué pasa?*" he asked, swinging down.

Francisco looked at his boots, Silvestre paced in a tight circle and Renaldo cut his eyes to Silvestre, and then back to Eduardo.

"What did you do this time, Silvestre?" Eduardo asked, laughing sharply. "Get into a fight? Owe someone money?"

"Fucked a girl from town and got her pregnant," their father spat.

"Oh, you stupid…" He shook his head, sniffing at Silvestre. They'd never gotten along. Silvestre got along only with women, and only before he broke their hearts. The two brothers were as opposite as could be. Even in physical appearance, Eduardo was barrel-chested and broad-faced like their father and unlike Silvestre's lean, lithe form.

"What will you do, Papa? He cannot marry before Francisco." Eduardo ran his hand roughly over his head, clearly agitated. "You know that the contract you signed with the government to have this land was very clear about how it could be passed down to your sons. Silvestre cannot usurp Francisco's position, not when Francisco has worked by my side for almost twenty years. No business partner except for yourself is his equal."

Francisco squeezed his brother's arm.

Esteban sighed. "The girl is quick with his child, so we must act with haste. After the last girl he took—" Renaldo sagged back on his boot heels in shock. There were more than Patricia? "—it was explained very clearly that it would not be tolerated again, not by me, and not by the people of this town, who are fully aware of what kind of man my son has become."

Silvestre fell against a wall, slipping down to sit on the dusty floor, hands tearing at his hair. "Just let me marry her. Or," he said, looking up with panic and hope in equal measure. "Maybe she won't carry the child to term? There are ways, I know some—"

Esteban stalked to him and slapped him across his face. "You would compound this sin? Where is your great love for this child you begged only last night to be allowed to raise? You play with women like they are a bug on a string, a momentary amusement, and not people in their own right. Would you have me treat your mother with so little respect? What if one of the boys in the village had done such a thing to your sister? Where is your honor? I have never been so ashamed in all my life."

"Papa, please!" Silvestre begged. "Please let me make this right. Let me fix this. We don't even know if she's with child!"

Estebán ignored him and turned to his other sons. "We will speak to her family. We will make sure they know how we will honor their daughter, will ensure the baby will grow up without ever knowing want. That girl deserves better than what has been dealt to her by this fool." He glanced at Silvestre, then sank down on his haunches with a hand on Silvestre's shoulder, which he roughly shook once.

"You have been very foolish, my son, over and over again. You have been greedy and dishonest, and you have dishonored your family and Patricia's family. You only feel remorse for yourself. Have you considered that people might not want to do business with a family who would behave in such a way? All the land, all the money you hoped to steal for yourself, to steal away from Francisco, you could have lost it all, leaving all of us with nothing."

Silvestre's face was stony. All anger and fear were shut away as their father spoke.

"Sending you to the Church is the best way I know to right the many wrongs you've committed. Maybe if you dedicate your life to God and to others, you'll be redeemed. But I have failed you if this is who you have grown to become."

Renaldo ground his teeth. Silvestre was a rotten apple in the bunch, that was all. His brothers were good men; their sister was kind and smart.

Eduardo made a noise of surprise. "Papa! I sent the confirmation letter yesterday. What are we to do?"

Estebán stood with a groan, his knees popping and cracking. "Another mess to fix … Renaldo, come here."

"*¿Sí?*" he asked, coming to his father's side.

"Silvestre was to begin his training at the first of September with the *mesteñero*, Henry Burnett. He's just been sent for, something we've had planned for months." Their father looked at Silvestre once more with a sigh, and then turned back. "I cannot turn someone of his reputation away without possibly causing more damage to the family's name. You will have to take his place, as Francisco is with Patricia."

Renaldo blinked, not sure how to feel. He was going to leave his family? It was as if he was being punished along with Silvestre.

"After your brother was trained, you were to be trained next," his father said, "but we'll have to change the timing." With a gentle smile, he said, "You're a natural, *mijo*. You will do wonderfully. And, it might be nice to be away as we sort out this mess."

Silvestre kicked at a saddle stand, knocking it over.

Renaldo's stomach dropped as he watched Silvestre storm off; there went his hope for his life remaining just as it had been.

CHAPTER TWO

THE MEN—EXCEPT SILVESTRE—RODE INTO TOWN to Patricia's family's place of business, a tack and feed store that served as a way station for vaqueros and cattlemen as they moved their livestock. The Flores family lived in a modest apartment above their board-and-batten store.

Estebán, his hands crossed and resting on the pommel of his saddle, leaned toward Eduardo to ask, "Do you know if this girl has brothers, particularly any who are prone to violence?"

Eduardo snorted an amused sound just as *Señor* Flores came outside grinning, his arms wide in welcome, as they all dismounted and hitched their horses.

"*Señor* Valle! And your sons have come with you as well! To what do I owe the honor?"

Renaldo noticed how *Señor* Flores looked over all of their horses with eyebrows high, approving their mounts and fine saddles, and realized the wisdom of his father in putting his pistols inside a saddlebag and not in plain sight. There was no telling how this could go.

"*Señor* Flores, I would like to have a private word with you, if you would be so kind?"

"Oh?" he said, looking worried. "Is there something amiss with your account? Because—"

"No, no," Estebán soothed, clapping a hand to *Señor* Flores' shoulder. "Nothing of the sort! I hope to bring happy news."

Señor Flores brought his hands together once with a sharp sound, laughing. "Ah! I believe I know what this is, then!" He looked past Estebán's shoulder and Renaldo knew he was realizing who was absent from their party. "Or... maybe I don't?"

"Please, let us go inside and speak."

Señor Flores held open the shop door, gesturing for them all to enter. Renaldo was the last and he noticed with a nervous jolt that Patricia's father was looking him over appreciatively. Renaldo knew that in looks he favored Silvestre over his other brothers, but surely *Señor* Flores wasn't that confused? No matter, their father would sort this out.

When they were settled in the small drawing room upstairs, Estebán began, "*Señor* Flores—"

"Please! Please! Call me Hector." He smiled at them all in turn.

Their father returned the grin, albeit with far less enthusiasm. "And you must call me Estebán. Hector, my sons and I have come to speak with you about joining our families."

"Ha, yes, I wondered if this day would come! I am shocked, however, that Silvestre did not come with you." Hector laughed, looking at each of them. "If he is worried that I will deny him my beautiful Patricia—"

"No, that is not why." Estebán sighed. "*Señor*, I must tell you that a union between Silvestre and Patricia is impossible."

"*¿Como? ¿Por qué?*"

"Because Silvestre is leaving this very day for Mexico, where he will train for the priesthood."

Hector stood gaping, seemingly at a loss for words. After a moment, he sputtered, "But… but this is insanity? I know that they are both very fond of one another—"

Renaldo bit back a wry laugh.

"—and Patricia and her mother both have assured me that a wedding between the two would certainly happen before fall."

"Did they, now?" Estebán said, eyes shrewd.

"Well, you know how mothers can be with these things, and Patricia takes after my wife Antonia; they are both very romantic, full of passion."

Renaldo couldn't help the tiny cough to mask his shocked laugh. Patricia was full of passion, certainly. At the sound of a squeaking door, they all looked toward it to find an older, matronly woman standing with her hands clasped and her face bright. Each of the Valle men gave her a tiny bow, which she followed with a curtsey. She urged a small girl who had been hiding behind her down the hallway and closed the door firmly after coming inside.

"Hector, *Señora,*" Estebán added, nodding at Hector's wife, "let me be clear. We are honorable men. My father, his fathers before him for generations, have always done what is right both by man and by God. And I am here to tell you that we will not let Patricia, hmmm, carry this *burden* alone."

Hector's eyebrows were climbing higher and higher as Estebán's words sank in. "Do you mean to tell me—"

Estebán nodded. "Yes. And I am here, Hector, to try and make this right. My son Francisco, whom you know, along with my son Eduardo, will not only inherit our land but will also take over my business when I retire, has offered to marry your daughter."

With a sharp cry of shock, Patricia's mother stormed into the center of the room, looking with disbelief from Estebán's face to Francisco's—her eyes going straight to the large brown mark that stretched from just above his eyebrow and down the length of his cheek—then glared at Estebán. "Him? You expect my beautiful, my precious and untouched Patricia to be turned over into *his* hands? Why not this young man?" she shouted, pointing at Renaldo. "He is more fitting for my beautiful Patricia instead of this one!"

Renaldo sensed Eduardo bristling at his side. Renaldo also grew angry that his brother would be reduced to something as trivial as a mark on his face, all of his accomplishments and merits ignored simply because he wasn't as handsome as Silvestre.

Estebán, however, did not react, just continued to speak. "Renaldo of course cannot marry before his brothers. And we will need to act quickly. I'm sure you can understand why delicacy and speed is of the utmost importance, *Señora*."

Señora Flores, nostrils wide and jaw tight, was silently fuming. Hector watched her for a moment before his face fell. "Oh, Antonia. You knew." Antonia said nothing but turned sharply on her heel and flounced out of the room.

Hector rubbed his face briskly with his palm. "I believe that Patricia should be honored to be accepted into your esteemed family, and with such an accomplished husband if he will still have her." He sent Francisco a rueful smile, and then held his hand out to Estebán, who shook it.

"I can assure you," Estebán said, "that Francisco will never let your daughter want for anything."

Francisco stepped forward. "*Señor*, you have my word that I will treasure the gift that your daughter is, will respect her and will raise the child as my own."

No one said anything for an agonizing moment—it was out, and there was no denying, no twist of language that could hide the predicament Silvestre and Patricia had gotten the family into.

Looking defeated, Hector held his hand out to Francisco and, with a tremulous voice, said, "You do us the honor, and I will be proud to call a man such as you son."

Finally, Renaldo could take a deep breath; he could sense his brothers and father relaxing as well, now that everything was clear. They all said their goodbyes, Estebán and Hector making promises to meet soon and discuss the plans for the ceremony. After they mounted and were outside of town, Eduardo said, "At least she only has sisters, eh, Papa?"

Their father laughed, but it was wry and bitter, far from his normal jovial, chest-rumbling mirth. Renaldo couldn't help but notice Francisco quietly whistling under his breath, looking quite excited. At least someone was.

As they rode up to their barn, they passed a gleeful Calandaría sitting on the wide front porch with a rifle in her hands.

"Mama said I'm to shoot Silvestre if he tries to come inside," she said, grinning at her twin, who couldn't help but match it.

"And where is he?" their father asked.

"Skulking about, but he's not inside. And," Calandaría said pointedly, "Patricia is inside with Mami."

Estebán nodded and rode on toward the barn. That was where they found Silvestre, who was beginning to look a little crazed.

"Antonia didn't agree to this farce, did she?" he asked, sounding sure of himself.

"*Señora* Flores had no choice," their father replied, his diction tight and clipped. "Her husband made sure of it. He's no fool."

Any confidence that this situation wasn't exactly the mess he'd made of it left Silvestre; his shoulders dropped and his hand rubbed roughly over his face.

"You and I will leave at first light tomorrow," their father said.

"Where will we go?" Silvestre asked.

"Fort Clark, where you'll stay the night until a group of their soldiers leave for the train at Ciudad Acuña in two days' time. And you'll have a guard until you reach Mexico City, where you will study to become a priest. You have brought this on yourself, *mijo*, and left us with no other options."

"That's ridiculous! You can let me marry Patricia! I cannot believe she would want to marry *him*," he said, nodding rudely at Francisco. "And are you the sort of man who would force a woman to marry against her will?"

"Are you the sort of man who would ruin a young lady's future? You only chose her because she was willing and attractive," their father spat. "Would you love her? Cherish her? Honor and protect her? Or would your head turn at the next pretty face, leaving her to care for a child on her own? Leaving her to believe her only value was her face and desirability? Francisco will love her, and in time I hope she will learn to love him as well. She will at the very least be cared for and respected, far more than she would ever gain from marrying you, though it pains me to say this about my own son."

33

"Silvestre," Francisco said, "I would never force myself upon her. I'm only ensuring her protection by giving her and the child she carries my name."

"That's all you'll have, a woman with your name and another man's child," Silvestre sneered.

"Papa," Eduardo said, glaring at his younger brother. "Is it possible to take him to Fort Clark today?"

"No," Estebán replied. "I am old, and the ride today was enough for my backside."

"I will happily go myself," Eduardo said, crossing his arms in front of his chest.

A pained expression on his face, Estebán shook his head. "No. This is something I must do. He is my son, and my indulgence has turned him into this… faithless man."

"Indulgence?" Silvestre spat. "How was I ever indulged? Left on my own so that you, Eduardo and Francisco could spend all day together, so you could teach them how to run the family business? Left with Mama to help when the twins came, and then sent off alone to school without a brother to introduce me to society?" He stood and crossed to their father. "Indulged? No. I was ignored, placated by my mother, left to make my own way—"

"Your own way?" Eduardo shouted. "Papa has offered you more than you can even wrap your fat head around. But nothing has ever been enough for you, you… peacock of a man."

"Enough," Estebán said, a hand on Eduardo's chest. "Silvestre, in time, you will be grateful that I did not saddle you with a marriage of which we both know you would soon grow tired, with a child who would demand your time and love, two things you have always struggled to share."

"Grateful, yes!" Silvestre said, a sharp, rueful laugh bursting from him. "To be permanently cuckolded by God, such a blessing!"

"At least you have known physical love in your life," Francisco said, his voice soft and low, yet all of the men became quiet, turning to him. "You have had women willingly come to you, desire you. For that, little brother, you should be grateful."

"Do not say one word more," Esteban said, a finger in Silvestre's face, who quickly clamped his mouth shut. "Eduardo?"

"*¿Sí?*"

"Will you stay with your brother while I have Mama pack his things?"

"Gladly," Eduardo said. He jerked his head to the side. "Come on. You can help me shoe the horses."

As they walked off, Renaldo watched Francisco staring at Silvestre's retreating back. He'd never thought of Francisco as being lonely; he was always smiling with the family, always willing to speak with the cattlemen and buyers, happy to spend time with Eduardo and his wife, Hortencia. But clearly he had been lonely and had hidden it behind his shyness with outsiders. Renaldo gave Francisco's shoulder a squeeze and turned him gently toward the house.

CHAPTER THREE

THE REST OF THE DAY passed with the routine workings of their ranch, but with the added excitement of Hortencia, Eduardo's wife, coming from their house at the edge of Vista Verde to help make dinner and visit with the women. Calandaría came to the corral late in the afternoon frustrated and clearly bored.

"Hortencia knows," she told Renaldo as he rubbed down Paloma. "I heard her ask Mama to let her take Patricia back home with her, but Mama wouldn't hear of it."

"Oh?"

"All afternoon she and Patricia have been discussing her trousseau, what is left to make, all of that boring lady talk," she said with a dismissive wave. "Mostly I think that Mama is worried she'll run her mouth when she goes home. She seems the gossiping type. Or a braggart, wanting to rub in the other town girls' faces that she is carrying Silvestre's child."

Renaldo nodded at that.

"Plus," Calandaría added, "I think Patricia is scared of Hortencia after she talked about finding three Mescaleros waiting for Eduardo back at their cabin, so to her I imagine staying here with Mama is far safer."

Estebán and Eduardo had worked for the past few years to build trust between their family and the Mescalero Apaches in the region. It was slow going, but Estebán maintained that the Mescaleros had good reason not to trust anyone not their own. *La familia Valle* not being Anglo certainly helped build that trust.

"You just want your bedroom to yourself," Renaldo teased.

"She cries all the time!" Calandaría slumped against the barn stall. "I had to put my pillow on the line this morning to make sure it would be dry by tonight."

Renaldo chuckled, going silent when they heard their mother call out, "Calandaría? *China,* where did you go?"

Calandaría made a shushing motion and crouched behind him. Juana Maria came inside the barn, hands on hips and skirts swirling around her ankles.

"*Mijo,* have you seen your sister?"

Renaldo continued to brush Paloma's side. "Who? Do you mean Calandaría?"

"How many sisters do you have?" she cried, throwing her hands up in the air and marching back outside. "Ugh! That child…"

After a moment, Renaldo unhooked Paloma from her ties and said, "You have to stop teasing Mama."

"I know." Calandaría sighed. "I just feel like this is the only freedom I'll have once that man she's so eager for me to meet comes to town."

"Do you really think it'll be so bad to be married?" He hadn't taken the time to consider it. Now, the mere thought of it left him unsettled and anxious.

"I don't know… I see what Mama and Papa have, how well-matched Eduardo and Hortencia are, and I think, maybe. I like the idea of a companion, someone to grow old with who isn't my brother," she teased, getting a small laugh from him. "But then I see Silvestre and how he is, and I don't know. Renaldo," she said, reaching out and lacing their fingers together. "Promise me you won't let me marry someone like him."

He kissed the back of her hand before dropping it. "Of course. I promise."

He put a little extra alfalfa in Paloma's feed while Calandaría watched, both of them silent. After a few moments, she asked softly, "What about you?"

"Hmmm?"

She tugged him away from the stall, pulling him to sit down next to her. "What about you? Marriage?"

He went still, forcing aside that untethered, fearful sensation for the sake of his sister's question, trying to picture that future. He could see children; he loved little ones, could imagine teaching a son or daughter, a niece or nephew how to love and respect horses as he did. He then tried to picture a wife at his side, tried to picture being with her sexually in order to make a family, and he couldn't. He felt just a vague emptiness, an ache like a bad tooth, a sense that he wasn't real, wasn't whole because he *couldn't* envision it.

Calandaría narrowed her eyes and nodded. "I don't know that marriage suits you, either. But not because you're like Silvestre, *cariño*."

His chest clenched at the sympathy in her eyes. They had always understood each other when no one else could. He supposed it was because they were part of one another in a way that their other siblings weren't. "I just can't..." He sighed harshly. "I can't picture it."

She nodded again. "I think I'm better suited to being trapped than you. I would make my fun of it, would enjoy teasing whomever I end up marrying, but I don't know that you could. And," she added, smiling softly at him, "I don't think that's wrong."

They sat in silence before Calandaría asked, "Do you remember the buckskin mustang that *maldito* trader tried to give Papa?"

Just the year before, a new-to-the-region horse trader had a freshly captured mustang that he couldn't control, an animal he'd dragged along almost the entirety of the Llano Estacado on its side. Rope marks were worn into the poor beast's neck and drag marks scored its flanks; its eyes bulged and its chest heaved with its panicked breathing. Their father had taken the poor animal just to get it away from the trader.

"The best *mesteñeros* know that if you must force an animal to come with you, you will never be its master," their father had explained to them at dinner that night. "You will never be able to train it, for they will always fear you, will never trust you. They will always know you as a brute, the one who stole their freedom, stole them from their family."

As Renaldo thought about it, he realized that would be just how he would feel if his father had chosen him to marry Patricia: stolen from his life. But then, hadn't Papa done that to Patricia and Francisco?

"There have to be consequences," Calandaría said, preternaturally knowing what her brother was thinking.

"Pray we don't make such bad decisions that we have such consequences thrust upon us," he said.

"Every single night, *hermano*." She laughed, nudging his shoulder with hers.

He thought back on that pitiful horse, the thoughtless trader and how careless he'd been with that poor animal. That was the summer Esteban had been introduced to Henry Burnett, who took the animal off his hands to be returned to the wild. The day after meeting him, Esteban had told his sons at dinner, "If we are to be the best in this business, we will do it *Señor* Burnett's way. You will learn how to be better stewards of God's creatures."

His father had made plans to apprentice Silvestre with him the following year, and here they were with those plans destroyed. Renaldo was to take his place, finally set to meet the famed *mesteñero* and leave his family for weeks, possibly months on end. His sister might be married and gone by his return.

"Do you think this man Mama wants to court you will be so bad?" he asked as his eyebrows came close together.

"I don't know. Mama wouldn't make me marry an ogre, and I don't think she'd marry me off to someone who would take me away from all of you, but… I don't know. I don't know *him*."

He rested his cheek on the top of her head and squeezed her. "Well, you'll have enough time to get to know him."

"I'll be sad that you won't be here to get to know him, as well. It won't feel right not to have you here."

His heart squeezed at the reminder that soon he, too, would be leaving and that this time, he wouldn't have the comfort of having his twin by his side.

"We'll both be getting to know strange men, I suppose," he murmured, kissing the top of her head and pulling away. "Come on, let's go inside."

"Renaldo," Calandaría said suddenly, grabbing his arm. "I… I don't believe in luck, not like Mama does, but I hope that all of this with Patricia and Silvestre is our family's bad luck done with. I want us to both meet good men. I want you to like this Burnett man."

The intense look she gave him stopped him in his tracks; a prickling sensation rushed over his skin at her words, sensing they meant more than just their surface. "Well," he started, unsure. "I want you to like the man Mama is bringing to meet you."

Eyes boring into Renaldo's, she chewed at her lip. "Yes, but I truly want you to like your man, as well, Renaldo. I want him to be good to you. Papa thinks very highly of him."

Oh. Renaldo sighed out a breath, lips quirking up at the end. "He does, yes. I don't think he'll be some awful taskmaster."

"That's not…" She huffed out in irritation, and then shook her head minutely, cupped his cheek with one of her small hands, brought their foreheads together. "*Cachorro*, never forget that no one knows you like I do."

"How could I?" he replied, grinning.

"And know that no matter what, wherever we go in this life," she said, her thumb working over his cheekbone, "*te quiero*."

"I love you, too, but what's brought this on?" he asked, holding her forearms and pushing her gently away so he could look in her eyes, which were shining with tears.

"Oh, I just feel like this… this stupidity with Silvestre is going to change everything for all of us, that's all."

41

They walked to the house, Renaldo with his arm around his sister's shoulders.

"It will, but we mustn't look at it as all bad. After all," he said with a wry laugh, "Mama will finally get her grandchild to spoil."

"And Francisco a wife," Calandaría said quietly. "I worry that Patricia won't realize how good and kind he is, how *lucky* she is to be paired with him and not Silvestre. And I worry that she'll be cruel to him."

Renaldo worried about that, too.

They didn't say anything for the rest of the walk.

"So we will have a large celebration for your birthday tomorrow," Juana Maria said to the twins, putting another serving of *machaca* onto Patricia's plate. "But tonight, I thought it would be best if we kept things simple."

The women looked at the men, standing at the door with plates in hand, their father holding an extra dish for Silvestre, who was waiting outside.

"Don't go to much trouble, please," Renaldo said, stepping back so his brothers could exit first.

"Please, Mama," Calandaría said, joining in. "We don't need anything extravagant, especially not with Papa sure to come home tired." She cast her eyes to Patricia, who was staring at her plate, moving the food but not eating.

"All the more reason to cheer him up!" Juana Maria said, shooing Renaldo to the door before tucking in to her dinner.

Outside, he caught up with the men, who were leaning against the rails of one of the corrals and talking.

"—Hortencia said she has the spare bed made up for him," Eduardo said, nodding toward Silvestre.

"Your home *is* on the way to Fort Clark," Estebán mused. "Silvestre, you can take your pick of the duns and ride with your brother at nightfall. I'll meet you both in the morning."

They ate the rest of their meal in relative silence. Francisco took Silvestre's dish when he finished and bent to say something only Silvestre could hear. Silvestre braced himself, but Renaldo watched his eyes go round and mouth fall open, nodding, then was shocked to see Silvestre clap his brother on the shoulder, give him a squeeze and mutter, "*Gracias, hermano. Muchas gracias.*"

"This is what I like to see!" Estebán cried out, his face wide with a smile. "Brothers forgiving one another, putting aside their differences for the sake of family. I'm proud of you both for this." He pulled each of them into his strong embrace and noisily kissed them on their cheeks.

"It's good to leave on such a positive note, my son," he said quietly, ruffling Silvestre's hair, but smoothing it back before Silvestre could bristle like a cat.

Silvestre wandered off, and before Renaldo could follow him to see where he was going, Francisco nudged his side and motioned for him to accompany him back to the house. "Let him say goodbye to our home in peace."

Calandaría, Patricia and Hortencia made quick work of cleaning up, and the older men settled in at the great table with a sigh, tired from a hard day. Francisco took Patricia by the elbow gently and asked, "Would you like to go for a walk outside? It's beautiful out, and I thought you might enjoy a little quiet and fresh air."

Patricia, shoulders tense and face a mask of misery, looked about the room. Their mother smiled at her eagerly. Without looking Francisco in the eye, she gave him a stiff nod and allowed him to wrap a thin *rebozo* around her shoulders to protect her from the dusty breezes that often cropped up this time of year.

As soon as the door shut behind them, Juana Maria clapped her hands and cried out, "See? God smiles upon us." She crossed herself, and then continued, "How anyone could not fall in love with my Francisco, I'll never understand."

Calandaría kissed her on the cheek and crossed the kitchen to get a well-worn pack of playing cards. "That is because you are a loving mother."

"Oh, it's so nice to have everyone getting along," she said, scooping up the cards Calandaría dealt to her and fanning them out to be sorted.

After several hands, some of which Renaldo played even though he was no match for his twin's competitive nature and deviousness, he realized Francisco and Patricia hadn't come back. Worried his brothers may have gotten into a fight but not wanting to disturb the peaceful evening the family was enjoying, he excused himself and went in search of them.

Francisco was leaning against the barn with his shoulders drooping and body sagging against the wood and his forehead turned away from the partially opened door, as if he couldn't bear to see… what? Renaldo looked around, and even though the moon hadn't fully risen, he could see there was no one nearby. He crossed the field quickly, and that was when Renaldo heard it: the unmistakable sound of Patricia's moans and Silvestre's passionate longings to stay with her coming from deep inside the barn.

"Francisco!" he cried, turning his brother to face him and shaking him a little. "How can you let this happen again?"

"Renaldo, please. She doesn't want me," Francisco said sadly. "I know this. We all know this. She wants *him*, and he's leaving for good in the morning. What can it hurt?"

"What can it *hurt*? What about you?"

"Oh, it can't hurt me, not really. Not when I never had claim to her heart in the first place, no matter how much I wish I did." He pushed off the wall, kicking at a stone on the ground. "It's my wedding gift to her."

Silvestre was grunting loudly, cursing under his breath as Patricia let out a high cry.

Francisco walked away from the barn as the sound of their lovemaking reached its crescendo. He stared up at the dark sky. "And it's an apology, I suppose. To him, for soon having what we all know would have been his."

"Until he grew tired of her and found another willing woman," Renaldo said, angry and disheartened. He wished he hadn't come looking, wished he didn't know this about his brothers' strange arrangement, and wished above all else that Francisco wasn't judged by his looks but by the type of man he was. "I... I cannot understand this."

"You don't need to. I know it's what is right. She will never look at me the way she looks at him, but maybe this way she won't despise me."

Silvestre came out then, tucking his loose shirt into his pants and looking thoroughly debauched with his hair wild and lips swollen. He stopped when he realized both Francisco and Renaldo stood there. He narrowed his eyes at his younger brother. "Well? Aren't you going to run to Mama and Papa?"

45

"What good would that do?" Renaldo said. "This isn't my business."

"You should take him back to Eduardo," Francisco said, walking toward the barn where they could all hear Patricia softly weeping. "I'll make sure she gets inside safely so that no one suspects."

"*Paco*," Silvestre said. "I—" He ran his fingers through his unruly hair before squaring his shoulders and holding out his hand. "You'll be kinder to her than I would. She deserves that."

Francisco stared at the hand being offered before brusquely shaking it and walking away, pulling a handkerchief from his pocket. "I know."

CHAPTER FOUR

WITH SILVESTRE, EDUARDO AND THEIR father gone the next day, their mother begrudgingly allowed Calandaría to help Renaldo with the animals while Francisco returned to his half-finished cabin, intent on preparing it for a new wife in order to make Patricia as comfortable as possible. At present, it was simply a half-finished bachelor's sleeping quarters used when he and Eduardo were tagging or rounding up livestock.

Estebán returned that night grim-faced and tense in the shoulders. Juana Maria flitted about the dinner table full of cheer and ideas, kisses for everyone and a tilt of her head to induce Francisco to sit next to his soon-to-be wife. Renaldo noted that while Patricia didn't frown or give any outward appearance of distaste as Francisco murmured a *"buenas noches,* Patricia" to her, she still sat ramrod straight, looking only at her food or Juana Maria.

Well, it *had* only been a single day since Silvestre had gone.

Neither Calandaría nor Renaldo wanted a special celebration for their twenty-first birthday— Calandaría had been given a beautiful set of leather-bound books and Renaldo, to his shock, had been given Paloma, with his father explaining she was now his to have or to sell. Grateful for the chance to keep her, Renaldo happily encouraged their mother to focus on the wedding, which she did with glee. Calandaría was grateful to have attention diverted from herself for a brief period of time.

Antonia Flores, Patricia's mother, arrived shortly thereafter with a large trunk of Patricia's things. The men were shooed out of the house, for which Renaldo was especially grateful. Ladies' underthings and… whatever else he assumed were in the steamer trunk held no interest for him. He did notice how *Señora* Flores seemed pleased with everything, despite the groom not being the one originally intended for her daughter.

He woke earlier than normal to finish his chores with their livestock in order to pitch in with the construction at Francisco's. It took a fair amount of time just to ride through the canyons along the river to the site, and they had no time to waste. Renaldo threw himself into helping his brother, completely forgetting that after the wedding took place, he, too, would be leaving the family home. The first time he remembered that, riding home with the sun setting behind him, pleasantly tired from a hard day's work and enjoying the quiet of the open land, he wondered about what sort of man this *mesteñero* would be.

The only one he'd ever known was an old man the family had met soon after they'd first moved to Vista Verde. His face burnt almost copper from the sun and as stiff, cracked and lined as an old boot, Old Tom Garrison had barely managed to string together a sentence when the family had invited him to dinner all those years ago. His father later told them it was because Garrison preferred living with the horses out on the Llano Estacado, a mercilessly hard terrain to pass through, let alone to live on—only the Comanche and Mescaleros truly thrived there. But Garrison had spent an entire decade on his own, dodging native uprisings, Anglos on their way west, soldiers taking what they'd wanted. He'd become wary toward humans and had grown to dislike civilization.

Renaldo thought about his teasing, clever sister; his kind, generous brother; their sarcastic and strong oldest brother. He thought about their dinners accompanied by laughter and stories, about his parents sharing their love for one another so openly. He thought about Garrison answering with grunts and nods if he bothered to answer at all. He thought about Garrison's harsh ways with the wild mustangs of the prairie, even if he did manage to bring most back in one piece, and worried that spending time with such a man would sour his love of their life out on the prairie, would steal the peace and joy he felt working with horses, would ruin the simple pleasure Renaldo took from being miles from anyone as the susurration of the wind through the gamma grasses perfumed the air with cenizo and sage.

But why think about some bent, sun-hardened, surly *mesteñero* set to take him away from his twin and his family, and all to teach him something he already knew? He'd grown up around horses, had trained them himself. He wasn't looking forward to being apprenticed, trapped on the high plains with some unpleasant old horse master, and so instead he happily lost himself in the routine of the ranch and working with his brothers.

The day before the wedding, a visitor arrived at Vista Verde an entire week early. Renaldo, ready to wash up and eat dinner after a long, hard day—his side ached from roping cattle as a part of Paloma's training, his hands were full of bits of raw hemp from the stock lassos, and one of the calves had kicked him high on the thigh—walked back from the barn using his hat to slap at the dust on his chest and thighs. He noticed a tall, striking young black man standing at the door to their home speaking with their father. They didn't see many black men this far from civilization—with the Civil War ending so recently, many were staying close to where they'd been forced to live, were heading far out west where there were more opportunities to make a new life or were going north seeking less hostile society. Who he could be?

He was about as tall as Renaldo, maybe an inch or two more, broad-shouldered and whip-thin, dressed in well-worn, simple clothes. He had a close-cropped beard, but instead of hiding the shape of his jaw, it accented its sharpness. His light eyes, almost luminescent even at this distance and glowing like amber, were ringed with thick lashes, nearly to the point of being girlish, but there was nothing feminine about the man. With his lean but strong-looking chest, muscular arms and curved backside, he managed to carry himself with a confident air while standing idly; his body was still, but in a way that made Renaldo think of a raptor sitting on an abutment, watching and waiting.

"Oh, here he is," Estebán said, motioning for Renaldo to join them, saying, "*Señor* Burnett, allow me to introduce to you my son, Renaldo."

This? This was the legendary *mesteñero*, Henry Burnett? He couldn't be much older than Renaldo, who realized his jaw had dropped. He closed his mouth quickly and moved toward them as if drawn like metal shavings to a magnet.

Burnett, however, looked amused, as the edge of his mouth quirked up. "Pleased to meet you," he said, his voice deep and husky.

Renaldo couldn't look away, shocked that his expectations couldn't have been more wrong. This was a vibrant young man. But... *this* was the man he would be alone with on the prairie for months? His stomach twisted at that thought, and at how unexpected it all was, causing his heart to race and face flush. Yes, it was unexpected. That Burnett had come so much sooner than they'd expected had to be why Renaldo couldn't find his voice and felt so upended.

"*Mijo,*" his father said sharply.

Renaldo shook himself slightly, and then nodded, saying, "*Señor* Burnett, it's very good to meet you, finally. Please forgive my shock, as I don't believe we expected you so soon."

Burnett laughed, a rolling, melodious sound, and replied, "Well, then just imagine my shock when I come here all the way from Nacogdoches expecting one Valle man, only to find him gone and you in his place." He smiled. "Your *padre* seems to think you're a better match, so that works for me."

That smile, bright teeth framed by full lips, eyes crinkled at the corners, helped lessen some of Renaldo's shock and, if he was being honest, some of the worry that he carried about spending a lot of time with a hard, taciturn man Renaldo knew he would be unable to please. At the realization that *this* was who he would be with on the plains, just the two of them with no one else for weeks on end, Renaldo became excited, finally looking forward to this task. A young man with an infectious grin wouldn't be such a chore to be stuck with after all.

Except, that was just it. He was a young man. He couldn't be older than Renaldo, or not by much. And while it was a pleasant shock not to be confronted with a wizened, grumpy old Anglo, he still didn't understand what this young man could teach him.

"Pardon my asking," Renaldo said, squaring his shoulders. "But you don't seem old enough to be worthy of the legends my father has told me."

"Renaldo!" his father said. "*Señor,*" he pleaded to Burnett, "please forgive him. It has been a trying stretch of time here—"

"No need," Burnett said, smiling, yet not as easily as before. "Your son here ain't the first to question me, ain't gonna be the last."

"*I* am not questioning you," Estebán emphasized. "I am well aware of your talents and hope you can pass on your gift in any capacity to my son."

"Well, I'll sure try," Burnett said, sizing Renaldo up. He huffed an amused noise, and then asked, "*Señor* Valle, is there a place where I could wash up?"

"Of course, of course," he answered, motioning toward the house. "Renaldo will see to your horse," he added, fixing Renaldo with an irritated glance while tossing the reins toward him. Estebán climbed onto the porch, opened the heavy front door, motioned for Burnett to enter. "And of course you will be our guest of honor at my son's wedding…"

Renaldo watched Burnett turn away and enter their house without a single backward glance, his gait sure and his shoulders proudly set, nothing like the hunch-backed lope of Tom Garrison.

He was nothing like Renaldo had expected, but then, nothing this summer seemed to be what any of them had expected.

"AND AT NAVIDAD, THE PRIEST will come and bless your marriage properly," Juana Maria chirped to Patricia, patting her hands. Renaldo twisted on his mount to look at his mother, Hortencia, Calandaría, Patricia and her mother and sister riding in the wagon, with faces ranging from pleased, to bored, panic-stricken and elated, in that order. Patricia's face was covered by an ornate veil, one her mother Antonia claimed Sister Margarita of Jesus had once touched.

Renaldo, Henry Burnett, *Señor* Flores and Estebán accompanied them on horseback, all headed to the presidio. He could see Eduardo and Francisco where they were mounted, bringing up the rear of their procession.

There were no longer Franciscan missions in the region, not after many wars had torn through the countryside, so Francisco and Patricia would have a civil service at Fort Clark, and appease both mothers by having it blessed properly by a traveling priest this winter.

Renaldo did all he could to stay out of the way yet keep an eye on his family as they passed through the gate of Fort Clark; it was a bustling marketplace as well as the home for almost two hundred soldiers. The group was directed to the private quarters of Captain John Wilcox, who greeted the fathers with handshakes and smiles and offered small bows with enough flourish to please the mothers.

"Feel like I've been dropped into some big city," Burnett murmured, startling Renaldo with his proximity. "Bit too busy for me."

"Ah," Renaldo said, flustered. "Yes. For me as well." He kept his eyes on how Calandaría held Patricia's long skirts off the hard-packed ground, catching how his twin's eyes darted to him and to Burnett, he presumed, before Renaldo turned forward once more.

"He isn't who she wanted, is he?" Burnett said again, leaning close enough that Renaldo could feel the warmth from his body.

Renaldo looked at his brother, standing a respectable distance from Patricia at the ornate desk where the captain was filling out their marriage certificate. Francisco kept cutting his eyes to Patricia, and even with those brief flashes of his profile, Renaldo could see the nervousness on his brother's face, the determination to make things right.

The captain indicated that Francisco could raise Patricia's veil, pronouncing them man and wife. Juana Maria and Antonia cried and held one another, and Renaldo watched as Patricia, stiff and frightened, relaxed ever so slightly as Francisco, instead of kissing her lips, took her hand and kissed the back of it passionately.

"No, he isn't. But it doesn't matter," Renaldo whispered back, shaking his head.

"Doesn't it?" Burnett replied. And seemingly to himself, he muttered, "Seems like that's the whole point," but said it just loud enough that Renaldo was able to hear. He wondered about that the entire ride back to Vista Verde.

Back at the ranch, Renaldo excused himself from the noise inside the house as the men congratulated themselves and the women fussed over Patricia, who seemed far more relaxed as everyone petted and praised her. He wandered out to Paloma's stall, where she greeted him with a whinny and friendly nicker. He let her snuffle all over his hair, looking for the sugar cube she knew he had for her.

"She's a beaut."

Renaldo startled once again, turning on his heel to find Burnett standing in the shadows, rolling a cigarette. Belatedly he realized that Paloma hadn't startled. "What are you doing here?"

"Didn't seem like that celebration was the right place for me," Burnett said, eyes on Renaldo as his tongue darted out, deftly wetting the paper and pressing it back. "I'm more comfortable with these folks, anyway."

Renaldo huffed out a laugh. "You mean the horses?"

Burnett grinned, his teeth brilliant, pushed off the wall and strolled outside. He lit a match off the heel of his boot and took a deep draw from his cigarette, its red glow prominent in the deepening twilight. After a moment, he asked, "That horse like you when you two met?"

Renaldo flashed on his father bringing a wild foal to the ranch, fighting and pulling on her lead, voicing her displeasure at being taken from her herd. His father had been as gentle as he could, smiling at her long legs and laughing at her spirited kicks. "She'll be good for you, *mijo*!"

At sixteen and about the same proportion of limbs to trunk as the young horse, Renaldo had climbed into the corral, smiled and stood completely still as the foal snorted, her ears high and forward as she took him in. She'd feinted and charged him again and again until finally walking around him in a careful circle, smelling his armpit, his chest, his ear. He'd held his hand out until she became curious enough to lip at it, allowing him to scratch her nose and rub the side of her face.

"She wasn't sure about most people," Renaldo said to Burnett, smiling at the memory, "but she was about me."

Burnett looked back at the house, took a deep drag from his cigarette, nodded and stubbed it out.

"That's good. I prefer 'em liking me right off, too, but sometimes you have to gentle them into believing they can trust you. If you have to force 'em, they'll fight you the whole way. You'll never be any good together."

Renaldo heard the loud sound of his father's laughter from inside the house, followed by the sound of a toast. He wanted to support his brother, but the thought of being in that noise, seeing Patricia's mother as she preened over marrying her daughter off to a wealthy family by any means necessary, watching Francisco's hopeful glances at his unwilling bride—and no doubt the unhappy looks she'd return—kept him rooted to the spot.

"Yep," Burnett sighed, looking up at the stars as they came out in winks and blazes. "It's never a good idea to force it."

"BUT I'VE LOST TWO SONS already! You can stay one more day," Juana Maria cried, fussing with Renaldo's hair and cupping his cheek.

"Mama." He laughed, carefully pulling her hands away from his face and kissing them. "You didn't *lose* Francisco! He's out with Papa culling the sheep."

"Oh, you know what I mean," she said, swatting at his arm and turning to Henry Burnett, seated at the long table with a cup of coffee, saying, "You can stay one more day. Could use some fattening up, I think." She nodded as if it was decided.

Burnett watched her bustle about the kitchen, and then pushed to standing, taking the remaining breakfast dishes to be washed. "Ma'am."

"Such manners!" she replied, grinning and scraping the plates. "Him, I like. You may stay as long as you'd like, *Señor* Burnett."

Burnett chuckled, a deep rolling sound that made Renaldo's insides twist pleasantly.

"She's right about fattening us up," Burnett said, handing over the last of the dishes and calling over his shoulder to Renaldo. "I've put out some provisions for us along the way, but you never know who might find those stashes before we get to 'em. Eat your mama's cooking while she's still willing to make it for you."

"*Señor* Burnett, you will take care of my son, won't you?" Juana Maria said, laying a hand on the man's forearm to look deeply into his face. "I don't even know how long you will be gone!"

"Well," *Señor* Burnett said, rubbing the back of his neck and looking sheepish at Juana Maria's intensity. "We'll be gone a spell. Prob'ly a few months. We'll take our time crossing the high plains until we get up near Colorado Territory. That's usually where you can find the mustangs 'bout this time of year. They're just about all that's out that way, if you're worried about us running into... less friendly sorts of folks."

Renaldo felt a thrill go through him. Never had he been out on the wild prairie for so long. He was excited, yet also terrified, at the thought of being out on the harsh plains, baking in the sun with nothing to eat, no water to drink. But surely Burnett had done this enough times that he had a system?

"I'm holding you personally responsible for my baby's life, *Señor*," Juana Maria scolded.

"Ma'am, I understand completely," *Señor* Burnett replied, his voice solemn and sincere. "He'll be safe with me. Not much out there but scrub brush and dust, anyhow."

Renaldo's mother smiled at him and pressed a cookie into his hand, shooing them out of the house.

Burnett took inventory of the horses he thought would be best for Renaldo to bring; they would each need a spare horse to change out riding in order to keep them from getting too tired. Francisco brought over a tobiano on a lead; the white, round markings down her neck and across her back were striking against her chestnut body.

"Abuelita is a good choice," Francisco said to Burnett, nodding toward the horse. "Gentle, good instincts."

"Abuelita?" Burnett asked, looking between the two brothers.

"Little grandmother," Renaldo said, grinning and running his hand along Abuelita's copper flank. "She mothers the other horses and watches out for the foals. *Gracias,* Francisco."

Francisco nodded. Renaldo noted that he looked tired, as if he hadn't slept. Renaldo wondered if Francisco had slept outside to keep Patricia happy. Given the dark circles under his brother's eyes and his rumpled clothing, he assumed so. He gave his brother's shoulder a squeeze.

"That's good thinking," Burnett said. "Could help us out there. *Gracias.*"

The brothers looked at each other, amused at Burnett's American-South accent as he attempted to pronounce Spanish. Burnett caught that, rolled his eyes and took the lead, walking Abuelita to where she could join his horses in one of the corrals.

"Be good, eh?" Francisco said quietly, ruffling Renaldo's hair with a wry grin that didn't quite meet his eyes, and headed off to where his work horse was tethered. Renaldo watched him swing up easily and ride to meet their father where their sheep were grazing.

After a day of working the animals, and then packing rope, blankets and sundries for Renaldo to leave the next day, the men all fell ravenously to their dinner. Silvestre was gone and Patricia had not joined them, so dinner was far more relaxed than it had been of late. Calandaría looped an arm through her twin's, asking him to join her for a walk shortly after *Señor* Burnett had thanked their mother and left to have a smoke outside.

"I'll miss you," she said softly, leaning her head against her twin's arm.

His eyes stung, so he blinked rapidly to dispel the sensation. "I won't be gone forever, just a few months."

Calandaría clutched at his bicep, her voice trembling as she said, "I know, but we've never been apart from each other before."

He cleared his throat, looking up at the sky as the stars came out. He didn't even know who he was without his brothers at his side, let alone without his twin.

"Are you afraid?" she whispered.

"No," he replied, drawing out the word as he allowed himself to think about it. "Nervous, excited, a little worried about us not being able to find water or food... maybe never finding the *mesteños*, or angering *Señor* Burnett, but I don't think I'm afraid."

She nodded. "That's good. I'm glad, *cariño.*"

He rubbed his hand up and down her back and felt her begin to shake.

"Because I am," she said, her voice soft and wavering.

"But why?" he asked, turning and holding her by the arms so he could see her face.

"I don't think anything will be the same when you come home. And … I don't think I want to meet this man of Mama's."

He pulled her into a hug. "But what if he's the most handsome man you've ever laid eyes on? What if he thinks you are the most beautiful woman he's ever seen? Mmm?" She sniffed, so he rubbed her back some more. "What if he thinks you're the cleverest of women and values your thoughts? Calandaría," he said, pulling her away again and bending down so they were eye to eye, his heart clenching at the tears on his twin's face. "What if he loves you?"

She inhaled slowly, shaking and with trembling lip, and replied, "But do you think anyone *could?* Mama says I'm so coarse and—"

He scoffed to stop that line of talk. "Of course I do, *chiquitita*. And you're just as you should be. Any man who cannot appreciate that doesn't deserve you."

They stayed there for several moments. The only sounds to be heard were the horses whickering to one another in their barns and the plucked-string noise of bronze frogs calling for lovers to join them on the banks of the spring. It seemed impossible that he would leave this place that he loved so much. He began to understand why Calandaría was so upset.

Turning to him, she wiped her cheeks with the edge of her *rebozo* and plastered a smile on her face. "At least I'll know that you'll be in good care. *Señor* Burnett seems to be a good match."

Renaldo looked off toward the southern barn where Burnett was keeping his horses and where he had insisted on bunking. "I think our personalities will match well."

She snorted. "Yes, I think more than that will match."

"What do you mean by that?" His stomach twisted for some unknown reason.

Before she could answer, Burnett stepped out of the barn with a cigarette between his lips and his shirt open, exposing his lean chest. As soon as he saw the twins standing there, he muttered something to himself and turned away, doing up his buttons.

"Apologies, miss," he said, nodding at her without making eye contact. "I didn't know any of you ladies would be out here this late."

She laughed, though. "With four brothers, I can assure you, señor, that this was the most modest of accidents."

"Still," he said, rubbing a hand over his closely shorn hair.

"Don't you have any sisters?" she asked.

He studied her as he lit his smoke, shaking out the match and flinging it far away. After a moment, he shook his head. "No."

Calandaría asked, "Any family? Here or maybe back east?"

Burnett kicked the heel of one boot onto the ground as if he was knocking off mud while tapping off the ash from his cigarette. "Only family I have left are with the *Natages*. 'Course, I'm only adopted, but they were good to me."

The twins looked at each other. Finally, Renaldo asked, "*Natages*? Mescaleros? You lived with—"

"Kiowa, at first," Burnett answered, cutting Renaldo off, but not with impatience. "They traded me off to the Apache when I was about fourteen. Could have been worse; they could have sent me to the Comanche. Lot rougher to outsiders, and living out here you'd know that pretty well, I'd expect."

Renaldo cringed at the thought of being traded at all, as if Burnett had been nothing more than livestock. It must have

61

shown on his face as Burnett chuckled in his warm, rolling way and said, "No, it's not like that. Kiowa found me when I'd just turned thirteen, helped me out of a tight spot and cared for me. Lucky it'd been them; a band of Comanches had just come through on a raid, killed a few people. The People call them Aná Tiúnî, Many Enemies." He tapped off the ash and said, "I proved valuable to the Kiowa, so they sent me off with the Apache for training, got themselves a healer in return."

He took a long draw off his smoke, blew it away from the side of his mouth and said, "'It's about the same as I'm doing for you, the training. Except we'll make sure you get home where you belong, and I'll have some coin in my pocket from your *padre*."

Calandaría didn't seem to find anything amiss with this tale, as she asked, "You lived with the Apache? Is it true they let their women choose their husbands and get rid of them just as easily?"

"I don't know that there's anything easy about getting rid of someone, especially if they're determined to stay," he said, winking at Renaldo, which sent off what felt like a multitude of butterflies in Renaldo's stomach. "But they don't have as many rules as other folks do. They have 'em, just not the same."

Calandaría took a breath that Renaldo knew meant that she had about a thousand more questions for him when Burnett stubbed out his cigarette and nodded at them. "Got an early start in the morning, so I'm going to turn in." He nodded at Renaldo, and grinned at Calandaría, tipping a non-existent hat. "Ma'am."

"*¡Buenas noches!*" Calandaría cried out, twisting on her heel as if she could peer into the barn from where she stood.

"Well!" she exclaimed, beaming up at her brother.

Renaldo had no idea why she looked so smug. "That was incredibly rude to pry into his past. You don't know what he may have been running from to end up out here," he chided. That would explain why *Señor* Burnett had told Juana Maria that he wasn't worried about who they may run into out in the vast, empty prairie—he'd lived with the Mescalero and Kiowa.

"He's fascinating!" She sighed, looping her arm through Renaldo's and dragging him back to the house. "And he seems to be eager to get to know you," she said, her voice bright and amused. "He's very interested in how you look."

"W-what?"

"Haven't you noticed? His eyes never leave you when you're in the same place."

"That's… well," Renaldo said, grasping for what on earth his sister was driving at. "But of course he's going to want to get to know me if we're going to be stuck with one another for weeks on end." Renaldo had had the same thought. He wanted to know everything there was to know about *Señor* Burnett, especially why Renaldo continued to experience shortness of breath and excitement at the thought of them all alone on the prairie for weeks on end. Excitement over the training, surely. It was thrilling to think of being on his own for the first time; that was all.

"Precisely my point. I think I'll be able to endure missing you for the sake of all the stories you'll have for me when you get back." She laughed, producing an incredibly unladylike snort. "Well, hmmm. Maybe not *all* of your stories, *bobo*."

"What are you *talking* about?"

She glanced at him before they climbed the front porch. "I— Hm. You don't see…?" She stopped, chewed her lip and then glanced up at him while shaking her head. "I suppose it just might be possible that you may not have those stories for me after all, which would be a shame…"

Her gaze turned scrutinizing, staring deeply into Renaldo's eyes. She must have found whatever she was looking for, since it softened and her shoulders dropped slightly. "Maybe you just need to be away from all of this to see."

"See *what?*"

"Just remember what I told you," she said, her hand on the front door knob. "No matter what, you are a part of me, *cariño*, and I will always accept and love you."

And with a brisk kiss to his cheek, she swirled into the house, leaving him standing there wondering what on earth just happened.

CHAPTER FIVE

"EACH ONE OF YOU WHO leaves me is tearing a piece of my heart out," Juana Maria cried, fussing with Renaldo's hair and collar as they said their goodbyes just outside the house. Hat in hand, he quietly endured it, knowing how hard it was for his mother to have yet another child leave.

"I'll be home eventually, Mama," he said, kissing each of her cheeks.

"Juana Maria, *mi amor*," Estebán chided, coming from the barn. "He's a grown man. Leave him be."

"*You* leave me be!" she said, dabbing at her eyes with a handkerchief. "Silvestre, now Renaldo, and soon Calandaría will be married... Who knows where my family will be scattered in a year's time?"

Calandaría rubbed her mother's back as their laughing father pulled Juana Maria into his arms, shushing her gently and kissing her. Francisco, there to see his brother off, nudged Renaldo's shoulder. Renaldo noticed that the smile his brother offered still didn't manage to meet his eyes, and that Francisco appeared diminished, drained and tired and less energetic than he normally would be.

"Mama! You didn't make such a fuss when I was sent to San Antonio for *universidad*," Eduardo teased.

"Because I had four other babies needing my care," Juana Maria mumbled from their father's chest, who was now rocking his wife side to side, singing her favorite song softly and smiling into the heavy braid she wore wrapped atop her head.

Renaldo, remembering with a flush of embarrassment that they had a guest present, looked to Burnett to see what the man made of this scene only to find him out of hearing range with his back turned, kicking at small rocks on the ground, hands jammed deep into his pockets and hat pulled low. Realizing that he looked very childish with his mother fussing and crying over him, Renaldo was glad to be off, glad to be away from Patricia's rages and Francisco's sorrowful eyes following her wherever she went, and from his mother's overzealous affection.

He could be free of it for a while, free to stop worrying about everyone and have time to focus on himself, to learn a valuable trade from a respected man. It was exciting to think of having a little peace and quiet for once. He was under no illusions that roughing it on the prairie would be easy, but he finally felt that he was ready to experience new adventures. Watching Burnett walk off to where their horses were corralled gave him a thrill for what was to come, even if he was still slightly mortified by the thought of what Burnett must be thinking of him.

His mother took him by the upper arm, tugging him to kiss his cheeks again. He smoothed away the tears on her face with his thumb. "Mama. Please don't cry. I'll see you soon."

Juana Maria nodded, turned briskly on her heel and flew back into the house.

"Oh, let her have her cry," Estebán said. "She earned it." He then pulled Renaldo into a hug, clapping him on the back before holding Renaldo's face in his hands, giving it a little shake side to side. "I expect you to be your best, you understand?"

"*Sí*, Papa."

"And no matter what you may think, *Señor* Burnett is a great man, and he has much to teach you. I have the utmost respect for him and will not stand for you back-talking him."

"Papa!" Renaldo cried. He'd never talked back to anyone in his life, not even Silvestre, who had so often deserved it.

His father nodded grimly. "Very well, then. I love you, *chiquito*."

"*Te quiero*, Papa," Renaldo replied.

"Go on, now. You do as you're told and you'll do just fine."

His heart clenched momentarily as he watched his father's bent yet still strong body lumber off and his brothers nodding and calling out, "*Hasta luego, hermano*," as they, too, headed out for their work. His breath caught painfully in his throat at the sight of Calandaría standing on the porch, clinging to the support post as if it was all that was holding her up; her smile was watery and wavering, yet still there.

"*Te extrañaré muchísimo*," she said, knuckling away the moisture under her eye.

He tried to swallow the hot lump choking him. "I'll miss you, too," he replied. "But I'm only leaving for a short time. I'll be home before *Navidad*."

"I'm holding you to that promise." Calandaría laughed suddenly, turning back to the house as if she could hear something inside. "You better go, or Mama will come and drag you back inside, swaddle you up and rock you to sleep."

He laughed, glancing down at his boots and nodding. He couldn't look at her, so he donned his hat, turned and loped to the horses, finding Burnett stroking Paloma's gray-dappled neck and whispering softly into her ear. Paloma, who usually didn't tolerate anyone touching her except Renaldo, stood perfectly still with her head pushing up into Burnett's touch.

Burnett said something else to her, then adjusted the pack draped across her back, and Paloma whickered happily, nodding her head. Renaldo approached her, but she turned toward Burnett's retreating back and followed him, lipping at his ear and burying her nose under his armpit.

Renaldo went completely still, his hand outstretched for Paloma's lead. He didn't know if he felt amazement at Paloma's ease with a veritable stranger or jealousy. He shook his head and swung onto the saddled Abuelita. Burnett, mounted on his own buckskin, a pretty mare named Lady, tossed Paloma's lead to Renaldo. Burnett already had his pinto, Cloud, standing patiently at his right side with its lead temporarily dallied to the pommel of Burnett's saddle.

"You ready?" he asked, eyes cutting back to the house and then back to Renaldo. Renaldo could see no judgment of the emotional send-off his family had given him or for the moisture he could still feel stinging his eyes. He nodded briskly. Burnett nodded back, then clucked his tongue to get their small *remuda*—their mounts and their change in horses—moving.

Burnett took off at a brisk pace; their horses' hooves thundered across the late-summer hardpan with ease.

"We'll take our time finding a good place for the horses to cross Río del Diablo," Burnett said. "No offense meant, but the part closest to your house I hear is skunky, so I want to get to where the ladies can drink their fill before we hit the plain."

Renaldo laughed, earning him a slightly irritated look from Burnett. "No," Renaldo said, waving his hand in apology. "It's just that I'm glad to hear it worked." At Hank's continued look of confusion, Renaldo added, "That people believe the water to be bad here."

"What do you mean?"

"With all the Anglos moving out west, the wagon trains coming through, people letting their cattle graze on private land like ours," Renaldo said, "Eduardo had the idea of saying to folks in town, to the people he sells his longhorns, that it's so very unfortunate that the mineral springs and the creek at the north end of our grant lands were sulfuric. Completely nonpotable, can't even get near it without our eyes stinging and the cattle stampeding to get away."

Renaldo laughed to himself. "He really played up how much of a trial it was to move to the south, which of course is where the public lands are closer to the Rio Grande."

"So, you're saying they're not?" Hank asked, scratching under his hat.

"Not at all. In fact, it's perfect. There's a hidden falls that has the most beautiful, amazing water I've ever seen or tasted. But don't tell," Renaldo said, grinning. "The last thing Mama needs is a bunch of strangers asking to stay on our land and water their herds if Papa and my brothers are away tending our animals on the prairie."

Hank seemed to think that over, and nodded. "Then we'll cut straight north." The corner of his mouth crooked up in a grin. "That's real smart. Helps your mama, and sister, too, I expect."

They took their time watering the horses when they reached one of the tributaries of Devil's River, cut across at a narrow bank a mile east of where the river rapids could be deceptively treacherous, and began to travel northwest through the canyons. When they began climbing from the fecund lands along the hidden natural springs and onto the grass-covered tableland of the Llano Estacado, the only sound that could be heard was the metallic jingle from their saddles and the horses' hooves on the sun-baked ground.

The sun was high in the sky, the vast high prairie spread out before them, and the weather was perfect, not too hot for Renaldo's leather vest, which he wore over a fine linen shirt and union suit. He had his best hat on, light-colored to protect from the heat of the sun, and broad enough to shade most of his face. It had been a gift from his father on his sixteenth birthday; the hand-stitched handkerchief tucked into his vest's pocket was a gift from Calandaría. He adjusted it so it set just so. Propriety still mattered, of course, and his mother would have been horrified if he'd left in anything less than proper attire.

Burnett similarly looked at ease in the saddle; he wore a light brown hat with a rounded dome, his rough shirt was rolled up at the sleeves, and the X of his suspenders framed his broad shoulders and narrow waist. They'd both done without *armitas*, the short leather coverings better suited for their type of horse work than full-length chaps, although Renaldo had his rolled up in one of their packs, should they encounter rougher terrain.

They hadn't spoken much, no communication beyond nods to one another and clucks of their tongue to their horses to urge them on. At first it was pleasant. Renaldo enjoyed the peace—it was rare for him to have a moment to himself back home. But once the landscape became an endless-seeming vista of grasses, some as high as their horses' bellies (which Paloma seemed delighted by, given the way she pranced through the patches with her ears forward), he let his mind wander. Their current location was devoid of any trees or shrubs, so there were no landmarks to memorize.

With nothing else to occupy his mind, he flashed to Burnett's reaction to his family saying goodbye. Renaldo surmised that Burnett had turned and walked off in order to avoid seeing a grown man break down in his mother's arms. Embarrassment twisted his guts at seeming so immature to someone who had been on his own for half of his life; he worried that Burnett would see him as a burden, someone who couldn't do what needed to be done.

"About my family..." He said, riding up beside his partner. "I'm sorry about all of that commotion back there. They're very emotional, my mother in particular, and it can be..." He let his voice drift off, and then briskly said, "Well, I'm happy to be free of them for a time."

His sheepish grin froze at the fierce look Burnett shot him before turning back to stare at the terrain ahead.

"Don't. You shouldn't ever apologize for having people who care about you."

Renaldo couldn't think of a response, so he said nothing. And just like that, the peace and excitement he'd felt was gone. He settled into his saddle with the strong, proud line of Burnett's shoulders directly ahead.

They didn't speak.

BURNETT LED THEM TOWARD A waist-high pile of stones. As they got closer, Renaldo could see it was cemented together with dung—from the looks of it, that of cattle or buffalo.

"We'll camp about a mile west of here," Burnett said, circling the low marker and cutting due west.

Renaldo pulled his hat low to cut the glare of the setting sun as they rode in silence, save the steady clop of horse hooves. The ground sloped downward until they reached what looked like a rift in the hardpan, but was actually a gorge. Burnett dismounted and peered down, clucking his tongue at his horses to follow him as he led them to the edge. He swung back up onto Lady, twisted in his seat and said sharply, "Watch yourself, and watch that pretty girl, too," nodding at Paloma, whose ears flicked forward, as if she knew she was being addressed.

Lady stepped over the edge. Burnett easily kept his seat as she picked her way down the escarpment. Cloud followed with plenty of lead on her reata to keep the horses from trampling one another.

"You heard the man," Renaldo said to Abuelita, stroking and patting her neck. As he approached the edge, he struggled to see just where Burnett had crossed down. The dust the two animals had kicked up was nearly impenetrable. Renaldo turned his head slightly, lips pursed tightly against the cloud of dust, and gave Abuelita her mouth, letting her guide them. She stepped nervously in place, and then moved forward after Renaldo nudged her sides. The path was steep, the cutbacks turning sharply after only a few paces, so Renaldo paid out plenty of length on Paloma's reata to ensure his girl didn't get tangled up in the more cautious Abuelita's footsteps.

After several nerve-wracking moments, they made it to the bottom of the narrow gorge, where Renaldo found Burnett dismounted, hobbling his horses' front legs with softened bits of leather rope as they drank from a small natural spring.

"How on earth did you ever find this place?" he asked, slipping to the floor of soft sand. It felt several degrees cooler here, since the high, sheer walls blocked out most of the sun.

"Didn't. Other folks did, and they shared it with me," Burnett replied, unsaddling Lady and all but ignoring Renaldo. Where had the jovial, friendly man from the ranch gone? His brusque demeanor left Renaldo feeling like a burden instead of a welcomed apprentice.

When nothing else seemed to be forthcoming, Renaldo decided to follow Burnett's lead and take care of Abuelita, leading his girls to the spring before removing saddles and packs.

"You know how to make a fire? Cook?" Burnett asked, pulling small oiled pouches from one of the packs.

"*Sí*— Uh, yes, I mean," Renaldo replied.

Burnett chuckled to himself. "I know what *sí* means, and some other words besides, so you don't have to speak only English with me. If I can't understand you, I'll ask."

Renaldo smiled at that, but still he wondered what had brought on the sudden discomfiting change in his mentor. "*¡Bien! Me pregunto… ¿Puedes entender por qué estoy confundida a tu comportamiento tan brusco?*"

Burnett narrowed his eyes. "Now, don't go showing off," he said, "or I'll start talking in Jiqarilla. You ain't the only one who knows other languages."

Renaldo laughed, the sound sharp as it bounced off the sandstone walls. "Fair enough. But please, put me to work. Especially if it means we'll be eating soon."

Burnett turned back to the pack and tied it closed. "Told you to fill up on your mama's cooking, didn't I?" He tossed one of the oiled bags at Renaldo, nodding toward the switchbacks they just climbed down. "There's a notch in the cliff wall over there. Make us a fire by it; that'll keep the heat focused on where we'll bunk down later."

"*Sí, Señor,*" Renaldo said; the small grin the honorific brought to Burnett's face made Renaldo feel less like a pesky younger brother.

AFTER EATING, CLEANING UP AND getting their bedrolls down alongside the slowly dying fire, they settled in for the night. Burnett stretched out his lean frame and covered his eyes with his hat. Renaldo began pulling his boots off when Burnett made a noise.

"You'll wake up with a hell of a surprise in there if you do," Burnett said, not bothering to look at Renaldo, who paused, his foot half-way out of his boot as he looked around, worried that a snake would appear, if not ready to leap into his boot, then near Paloma. If that happened, it would leave her nowhere to run away; she might hurt herself. He rolled his eyes at himself; Paloma was far more used to spending the night outdoors than he was. And as touchy as she could be, she'd alert them well in advance of any danger.

He pulled his boot back on and tried to get comfortable on the cool, sandy ground, glanced at Burnett to catch him grinning under his wide-brimmed hat. Well, Renaldo could deal with teasing far better than having someone be irritated or even angry with him.

Renaldo took a moment to enjoy the stars as they came out; the walls of the canyon boxed them in like a picture frame. He wondered how Calandaría was faring, if Francisco was still hovering at Patricia's heels, if his mother had set out his dinner plate from habit, as she'd done for Silvestre. He wondered if it was unmanly to be so attached to his family and what someone like Burnett would think of Renaldo if he knew.

"'Night," Burnett murmured.

"Oh, yes, *buenas noches,*" Renaldo replied. It still seemed so early to him. His family was most likely playing a game of cards at their great table.

Just when he thought surely Burnett was asleep, Burnett said, "First night away from your people?"

"No," Renaldo replied, rolling to his side to face Burnett. The man hadn't moved an inch. "I spent four years in San Antonio at school when I was a boy."

Of course, he'd had Calandaría with him then, so this wasn't quite the same.

"Bet your bed was a mite comfier than this, hmm?" Burnett said, his voice on the edge of laughter.

"*Sí,*" Renaldo said, grinning. "Food was better, too."

Burnett's chuckle was low and made his belly shake.

Renaldo turned to his back, hands laced behind his head. "It is good to be away. I don't often get the chance to escape from them," he laughed, wanting to convince himself of his statement's truthfulness as much as he wanted to convince Burnett that he could do this, that he wasn't some child who needed tending. "They can be, well," he said with a laugh, "a bit oppressive, I'm sure you noticed. I'm sure it's nice to have such freedom as you do."

Burnett didn't say anything for a long time, long enough for Renaldo to realize just how foolish that had sounded. Hadn't Burnett brusquely chided him for complaining when they'd left Vista Verde? And after all, he didn't know why Burnett, a black man, called the Apache his family. Where was his real mother? His father? It was incredibly insensitive, Renaldo realized, as well as a sign that he apparently couldn't learn from earlier mistakes.

Finally, with a tight voice Burnett said, "You shouldn't talk about things you don't know, especially with us just getting to know each other."

"I'm… I'm so very sorry," Renaldo said, his face hot. "Of course it was rude of me to assume anything about you. Please forgive me."

Burnett grunted, and then said, "Better get some shut eye. That morning comes quicker'n you expect."

It was as clear a dismissal as he was going to get. It took him a while to fall asleep, thinking of the quiet man next to him and what his life must have been to lead him to where he was now.

CHAPTER SIX

RENALDO AWOKE WITH A START, possibly because Burnett had just banged a spoon against the metal coffee pot.

"You gonna sleep all day?" Burnett asked, pouring coffee beans into a small hand-crank grinder.

Renaldo stretched, yawned and shook his head. "Sorry. I'm up." It took him a moment to clear his head after standing. He looked around but couldn't see the horses.

"They're down the crick a ways. Found themselves some wild asparagus." Burnett poured the fresh grounds into the blue-speckled pot and then walked to the spring. He called over his shoulder, "Hope you like your coffee strong, because it's the only way I make it."

Renaldo nodded, grinning around another yawn. "*Gracias.*"

"*De nada,*" Burnett replied. "I like my salt-pork well done, nice and crispy, if you please," he said nodding toward the campfire, which had died down almost completely. Renaldo had his job list for the morning; fair enough.

They made quick work of eating, stowing their gear and resaddling the horses. As Burnett led their small procession to the switchbacks leading up and onto the tablelands, he said, "We'll be out longer today than yesterday, so pace yourself…" He patted one of the water-skins dangling near his hip.

He clucked his tongue, dug his toes into his stirrups, and Cloud leaped forward, her powerful body climbing up the path easily. Lady followed quickly. Renaldo leaned forward, patted Paloma's neck and said, "Let's go, *mi querida*," leaning forward as she, too, took off like a shot, whinnying and tossing her head as she chased the others with Abuelita at their heels.

Burnett led them back to the stone marker, using that to turn northwest.

After almost a full day of complete silence on the trail, Renaldo decided he might go insane if they never spoke beyond giving one another instructions, or Burnett pointing out what he considered landmarks along the dusty trail, but which seemed to be no more than piles of scree or unremarkable dry riverbeds to Renaldo. He thought back to how much friendlier Burnett had been when they'd first met and wondered what he'd done to cause such a rift between them.

Was the man *that* unforgiving of a slip of the tongue? Or… he realized with a sickening feeling, had he touched on a subject far too sensitive for someone of such short acquaintance, given how little he knew of Burnett? Renaldo was determined to repair the damage.

"Did you train Lady and Cloud yourself?" he asked, riding alongside Burnett.

"Mmm-hmm," Burnett replied, looking ahead.

Renaldo sighed. Paloma tried to edge in front of Lady where she was being ponied on Burnett's right until Renaldo pulled gently on the reins to make her stop and behave. Apparently he wasn't the only one trying to gain Burnett's favor.

"Have you had them long?" he asked, determined to have an actual conversation.

"I've had Lady 'bout three years, found Cloud early summer up near Kansas."

"Bought?" Renaldo asked.

Burnett shot Renaldo a dry look. "*Found.* She'd gotten separated from her herd; been on her own and getting panicked from the looks of it by the time I came around. I was out scouting. Me and Lady made her acquaintance, and I guess she thought we'd make a good family. Been working with her since, oh, mid-June I think it was."

Renaldo gasped. It was the first week of September. "You... *this* June?"

Burnett sucked his teeth, still keeping his gaze locked on the distance ahead of them. "Well, I guess that means the stories your *padre* told you about me just might be true after all, then, huh? How 'bout that," he muttered to himself, a pleased grin on his face.

Dumbfounded, Renaldo bounced along in the saddle as Paloma plodded along. That a wild horse could be so well behaved—saddle-broke and trained on a bit—in a few months was absolutely unheard of in his world. "That cannot be," he muttered.

"You calling me a liar?" Burnett said, his voice even, cold and on guard, his gaze piercing.

"No, no. Not at all. I'm just shocked. It took me months just to get Paloma to wear a saddle for more than a few moments."

Burnett chuckled. "I wonder if that's why your Pa thought you might could learn a thing or two."

"I don't know how it can be done," Renaldo said, his index finger firm on Paloma's reins as he directed her away from where she continued to butt in front of Lady. "It's just a shock to me, that's all."

"Well," Burnett sighed, "You not knowing how it could be done is why we're here together, I suspect." He turned to flash his teeth at Renaldo before settling back comfortably. After a moment, he said with a voice a bit softer, less biting, "It's a shock to most folks, truth be told. I do know that. And I guess that's why I keep getting work, if not for what I can do, but for folks to see if I live up to legend. Get their proof."

Renaldo's face went hot; he was glad Burnett wasn't looking at him. After a moment, he cleared his throat and said, "I want you to know that I consider it an honor to learn from you, *señor*."

"Well," Burnett sighed. "That's if you *can* learn, of course. We'll find out, though, won't we?" He clucked his tongue, encouraging Cloud to pick up her pace, forcing Paloma out of the way of Lady before the horses became entangled.

"Stop trying to make him like you," Renaldo whispered in Paloma's ear. For a second, he thought he heard Burnett chuckle.

THAT NIGHT THEY SLEPT OUT in the open near a shallow pool of water the horses eagerly drank from. Instead of building a fire, they ate jerky, some other dry goods and corn cakes.

"No sense in signaling to just anyone passing by, letting them know where we are tonight," Burnett said, dropping down to his bedroll and putting his hat over his face. "Won't get too cold up here anyhow."

Without coffee or the need to cook a breakfast, they were able to get back on the trail quickly the next morning. And so it went for several days: sometimes finding water on the prairie and stopping for the day or Burnett finding a marker that indicated where a gorge could be found, a quiet, uneventful ride along the prairie as they pushed north.

Renaldo spent those long, quiet hours studying every minute movement of Burnett's hand or foot while guiding his mounts, the gentle way Burnett and his horses seemed to understand one another, the team Burnett, Lady and Cloud had made built on respect and care. It was as if Burnett and his horses were equals, not he their master.

That must be how he gains their trust and attention so quickly.

After several days, they'd fallen into a steady rhythm, Renaldo watching and learning how to set up and break down their camp efficiently, changing horses daily, the monotony of the Llano Estacado somehow becoming pleasant for its repetitive vistas, comforting. Renaldo decided after that uncomfortable discussion with Burnett when they'd first set out that he would let Burnett lead any future conversation, if only to avoid irritating the man into an even more taciturn state.

Of course, that meant that there wasn't much in the way of conversation at all. Renaldo's hair was a wild mess under his hat from where he tore at it every time Burnett gave a single word's instruction, only to become completely silent once again.

81

Renaldo was determined, however, to prove that he could learn, could be patient.

He hoped he could continue to be patient, at the very least, but his traveling companion certainly wasn't making it easy.

One day, they rode on until the sun was well overhead. There had been no breeze the entire day, and in mid-September, it was unseasonably hot. Renaldo had given in midday and stowed away his vest, then rolled his shirtsleeves as high as they could go to find some relief. As they continued, Renaldo could see the water vapor rising from the hardpan in shimmering waves. The horses' heads began to droop as they plodded along, but Renaldo didn't want to ask if they should dismount to give the horses respite. He didn't want to appear as if he questioned Burnett's know-how, especially since, up until now, they hadn't encountered any problems.

He would wait. He would trust in Burnett to keep them alive: a litany he repeated in his head over and over as still they plodded on.

Fortunately, Burnett spotted another of those strange waist-high markers made of stone and buffalo dung, except this time, he dismounted at it. He tossed Renaldo the reins and stalked over to a squat blue agave a few feet beyond the marker. From his saddle, Renaldo could see a pile of rocks and bones, which Burnett seemed to be studying while hunkered down next to it.

Burnett pulled off his hat and used his dusty kerchief to wipe over his closely shorn hair and the back of his neck. "Well, that's a bit of a mess," Renaldo heard him say quietly.

"Everything all right?" Renaldo called, forcing Paloma to stay put. Abuelita was patiently waiting at their side, clearly nearing exhaustion.

Burnett pushed off of his knees to stand up, groaning as he did. He clapped his hat back on and walked next to Cloud, patting her neck absentmindedly and looking off into the distance.

"You might want to pour a little water on their heads," Burnett said, pulling a canteen glistening with condensation off his saddle. He rubbed its side with his kerchief before wrapping the damp kerchief around his neck, saying, "We have to go a bit farther to hit water than I planned."

Renaldo dismounted and grabbed his own canteen, watching as Burnett poured a thin trickle over both Cloud and Lady's head before holding his hand out and pouring a little water in his palm for them to drink. Paloma and Abuelita, however, didn't seem to understand why Renaldo would do such a thing and voiced their displeasure, blowing and stamping.

"Now, now, ladies," Burnett said, taking Abuelita's lead and holding his hand out for her to drink from as Renaldo poured a little water into it. "We have to get a bit farther down the trail, so you need to take your breaks where you can. We'll get you somewhere cool soon enough."

Paloma stomped in place, jerking her head away from where Burnett was trying to get her to drink, but instead of acting frustrated, he laughed that low, belly-rumbling chuckle of his. "I know, I'm a terrible guide today. My apologies, Miss."

"How much farther?" Renaldo asked.

"'Bout an hour more. Do me a favor. Go break off some of them prickly pears and bring 'em over here, if you would."

Renaldo headed to the blue agave and looked at the pile of stones and a bleached jaw from a small animal, but couldn't understand what message they were supposed to convey. They just looked like a pile of stones and bone. Behind this, though, was a sprawling prickly pear, its broad, green pads covered in wicked spikes with multiple pink "pears" growing along the curved edge of each pad. He kicked them off with the toe of his boot, and then pulled off his wide-brimmed hat and flipped the fruits into it with his shoe until it could hold no more. He carried the whole lot to Burnett, who dropped a few fruits on the ground in front of each of the horses.

Paloma ate hers quickly and started nosing Abuelita away from her pile before Renaldo whistled high and sharp. "Greedy little girl!" he chided, leaning against her side and pushing her away.

"She's been living the good life too long," Burnett said. "She forgot how hard it was to live out here with her kind."

Renaldo looked over at Lady and Cloud, who were both eating their pears quietly.

"Your pa's a good horseman and a better cattleman, but I think he indulges his horses like he does his children," Burnett laughed.

"He doesn't indulge us," Renaldo snapped. The heat, the worry about his horses, and the sweat and dust caked and baked into the cracks and crevasses of his skin left him feeling as cantankerous and prickly as a cactus. "And Paloma has always been my horse, not his."

"Is that right?" Burnett said, shaking any remaining bits of vegetation from Renaldo's hat before handing it back. "You raised her from the start?"

"Of course," Renaldo replied, slapping his hat on before taking Abuelita's reata and swinging up into Paloma's saddle. "I assumed you knew that to bother taking me on."

Burnett slowly shook his head, eyebrows knit together. "Thought you'd pitched in, is all. Huh." He didn't say anything else, just climbed into the saddle and took Lady's lead. "Well, let's head out. Sooner begun, sooner done."

They rode in almost complete silence. The day was so hot that no other animal—not even a bird or an insect—could be seen. To Renaldo, it appeared the sun stayed permanently affixed high above as they continued on; nothing changed in the landscape until they once again reached a large rift. Now, however, Renaldo could hear the sound of running water. The horses could as well; their ears flicked forward and their steps became livelier.

They made their way down to the floor of the gorge where a fast-paced stream tumbled and burbled over smooth stones. It was the first body of water they'd encountered since crossing *Rio Diablo* that was deep enough to swim in. The canyon floor was wide enough to support a variety of agave and a few scraggly juniper trees in addition to billowing feather and gamma grasses along the water's edge. They quickly dismounted and relieved the horses, their hides soaked and foamy, of their saddles and gear.

Paloma made off like a shot to the water, kicking around and whinnying happily. Abuelita, always more cautious, picked her way along the water's edge carefully and, after finding it to her liking, let out a joyous noise, her tail swishing as she drank and splashed about toward a deeper pool where the water lapped against her belly. True to her nature, she kept looking over her shoulder to keep track of Lady and Cloud, as well as Paloma.

"Hoo-boy," Burnett sighed. "Definitely time for a wash." He pulled off his boots, then tossed his hat on top of them with a supple flick of his wrist. He waded out fully clothed into the river, sank down and sighed loudly.

"Pal, I can smell you from here," he called out, kicking his feet up and floating on the surface, briefly caught up in the current, "and it ain't the sort of perfume folks enjoy. I suggest you take advantage of our present circumstances, if only for your own well-being. Or mine."

As Burnett floated placidly on the surface, Renaldo couldn't help but stare at how Burnett's shirt clung to his chest; the linen was fine enough to allow his underclothes and the darkness of his skin to show through. Renaldo blinked a few times, his heart beating as if he'd just walked in on something he wasn't meant to see. It was ridiculous to think like that, considering that Burnett clearly had no problems with his state of disarray, but Renaldo couldn't help but wonder just how one was expected to get clean while fully clothed.

He wasn't fully comfortable with the idea of stripping down to his *chones* in front of anyone but his brothers, either. As soon as he had the thought, however, he snorted at himself. If Burnett had been old Tom Garrison, Renaldo wouldn't have cared. He shouldn't care now, he decided, pulling off his boots and carefully lining them up. He glanced sideways to watch as Burnett tugged his soaking wet shirt over his head, unbuttoned the top of his union suit, and shoved it down around his waist. He then stood up, turned his back and began slapping his soaked shirt against a rock.

Renaldo was mesmerized by the many parallel, thin, dark lines that ran down Burnett's lean back, scars that resembled… claw

86

marks? Either Renaldo must have made some kind of noise or Burnett expected comment on them, as he could see Burnett's shoulders tense, his body go rigid as his back was exposed. Renaldo turned away and began whistling. Growing up with Francisco meant he knew how sensitive people could be about scars and perceived disfigurements, things people believed to be imperfections, or worse, deformities. In Renaldo's eyes, Burnett had nothing of which he should be ashamed. His body worked as it should, was healthy and strong and capable; what did it matter if there were visible signs of a hard life lived?

And as to how the marks came to be there, Renaldo would wait until Burnett chose to talk about it.

Renaldo wanted to assure Burnett that he wasn't disgusted or bothered, so he took a fortifying breath and whipped off his hat, tugged his dusty—and yes, it was more than fair to say it was smelly—shirt over his head, and untied the laces of his trousers; they quickly puddled around his ankles. He kept his union suit on, but followed Burnett's example and pulled the top down around his waist, leaving the bottom intact for modesty's sake. He grabbed the pile of clothes, tucked them under his arm and quick-stepped into the water, sighing in pleasure at how pleasantly cool it was against his sun-baked skin.

The mud sank between his toes as he walked along the shore to find his own deep pocket to soak in, laughing when he felt Paloma come up behind him to snort over his bare shoulder and sniff his armpit.

"I know, I know," he said, gently pushing her head away. "Let me bathe in peace, *Palomacita*."

"Told you you needed it," Burnett said, his eyes sparkling and the corner of his mouth twitching.

Renaldo rolled his eyes. Burnett stood in the almost waist-high river, water pouring off his chest and his trousers clinging to his body, and Renaldo's face burned with heat as his pulse quickened at the sight. He had never seen so much bare skin on anyone who wasn't his family. It was … it was simply shocking, that was all. That was the only reason he reacted in any way. He blinked, forcing himself to look away from how the water had made Burnett's union suit all but transparent; the curves of his backside were prominent and mesmerizing, the bulge in the front….

He sank low in the water, his cheeks aflame.

He had filthy clothes to tend to, so he began imitating Burnett, soaking the pieces of cloth and slapping them against a flat rock.

"Take a handful of sand and rub it on there good. It'll take out most of the dirt and stains," Burnett said, doing that very thing.

"*Gracias*," Renaldo, murmured, wading toward a patch of clean, light-colored sand.

"*De nada*," Burnett replied. Renaldo glanced at him to find Burnett striding through the water toward their gear, wet clothes on his arm. "Watch out for that mesquite tree 'til you get your boots back on," he said, nodding at where the horses were grazing near a lone tree. "Then again, some of those prickers'll go through your boot, too."

"When Calandaría and I were, oh, about six years old, I believe," Renaldo said, washing and wringing out his trousers, "we found a sprawling mesquite tree all by itself in a field where my father had planned on grazing cattle. One of the spines punctured the calfskin sole of her shoe and got twisted up into the arch of her foot."

Burnett whistled in sympathy. Renaldo smiled at him, and then turned back to his task.

"I tried to carry her back to the house, but I was too little. Francisco found us," he said, laughing sharply, "probably because of Calandaría's screaming, or no, maybe it was because *I* was screaming *because* she was hurt."

Burnett smiled at that, a faraway look in his eyes.

Focusing on the yellowing stain in the armpit of his shirt, Renaldo continued, saying, "Calandaría never cried; that was more frightening to me than anything else, even her agonized face." He shook his head to rid himself of the memory.

"Francisco carried her back to the house with me holding her hand the entire way, sobbing and terrified until we reached home. *Mi madre* made me go back to the tree by myself to scrape off the gum from the bark to make a *tintura*, a … a tincture." He looked at Burnett to see if he knew what he meant. At Burnett's nod, he continued. "I was scared of stepping on a spine myself, so Francisco let me put his boots over my own."

He smiled at the memory, how Francisco had helped pull the stiff leather over Renaldo's considerably smaller boots, ruffled Renaldo's hair and told him to be quick for Calandaría's sake.

"I can remember how quickly my sister's foot swelled up," Renaldo said, "red and hot to the touch. The tip of the spine had broken off deep inside her foot. Mama made a poultice with the gum, and I held Calandaría's hand while Mama heated up her big darning needle."

He gathered his clothes and stepped onto the soft sand, remembering how Calandaría had pressed her tear-stained face into his neck, her whole body shaking with pain as he, too, cried for his twin. He'd worried she would have to lose her foot, that

89

the grim expression on their mother's face—their sweet mother who always had nothing but smiles and hugs and kisses for the twins—meant that she could not help Calandaría heal.

When the twins had been young, they'd both believed that one twin's pain was the other. If Calandaría had to lose her foot, that meant he'd have to lose his, too, and he was ashamed of how afraid that made him. His sister had always been braver.

"I think she wanted me to hurt as much as her foot did, she squeezed my hand so hard," Renaldo chuckled. "When the little bit of thorn was out, Mama wrapped her foot in a cloth soaked with the *tintura,* and I had to do Calandaría's chores for three days until the swelling was gone."

"If I didn't know how much those hurt," Burnett said, "I'd think she'd done it just to get out of work."

Renaldo laughed. "No, she's too smart to actually hurt herself."

"She sure struck me as a woman who knows her own mind."

"That she does," Renaldo agreed. "She knows her mind, to be certain. And she'll tell you that she also knows mine, and each of my brothers', our father's," he said, chuckling. "The only person who can truly challenge her is our mother. I think they both like that, even though they have their little arguments. I'm certain that if our mother would stop insisting she wear her corset, Calandaría would concede on every other issue they persistently argue about."

"I can't say as I blame her there," Burnett laughed. "I wouldn't force a dog into one, let alone a nice miss like your sister."

"We are *definitely* lucky to have been born men," Renaldo said, "if only for lack of hair pieces." He drifted off with the memory of his sister coming to the barn in order to remove her heavy artificial hair, of massaging her neck and head when she complained of a headache, of hiding her from their mother until Calandaría could put the hairpiece back on.

"You're sure lucky to have each other, you know," Burnett said, turning away to gather wood.

From the tone of his voice, Renaldo got the impression that Burnett believed Renaldo wasn't aware of just how fortunate he was. Miles away from his family, from his sister and her teasing, her encouragement and easy affection, he realized just how lonely he was, how lonely he'd been since riding away from Vista Verde. He missed her terribly, missed her hugs and smiles, missed having a connection with someone who enjoyed his company, someone who cared about him.

Renaldo rubbed at the ache building in the center of his chest. "I *do* know," he replied. "I *cannot* imagine growing up without her. My brothers were too old to fuss with us by the time we came along. Oh, they looked out for us. Francisco always took great care of us, especially when we were very little. Hmmm, but then again, Calandaría," he said, unable to help the rueful tone, "she was definitely the one who always got us in the most trouble, so maybe not having her as my sister would have been for the best. For my backside, at least."

Burnett snorted at that, and then pulled out his flint and steel from a saddlebag and hunkered down to light their fire.

"*Señor* Burnett," Renaldo began, only to stop when Burnett turned toward him, the expression in his eyes indiscernible.

"Just how old are you, exactly?" Burnett asked.

"Oh, *tengo ventiún años.* Or as you'd say, I am twenty-one years old."

Burnett muttered *ventiún* under his breath. "That's the number?" At Renaldo's nod, Burnett continued. "Since I only have

91

a few years on you..." He counted under his breath and said, "Uh, *tengo veintiséis?*"

Grinning, Renaldo said, "*Tengo veintiséis años, sí. ¡Muy bien!*"

"*Gracias,*" Burnett replied, his teeth flashing in return, "But that means you don't need to call me no *Señor.*"

"Then... should I just call you Burnett?"

"Well," Burnett said, standing with a groan. He took a deep breath and said, "My name's Henry."

"*¡Órale!*" Renaldo replied. With precise, Anglo-style enunciation, he said, "Henry Burnett."

"No, that doesn't sound right coming out of your mouth," Burnett said, shaking his head and chuckling. "It's the accent. Makes me sound like a white businessman or a politician the way you say it." He stood and regarded Renaldo before saying, "Hank. That's what I tell my friends to call me."

"Hank..." Renaldo said, grateful to be considered a friend and liking the sharpness of the nickname, the abruptness. It was immediate and piercing, fitting for someone who reminded him of a raptor.

"Now, don't puff yourself up about it, it's just a name," Burnett said, jamming a large stick into the ground next to the fire. He draped his sopping trousers over it.

"Names are important," Renaldo said, hunting for his own stick.

"Sometimes," Burnett said. "Sometimes not."

Renaldo cocked his head, not sure he understood. Burnett saw that and said, "When you're like me, the name you make for yourself means more than a name you've been saddled with just by being born."

"Is… Hank the name the Kiowa gave you?"

Burnett laughed, a deep rolling noise. Still shirtless, Renaldo could see the muscles in Burnett's chest and belly flex from the force of it. "Not hardly. They called me *ta-á-tso*, stranger. But I was, so I didn't mind it none. I like the truth of the thing in N'dee names. "

"When you joined the Mescalero? Did they call you that, too?" Renaldo asked, getting the frying pan out to start their dinner.

"Maybe get some of them screwbeans out of the other bag for tonight, if you please," Burnett said. "And they named me *It-sá*. That's what they call a hawk. Guess they heard me say 'Hank' and got it tangled up."

Renaldo tossed the finger-length, stiff screwbeans into the pan with bits of salt pork to soften them up. "It's fitting, though."

"But don't let me catch you calling me that," Burnett said, chucking a pebble at Renaldo's shoulder. "Only N'dees are supposed to use their language. Very disrespectful for folks to go butchering it like they do."

"*Bien, bien*," Renaldo replied, tipping the screwbeans—their inherent sugars now caramelized with the pork—onto a chipped blue-speckled plate. "I will only call you Hank."

Burnett smiled to himself, and then said quietly, "That's just fine."

"Or *chico. Chiquitito!*"

Burnett chucked another pebble at him, but Renaldo easily dodged it, tipping his chin toward the plate he held out, filled with the sweet and salty toasted pods.

"Thanks," Hank said.

"*De nada.*"

A tightness he hadn't realized he'd carried in his chest since they'd left Vista Verde melted at the sight of Hank's easy demeanor as he settled to eat the food Renaldo was preparing. It wasn't that Hank had been rude for these past several days, just... distant. The more Renaldo thought about it, the more it made sense; they didn't know each other, and Hank had clearly had a difficult life, far more difficult than anything Renaldo had ever experienced.

He longed to know what those experiences were and, now that they seemed to have made peace, Renaldo hoped that would be possible. He wanted to know everything he could about Hank Burnett.

"'S'good," Hank said, nodding up at him as he bit into another of the long, pale-green screwbeans, crispy brown bits of salt pork clinging to its curves. Heart light and cheeks aching from smiling, Renaldo put another piece of fatback on to melt.

This was what he'd hoped their trip could be: the comfortable teasing and companionable ease finally settling between them not unlike what he shared with his brothers.

Hank twisted, reaching for something in one of their saddle-bags; the lean muscles in his shoulders and arms were prominent where they worked and moved under his deep brown, silky-looking skin. Renaldo had the wild idea of touching him, tracing the definition in those wiry, strong arms with his fingertips all the way across the flat plane of Hank's back, wanting to know how the raised lines of scar tissue felt, wanting to know if they still hurt, wanting to know what all of that skin would feel like against the palm of his hand, how warm it would be, how smooth.

His hands shook as he realized that no, this was nothing like the camaraderie he shared with his brothers. The thoughts he was beginning to have were nothing like the way he thought about his brothers. He hadn't had those ideas about anyone since he was in school, and had assumed that all young men were consumed with lustful thoughts about anyone, male or female, their bodies in flux as they grew into adults. Those fantasies had been meaningless, hurried and dispassionate in the cover of night so he wouldn't be overheard, knowing the other boys at school did it as well.

But touching himself while thinking of general things—hands on him, faceless bodies moving in time with his—was one thing. Imagining his traveling companion and mentor stretched out upon the ground, touching him everywhere, dragging the pad of his thumb along the lush curve of Hank's lips, pulling them apart with the barest of touches and replacing his thumb with his mouth... That was another, and nothing like the mindless thoughts of sex he'd entertained as a young boy.

Was this because Hank was different? Someone new? Renaldo had never had such a visceral reaction to someone, such a desire to touch so intimately, and he'd certainly been offered an opportunity to do so with Patricia, offensive as that offer had been with Silvestre still inside her. He shut his eyes as if that would erase the memory.

With the reminder of his brother, he felt ashamed. Here he was, staring at his mentor's body, looking at Hank in the same way Silvestre had ogled women in the village.

He turned away before he could be caught out, angry at himself for being so base. He was sure that Calandaría would be disgusted with him, given her reaction to their brother's deplorable acts with not only Patricia, but the other women of their town. He shook his head and focused on frying the last of their corn cakes and wondered how quickly their clothes could dry so they could put them back on.

Thinking of Calandaría made Renaldo wonder if this was all simply because he missed being close to someone, missed how easy with affection his family was. Now that it seemed Burnett was finally opening up to him, perhaps he was just confusing excitement about getting to know someone with inappropriate desires.

Whatever the case may be, he needed to tamp it down. He was here to do a job, not put himself in an even worse position than Silvestre had done.

CHAPTER SEVEN

RENALDO HAD BEEN SO CONFUSED by his strange, lustful thoughts that he'd barely spoken beyond simple answers for the rest of the evening. Hank hadn't seemed bothered by the lack of conversation and had fallen asleep almost immediately. Renaldo had envied his ability to sleep so easily. It must have come from living on the range for so many years.

He'd been kept awake with the thought that he had no idea how Hank would react to any outward sign from Renaldo, no indication that he would welcome any overtures—or be violently disposed against them. He'd lain on his bedroll for hours, wondering why he was having such an intense reaction to this man and wondering what there was to *do* about it.

Probably nothing. Most certainly.

"You ready?" Hank asked the next morning, swinging a saddle onto Lady.

Renaldo nodded, kicking a little more sand over the last embers of their fire. There wasn't anything close by that could catch fire, but it didn't hurt to be cautious.

Paloma had followed Hank around the camp all morning like a stray dog looking for scraps. Hank's laughter as she nibbled on his hat or shirt sent vibrations along Renaldo's skin. He turned his back on the two of them and scanned their camp, making sure he hadn't forgotten anything. Their canteens were filled and tied to their saddles within easy reaching distance, the horses had grazed and been watered, and Abuelita stood patiently waiting for him, saddled and ready.

Nothing left but to move on.

When mounted, Renaldo caught Paloma's lead when Hank tossed it to him, and they continued on, following the same pattern as they'd done for days, the rising sun behind their right shoulders, the bare rock and sage-strewn caliche cap rock endless before them. Today, however, he could see distant mesas due west: purple and gray and promising, a few days' travel to reach. They were easily covering twenty-five miles a day.

"Will we reach the Mescalero Escarpment soon?" he asked, spurring Abuelita to be abreast of Hank.

Hank, sitting easily with his hands crossed on the pommel, rolled his head to the side and smiled. "Thought you'd never been out this way before."

"I haven't," he said, amused by having surprised Burnett. "But I have seen maps, perhaps you've heard of them?"

Burnett chuckled to himself. "And the answer to your question is no. We'll cut north at Sulfur Draw, stay that direction until we find our friends."

"Our friends?" Renaldo asked, before grinning. "Ah, yes, our wild friends."

"Oh, there's wilder out there," Hank said, his gaze shuttered briefly.

Renaldo didn't respond to that; he didn't know how. After a while, he asked, "And when we find our friends, what then?"

Hank looked at him over his shoulder, and then turned forward. "You remember your little lady when she turned up at your place?"

Renaldo glanced at Paloma, trying to bite Cloud's tail. He clucked his tongue at her to no avail, so he gently tugged on her reata to pull her back. "Yes," he replied. "Very skittish, all nerves."

"And you?"

"Beg pardon?" Renaldo asked.

"Were you very skittish? All nerves?" Hank asked, grinning back over his shoulder. "You know by now that horses are a mite smarter than they're given credit. And a smart animal, be it horse or human, won't want to go with someone who ain't sure of himself."

Renaldo thought on that, knowing it was true.

"So you need to know."

Renaldo squeezed Abuelita's sides to move closer to Hank once more. "Know what?"

Hank didn't answer immediately, but pulled out a well-worn leather pouch from a saddlebag and rolled a cigarette. He lit a match off the pommel of his saddle, took a long draw and said quietly, "Yourself."

A STRONG BREEZE KICKED UP dust, forcing them to pull their neckerchiefs high over their noses. As the sun began its descent, Renaldo noticed another marker in the distance ahead. Hank pulled his bandana down and grinned; his teeth were bright against his skin, which was now covered in beige and gray dust.

Renaldo imagined he looked about the same; the winds had been relentless all afternoon.

"We're getting close."

Renaldo maneuvered alongside him as Abuelita stood patiently with her head turned away from the gusts and looked down at the stone and dung pillar, noting several bones that appeared to be the leg bones of a small animal: a fox or possibly a bobcat. At closer inspection, there also was what once had been an intact bird wing, but was now broken into two sections.

"What does that mean?" he asked.

Hank circled around him and continued north, Paloma already tugging on her lead, ready to follow. "Means we're getting close."

Frustrated, Renaldo snorted and spurred Abuelita on. "But... who is putting these markers out for you?"

"Can't give away all my secrets, now can I? You wanna run me out of business?" Hank was grinning, clearly pleased with himself.

"I'll figure it out," Renaldo said, huffing out an irritable noise.

"Sure you will," Hank replied. Clearly he didn't think Renaldo would.

After a half hour or so, they came to yet another river. This one, however, was barely a trickle; the water's surface would only come to Renaldo's ankles if he had a mind to walk through it, but there was water enough for the horses to drink and to refill their canteens. An oily bloom of algae shimmered over the surface of the low, slow-moving water, leaving him relieved that he'd taken the time to bathe the night before. He could see the wisdom in taking chances when they presented themselves.

As they set up camp, Hank began asking Renaldo about Vista Verde.

"Your *padre* been out there long?"

"Since Calandaría and I were very young." Renaldo put his flint and steel away, setting a few dried sagebrush stems near the small campfire he'd just built. "Calandaría's accident with the thorn was just after we moved there from San Antonio. Eduardo and Francisco were old enough to work side by side with my father, by then. They helped him build the house, the barns, dug the canal to bring the fresh spring water to Mama's garden. It would have been too much work for him alone."

"Mmm," Hank replied, pulling out a curry comb and working Lady over; the firelight picked up the flash of metal as he dragged the comb over Lady's buckskin coat. "Were your father's people ranchers? Er, *rancheros*?"

Renaldo grinned. "*Sí. Mi abuelo* had a large ranch in Mexico, one he inherited from his father. I've been told *mi tío*, my father's brother Jorge, lives there now."

"Told?" Hank asked, turning to look at Renaldo with confusion. "You didn't know him, then?"

"Oh, no." Renaldo took their bedding and began to unroll it. "My father's brothers are scattered from central Mexico to Chihuahua, all with large ranches of their own. Most of my mother's people, the Santos family, are well-established in Mexico City's society and will not come north. But then, for a time, it wasn't safe for anyone who wasn't Anglo. Still isn't, in many places, which is why my father was happy to take the *empressario* grant in Del Rio. San Antonio was becoming very dangerous for non-Anglos."

Hank huffed out a noise of agreement and went back to work on Lady's long, black tail. "Now that I do know a little something about."

Before Renaldo could ask him about that, could press to learn more details about Hank's life, Hank asked, "Is it what *you* want?"

Renaldo looked to his companion, startled momentarily. "Why, of course!"

"Not just something you're doing because you're supposed to do it?" Hank asked, patting Lady on the rump and getting out the worn leather rope he used to hobble her at night.

At that, Renaldo paused, thinking. It was a serious question and deserved a serious answer. It was also a question he had never entertained before. He looked over at Paloma, nosing at the wild grasses along the scanty, gravelly riverbed, and to Abuelita, standing between Paloma and the open space of their camp site. He smiled, amused by their personalities and grateful for their trust.

He thought about how he'd spent the late portion of his teen years earning that trust, developing his abilities to work with Paloma, wanting to give her the very best training, and he knew with certainty.

"No," he replied. "I cannot imagine another life. And I don't want to," he added, looking Hank directly in the eye. "This is what I'm meant to do."

Hank nodded, seemingly pleased by that answer. "We should meet up with a herd in about three days. They've settled in a valley not far from here."

"Oh?" Renaldo asked, intrigued. "Is that what your stones and bones have told you, then?" he added, waggling his eyebrows in a cheeky way.

Hank shook his head and banked their fire to keep it burning low and steady throughout the night. Dusk had fallen, the wind had dropped off to a light breeze, and the sound of insects was a pleasant backdrop to the calm evening. "You ain't gonna figure it out on your own," he said.

"We'll see."

Hank snorted, kicking Renaldo's boot as he passed to hobble Cloud; Lady was well-situated at a clump of grass. "You're darn right we will. *You* will."

By the time they'd settled in for the night, the only sounds to be heard were the horses quietly whickering to one another and the occasional questioning hoot of a distant owl. Renaldo lay on his bedroll, looking up at the stars as he was wont to do, and thought on how things had changed between them, how Hank had decided after some sort of test that Renaldo was worth speaking to, and he realized how one-sided the questions had been.

Emboldened, he asked, "How did you know that *you* had made the right decision to work solely with horses?"

"Just knew," Hank replied, his voice muffled by his hat, placed over his face for sleep as was his usual pattern.

Renaldo rolled his eyes. He decided to try Hank's tactic. "And how do you know it's not just something you believe you're supposed to do?"

There was no reply.

"If we're going to work together," Renaldo gruffed, "then it needs to be equal, don't you think? *We* need to be equals."

There was nothing but silence from Hank for several moments. Just as Renaldo was working himself into a fit of pique, Hank cleared his throat and said, "From the time I was able to speak, I've lived with horses. Lived," he said, pulling his hat from his face and fixing Renaldo with an intense stare. "Horses never judged me, never wanted anything from me other than basic decency. We have an understanding," he added with a nod. He put his hat back over his face and crossed his arms at his chest once more.

Renaldo asked, "What is it that you understand about each other?"

Voice muffled by the worn felt of his hat, Hank answered, "That we're all trapped in something larger than ourselves, so we need to find folks who'll leave us to make our own choices as much as we're allowed. That's what wild herds are, you know, chosen families. They're not all related, and that's why it works."

No, Renaldo didn't. He only understood the ordered dynamic of his family; messy and noisy and on top of one another though they were, they all belonged to one another because of blood. As much as it bothered him at times, he'd never felt *trapped*. He'd never felt as though he wouldn't be able to choose something different for himself, if he'd even had the *thought* of something different.

Something stuck out, though, so he asked cautiously, "Why did you live with horses at such a young age, Hank?"

Again, for several minutes Hank didn't speak. When he did, it was with a voice of finality. "Because I couldn't be with my real family if I wanted to stay alive. So I made one for myself." He shifted, then said, "'Night, Valle."

"*Buenas noches*," Renaldo replied softly.

"WHY DON'T YOU EVER TALK about that brother of yours who was supposed to come with me?"

Renaldo wiped off his mouth, capped his canteen and slipped it back into his saddlebag. It was getting to be late in the afternoon and the air was still, the heat oppressive. He and Hank had been mostly silent since breaking for lunch.

"Silvestre?" Renaldo asked. "Well… I suppose it's because he and I weren't close. He wasn't close to any of us, really." *Because he felt trapped, as you must have,* he thought. *Trapped by circumstance and by duty.* Even with that thought, he couldn't reconcile his brother's abhorrent, destructive behavior with the conscientious decisions Hank must have made. He couldn't imagine staid, steady and sure Hank acting recklessly.

Hank grunted, but didn't say anything more.

"Silvestre was never satisfied," Renaldo continued. "He was always looking for more. He never could be happy with what he had."

"How about you?" Hank asked. "You happy with what you have?"

Renaldo thought about their beautiful home, the peace of the springs at dawn with kingfishers darting for their breakfast, the wide grassy expanse of grazing land, the privacy from the townspeople. He'd always imagined building his own cabin on the edge of their lands, not unlike Francisco and Eduardo had done: their own places but still connected to their family.

"I can't imagine not living at Vista Verde, or at least nearby," Renaldo answered. "I don't want more land than I could manage, don't want more livestock than the land would support. I suppose the answer is yes, I'm content with what I have."

105

Hank made a noise of agreement and pulled out his tobacco pouch. "See, that's where folks go wrong. Always trying to make things bigger and better instead of smarter and more efficient-like. If you have a living that gives you enough to eat and a roof over your head, anything above and beyond that's just showing off."

"Do you have a ranch somewhere? A home?"

Hank crossed his arms and rested them on the pommel of his saddle, rocking with the movement of Cloud as she ambled along. "Nope. Haven't found just the right place yet." He tapped the ash off the end of his smoke and said, "Besides, it's not too easy for folks my color to just up and buy land. Your neck of the woods is a bit better about it than Nacogdoches or back east. Bit more open, too, sort of place I'm better suited for."

"You might settle in Del Rio?" Renaldo asked. Maybe Hank would find land near Vista Verde, or close enough to ride out for a visit on occasion. It was an exciting thought: Their nearest neighbor now was an old widower who raised sheep and kept to himself.

"Don't know. The only folks I know out that way are your family and that saddler in town, Longoria." He stubbed out his smoke with two wet fingers and slipped the butt end back into his tobacco pouch. "Haven't seen too many black folk through there. And you know as well as I do that black and Mexican ain't the same."

"I can't imagine it would be a problem," Renaldo rushed out. "My father does a healthy business with the Mescaleros, as does *Señor* Flores. The black Buffalo Soldiers have been welcomed in town without incident. The Anglos aren't as numerous back home as they are elsewhere, more Tejanos and Mexicans than anyone else, so they've had to learn to do business with all of us equally or suffer the consequences. The color of your skin won't matter there, not to us."

After a moment when it seemed Hank was thinking over Renaldo's words, he seemed to realize something. "Why don't you live with your Apache family, the Mescalero?"

"Well..." Hank took a deep breath and held it, blowing it all out in a rush. "The *Shis-Inday* were good to me, better than anyone else had been, but I didn't quite fit. They still call me *ndě-áz-dí-i*, which is like a family friend but deeper. Clan. Tribesman. Still," he said, spurring Cloud on from where she'd started lagging, "I never did fit into the role expected of me just right, so I thought I'd try my hand at living on my own and see if I could find a place where I could."

Renaldo sympathized with him, but couldn't quite understand what it must feel like to be so untethered.

"You're lucky your *padre* has gotten so well established. Helped you boys out more than you realize," Hank said.

"No, I do. I really do," Renaldo replied. He thought back on Silvestre's ingratitude, his thoughtlessness toward the damage he could have done to their father's reputation, to the sacrifices other people had to make to ensure that their family's business survived and that Patricia and her baby would be well-cared for. "I want to make him proud."

Hank looked off in the middle distance, lost in thought for a moment before nodding.

They rode on in companionable silence for some time until finding their campsite for the night. They spent extra time going over the horses, checking their legs and hooves for any damage or stress and found none. After they were finished and settled for the night, Hank asked, "So if your sister hitches up with this *hombre* your mama picked out for her, what then, you think?"

Renaldo tucked one arm under his head; his free hand rubbed at his chest where a deep ache throbbed. "I… I don't know. If he has a business that can't be moved, I suppose they'll live in San Antonio where he's from."

"No law saying a man can't go on a visit now and again."

Renaldo smiled, but it felt false. "Yes, that's true. But I wouldn't be able to often, and if she chooses to have children, neither will she."

"Does she even want that?" Hank asked.

"Hmmm?"

"Does she want to get married? Have babies? The impression I got," Hank said, his voice light and cautious, as if he was aware that Renaldo's heart felt as if it was breaking, "was that she'd just as happily strap on some six-shooters and ride the range, cussin' and tearing things up."

Renaldo barked out a laugh. "As long as she had a fine bed to retire to every night, I do believe that is the very life she'd choose for herself."

"Fine woman, your sister."

Renaldo turned to look at Hank, stretched out along the ground. Tonight he didn't have his face covered by his worn and dusty hat. Instead he was smiling up at the sky, watching as the stars came out. Was Hank… interested in Calandaría in that way? True, his sister was beautiful and intelligent, and she came from a well-established family, although Renaldo knew that Hank didn't care for things such as a family's wealth, not like Patricia's mother, at least. But the thought of Calandaría smiling up at Hank, of Hank taking her into his arms with that deep, rolling laugh of his...

Renaldo's chest twinged again, but he couldn't understand why. Of course he would want his sister to be well-matched, and Hank had proven himself to be a good man. One of the better men Renaldo had the pleasure of knowing, or at least, so far he'd proven to be so.

"Are you..." He cleared his throat. A flash of some unwelcome and sour emotion raced through him. "Are you asking about my sister because you're interested in her as a wife?"

Hank laughed, going so far as to put his hand on his belly as it heaved. "No. No offense, but I can admire a lovely creature such as Calandaría without wanting to marry her. My apologies if you thought I was being forward."

"No, it's quite all right," Renaldo said, relaxing back into his bedroll.

It shouldn't matter that Hank was or wasn't interested in Calandaría. He certainly didn't object to someone of Hank's demeanor seeking his sister's hand. His sense of control and focus was second only to Francisco, whom Renaldo admired above most men.

Hank yawned, and Renaldo shamelessly watched as he contorted himself, stretching and twisting to get comfortable, and in that moment Renaldo knew why he was so displeased with the thought of Hank marrying anyone, let alone his sister. He wanted Hank to want *him,* wanted Hank to smile and take *Renaldo* in his arms, wanted to feel the vibrations of Hank's body against his own as they laughed together, the solid warmth of Hank's back against Renaldo's chest as he held Hank close, both of them standing on a porch at night surveying the land they shared, wanted to experience it all every day and every night until he couldn't remember what his life had been like without Hank at his side. He wanted it so much his body ached for it.

But he couldn't have it. *They* couldn't have it. Or, if they could, Renaldo didn't know how. He had this, at least, this time, and he didn't want to squander a moment of it. He could enjoy what they had now, this blossoming friendship, even if it never became something more.

When his breathing had evened out, Renaldo said, "You know almost everything there is to know about my family, even the dirty secret about my sister-in-law that no one else knows, and yet I know nothing of yours. I thought we agreed to be equals?"

Hank lay there, not answering. Finally, he said in a rough voice, "I take it you want to know about my birth family?"

"I… yes," Renaldo asked. "Just what you can tell me about them, of course. I don't want to pry." He winced, realizing that he was doing that very thing.

Hank said, "Oh, no. 'Course not, because that would be rude…" Renaldo could hear the humor in his tone.

Stretching his arms above his head with a groan, Hank said, "My blood relations are all gone."

"Oh, I'm so sorry," Renaldo began, but Hank pushed on.

"Died a few years ago back in Mississippi, I heard. Only had my mother by the time I left."

"You were just a boy, right?" Renaldo asked, remembering the brief conversation between the twins and Hank before they'd left for the range.

"Mmm-hmm," Hank answered. "Left when I was thirteen. I had two sisters, me smack in the middle of 'em. The younger one didn't live a day, my older sister was sold to another plantation when she reached womanhood—that's what they call it when they get their monthlies," he explained, his voice tight and careful. "She wasn't much older than twelve at the time, so I don't know how they came to decide she was a woman, but then, nothing those people did or believed ever made much sense to me."

Renaldo couldn't speak. Calandaría at twenty-one was still considered a girl, even though their parents had decided she was just old enough to be married, should she make the right match.

"My mama," Hank continued, his voice soft and plaintive. "Beautiful woman, my mother. Skin black as night and smooth as silk, a long, graceful neck, and the sweetest face you ever saw. She kept her hair all wrapped up in these beautiful, bright bits of cloth," he said, motioning toward his own head as if he could remember touching his mother's head wraps.

"Regal, she was. She got grief for it. Some of the other ladies called her uppity for how she carried herself, but that was just her way. Mistress Burnett would come after her fierce, calling her proud, yelling about how shameful it was for her to strut around as if she was someone, black as pitch and all.

"Mama explained to her in a way that old Mistress could understand that because she was the first face folks visiting would see when they came calling, that it was a mark of how fine the house was to have someone standing tall and strong, even proud in greeting. That was the sort of thing Mistress Burnett could understand, but there weren't many. Oh, she hated my mother," Hank laughed, but it was sharp and ugly.

"What your mother said makes sense," Renaldo said, speaking carefully. "Who wants a quivering mess representing the house?"

Hank grunted his assent. "Mistress was just always looking for something to come after my mother for, looking for just the thing to toss her to the dogs."

Renaldo's hand spasmed against his chest. He knew what Hank was speaking of, wished that he didn't know what people could do to one another, and was so grateful that his family had been spared some of the atrocities committed against Tejanos and Mexicans after Texas declared its independence some decades ago.

"What Mistress hated most of all was me, of course. She got sick when she was a young woman and it made it so she couldn't have any babies. Mister Burnett… I don't know if he wanted babies or just enjoyed trying to make them," he said with a wry laugh, "but he wouldn't leave my mother be. She said she knew the moment she got to Heritage Hall that he'd be after her just as soon as the ink on her papers dried.

"Mama hid being pregnant for a good long while, almost up until she went into labor. Well, couldn't nothing be hidden then. She lied and said I didn't make it because she knew Mistress wouldn't let her keep me. Mistress had her eye on my mother, mostly, so it wasn't easy in the beginning. The other house ladies helped hide me those first few months, but Mama got caught nursing me while dusting the parlor. Well, she argued that none of her chores had gone untended, and she usually kept me hid away, so wouldn't she please let my mama keep me? If Mister Burnett hadn't been home on business hearing all their yelling, I'm sure I wouldn't be here today."

Renaldo cringed. "Then I'm glad he was."

"Thanks for that," Hank murmured. "Turns out Mama had kept me hidden from Mister Burnett, too. He knew who I belonged to, and from then on, made a point of taking care of me in little ways. He couldn't show the others that he knew about me, or they'd turn on my mama and me, say I was getting special treatment. Mama had it bad enough as it was, with all the other ladies knowing she was Mister's favorite.

"So he'd make sure I had decent shoes," Hank continued, "that I learned my letters and that sort of thing, but there was one thing that Mistress wouldn't stand for, and that was me staying in the big house once Mama weaned and trained me. So Mama stayed there and I was moved to the slave house out near the fields when I was around three years old."

Renaldo must have made a noise because Hank reached over and patted Renaldo's arm as if to comfort *him*. Renaldo wanted to grasp it, hold it in his own, squeeze it in sympathy, but he didn't.

"All the ladies, especially the older ladies past their childbirth years, looked after us little ones, so I had no shortage of mothers telling me what I could and couldn't do," he laughed. "But I was too little for real field work, so I followed the bigger boys around trying to stay out of trouble. They had me scare the birds away or pull weevils out of the cotton to keep me occupied, but Mister didn't like me out in the fields. He'd seen me combing out the horses' tails. Guess he figured I had enough sense not to get kicked in the head, so I'd have enough sense to put to better use. That's when he put me in the stables. Six is old enough to slop hogs and tend horses when they're tacked."

"You said that the Kiowa helped you when you were a teen," Renaldo said. "How... what happened?"

"Well," Hank said, stretching again, seemingly unperturbed by his story, but then, he'd lived it. "Mister Burnett always made sure I had a little extra—not much, mind you," he said, glancing over, "but more than the others had. An extra corn cake or two waiting back on my bedroll, or he'd have one of the house ladies slip me a cookie when I came to check on my mama, that sort of thing. Because of that I wasn't sickly like the other kids. I was in the stable out of the sun and heat, didn't have to bend over all day long in the field, didn't have to wear a hat all the time, so I grew pretty healthy-looking. And apparently I looked an awful lot like Mister Burnett."

Renaldo turned to his side, propping his head on his hand. As the campfire flickered, he looked his fill as Hank lay still, eyes closed as he told his story. Hank had wide-set eyes, a prominent arch to his nose, full, round lips. His cheekbones—visible above his growing scruff—were sharply defined. With the firelight flickering as it was, he could see the hollows of Hank's cheeks, a dimple on the right side of his mouth, another in his chin.

"Got the same smile, Mama told me," Hank said. "Same chin, same nose, same hairline. Evidently this—" He touched his hairline, and Renaldo could see it was almost a perfectly straight line with a small cowlick above his right eyebrow. "—is a Burnett trademark. All the men have it. It's how you can tell a Burnett brother or cousin from a stranger, the folks back home would say."

"But even with your skin's color you resemble him?" Renaldo asked. "Do you look that much like him?"

"Oh, Mister Burnett's as white as rice and I have my mama's hair because that man should be completely bald about now, but yep," he sighed. "Spitting image. Mama told me once she kept hoping my eyes would change, get darker, that maybe my face would be more round like her and her mama'd had. She made me wear a hat or a head scarf all the time, trying to hide this," he said, pointing at his cowlick.

"I assume his wife didn't care for that," Renaldo mused.

"That she did not, Valle," Hank said. "I took to hiding whenever she'd come around, just to ease her spirit, I called it, but there wasn't anything to ease in her. To be fair, her man was getting with ladies outside the marriage, and regular."

"To be *fair*?"

Hank shrugged, eyes slipping back closed. "But to be fair to *me*, I didn't see why I had to suffer because she had a cheating, no-good husband."

At "suffer," Renaldo remembered the thin scars down Hank's back.

"Did you run away, then?" Renaldo asked.

"No, didn't need to. Mister Burnett gave me my freedom when I was thirteen. It was that or Mistress was going to start taking out her feelings on Mama, and I wouldn't stand for it. It's one thing to start treating us little boys like men, punishing us like we were grown adults and not little children only eleven, twelve years old, but it's another to take that out on our mothers."

Burnett's voice was icy steel, but Renaldo was all sympathy as he listened. The thought of anyone laying a hand on his mother…

"So Mister Burnett, he come out to the stables one day just around when I'd turned thirteen, wringing his hands, all sorrowful like a damn undertaker before they get your money. He took me away from where the patty rollers were having their lunch, just having brought back some folk. He didn't want us overheard. He told me that I had to go, there wasn't nothing he could do about that, but he was going to make me a free man to make up for it. I thought they'd cat me again when I spoke up about Mama and Mistress Burnett taking a lash to her, but instead, he told me that I couldn't stay in Mississippi no more. I had to find my way on my own like a man.

"When I asked him if Mama was coming with me, he looked at me like I just said I'd seen a dog walking on his hind legs and smoking a pipe. Oh, he got all red in the face, talking about she was a fine woman, a good worker, and needed to be protected in a good, Christian home, and I knew right then that he meant she needed to be in *his* home, and that there weren't nothing Christian that he was thinking about when it came to my mother, and then I didn't want to talk about it no more."

Renaldo thought about Patricia being forced to marry Francisco against her wishes. She'd wanted a child, wanted a child with Silvestre, but both she and Renaldo's brother had been careless, reckless. And Silvestre hadn't wanted anything more than a dalliance. Silvestre wanted all the benefits of being with a willing woman and none of the responsibility that came after. He hadn't wanted to marry Patricia and certainly hadn't wanted to raise their child.

Was what their family had enforced upon Patricia not unlike the indignities the women in Hank's life had been forced to suffer? He looked upon Hank again, seemingly at peace with his hands folded at his chest, eyes closed, lips softly parted, and Renaldo wondered what Hank must think of his family.

He played Hank's words over in his head again, and frowned. "You said 'cat' you again? What *is* that?"

"It's when they strap you shirtless to a whipping pole, get one of them feral cats hanging around the barn all riled up, and drag it over your back. Kinder than whipping young boys and girls, is the thought."

"*Dios mio,*" Renaldo muttered, crossing himself. He knew that what his father considered "whipping" was nothing compared to what Hank had been subjected.

"You'll like this," Hank said, his grin bright in the darkness and out of place given the topic. "He told me once he handed me my papers that I could pick a horse for myself, that it was his 'gift' to me. Seeing as I'd hand-raised most of them, that was about as close to fair as I could expect. So I looked him square in the eye and told him I wanted Penny—that was his thoroughbred he'd brought out especial from Kentucky, just as bright and glossy-coated as a new piece of copper—because I knew he loved that horse more than just about anything. I wanted to see how much he wanted me to go peaceful-like, so I said it was the least a father could do for his only son."

"How did he take it?" Renaldo asked.

Hank laughed. "He chewed on his lip, ground his teeth, made his hands into fists so tight I thought I'd see blood dripping down. But eventually he nodded, gritted out that I made a good choice and said I needed to be gone by nightfall."

Shifting on his pallet, Hank grabbed his hat, tipping it to cover his eyes but not his mouth. He folded his hands back on his chest once more and continued. "I crept into the big house soon after and told my mama that I loved her and that I'd be leaving. When I asked some of the folks there if any of them wanted to come away with me, they all got scared. I understood why, of course, but it couldn't hurt to ask. I told Mama I was leaving on Penny, and she told me this was proof my daddy loved me.

"Daddy," he spat, snorting. "He wasn't ever that; he was Mister Burnett, and not a damn thing more. That was the only time I ever heard her call him that, and I'm glad. Turned my stomach," he sighed. "But she insisted it was proof he loved me, giving me his best horse and not letting Ole Mistress do what she wanted to me, which I guess was whip me to death in front of everybody.

"I got my papers, Mister shook my hand and told me to try my luck out West, that there were some folks even darker than me that were making their way, and then he said that he'd take real good care of my mama, so I didn't have to worry any." Hank snorted at that.

Renaldo was incensed on Hank's behalf. He was grateful that his father had moved the family to such sparsely populated land, and that those who lived there were like them: Mexican heritage and proud of thriving there for centuries.

After a few moments of quiet, Renaldo asked, "How did you end up here?"

"You don't give up, do you?" They were close enough on their pallets that Hank could knock the toe of his boot against Renaldo's. Renaldo smiled at the gesture, happy to see that even though Hank's face was still half-buried in his hat, Renaldo could still see his bright, dimpled grin. Renaldo so desperately wanted to know everything he could about Hank, about this quiet and gentle man who had come from such violent beginnings, and he couldn't seem to control his impulses where the man was concerned.

He was simply relieved that asking these invasive questions hadn't brought out another of Hank's sullen silences.

"Crossed from Mississippi into Louisiana, and only pushed on at night," Hank replied, "I slept in the swamp during the day. Oh, Penny didn't like that one bit, but the slave collectors could still get money catching and selling me—they don't care too much about paper out in Louisiana unless it's the money kind. And of course they'd see Penny and assumed I'd stolen her, and that's a hanging offense without question. They still had that big slave market out there in New Orleans, seeing as the war hadn't started up yet. There were lots of folks like me living out where you couldn't grow anything, hiding, trying to make their own way. Maroons, we call 'em."

The fire crackled, sending up a spray of red embers. Renaldo looked to see if it needed stoking, but it burned steady, its coals glowing white and orange.

"The Maroons helped get me through Louisiana," Hank said, "and by the time I got to Texas, I got caught up with a band of Kiowas. Take that to mean that they caught *me*. They took Penny," he laughed, "Oh, they took her right away as a gift to the war chief and gave me one of their wild, unbroke ponies, testing me, I think. I knew how to keep my seat even then, so they let me ride with them for a spell. They don't see thirteen as being a man, not like how the white folk see black children, and they treat their babies really well. They put me in with a nice Kiowa lady and her family to finish training me up."

"So you lived with them? For how long?" Renaldo asked, turning his head to keep his gaze on Hank. He was feeling settled; his limbs were heavy. It was very pleasant, the fire crackling, the horses making their quiet noises among one another, and Hank's deep voice as he told the story of his life.

"'Bout a year. That autumn the older boys took us young'uns up north to follow buffalo, deer, all that. They taught me how to track, how to blend in so you don't spook the animals you're hunting, how to live on what there is around you, how to make peace with the land. Then they swapped me for a healer the Mescalero had under their protection, and the Mescalero took over where they'd left off. Good people, they are. Made me feel like I belonged to them, not just trailing along."

He tilted his hat up and looked over at Renaldo with a crooked grin. "But when it came time for me to be a man—that's a whole big celebration they throw—they realized I didn't quite… fit the mold. They already had someone for the role they thought I wanted to play. And since I wasn't a true *Shis-Inday*, I couldn't be one of the *nde'isdzan*, a spiritual advisor. *Berdache*. That's what the French called them, but I don't like the word much. They say it like it's something nasty, and I don't like that, not one bit. Especially since the Mescalero don't see it as something wrong. To them, it's natural. It is to me, too."

He cleared his throat quietly, then said, "Anyhow, *Nde'isdzan* is closer to the real meaning." With a lofty and musical cadence, he said, "He who sees both ways and is neither and all."

"I don't quite understand," Renaldo said.

Hank took his hat off, pushed up on one elbow, and looked at him, the sort of intense evaluating stare that made Renaldo nervous, as if he needed to prove his worth to this man.

After a moment, Hank's gaze softened, and he said, "You don't, huh? I thought… well, maybe they don't have that word in Spanish."

"What word?"

Hank grinned, laughing softly to himself as his eyes closed again. "I think that's enough talking for today. You wore me out." He was still smiling, so Renaldo didn't take it as irritation. "We'll head out at first light."

"Hank?"

Hank hummed a, "Mmm?"

"Thank you for trusting me with... with this."

Hank smiled, knocking his boot against Renaldo's again. "Turns out you're easy to talk to, I suppose."

Pleased, Renaldo looked up at the stars, noting how the constellations were shifting as the season moved past summer and into autumn. He and Hank had turned a corner in their relationship, and he was grateful for it. Something about Hank left Renaldo wanting more: more time, more information, more conversation, all he could get.

He thought about how Hank had chastised him when they'd first hit the trail, how he'd wanted Renaldo to know how lucky he was to have the family he'd been blessed with. He thought he'd understood, but hearing all that Hank had gone through... he couldn't imagine Calandaría—brave, beautiful, willing to speak her mind—being given away as if she was a... chair, something without feelings. The thought was completely foreign to him.

The Americans' war had ended a few years before, but the repercussions hadn't. The reasons it had been fought in the first place were still evident; the people it had touched were still suffering in many ways. He looked over at Hank once more; his breathing was evening out in a way that let Renaldo know he would be sound asleep within moments. Was Hank suffering? He didn't seem to be. He was making a life for himself and on his own terms, too.

Hank didn't seek sympathy, didn't warrant pity and suffered no fools. Renaldo had the memory of his blistering silence as proof.

Henry Burnett was like no one Renaldo had ever met. He made Renaldo want to be on his best behavior, want to be respected and liked. With a pang, he realized that when this trail ride came to an end, he might not ever see the man again.

He resolved to be grateful for the time they had together, for all that he could learn. He flushed remembering how irritated he'd been when they'd first met, as if Hank's age was proof he couldn't teach Renaldo anything. Renaldo was learning more than he'd imagined, including uncomfortable truths about himself. And he had the feeling that not many people had been told Hank's story.

The fire broke apart again, a small shower of embers crackling above it. He muttered softly, "*Gracias por compartir tu historia conmigo,*" grateful for the honor of Hank's trust.

"*De nada,*" Hank murmured, his lip curling up in a grin before his face went lax with sleep.

CHAPTER EIGHT

THEY HIT THE TRAIL THE next morning bright and early. Renaldo was eager to arrive at the valley the *mesteños* were presently calling home. Hank's shoulders were loose, his smile easy and his gaze on Renaldo often. He felt warmed by Hank's regard, welcomed and accepted, and frankly, excited. It left him wondering if maybe Hank'd had thoughts similar to his.

He found himself openly staring at the long line of Hank's neck, at the prominent tendon when he turned his head, the tiny dark freckle just where Renaldo knew Hank's pulse point to be. The day was warm with a pleasant breeze ruffling the collar of Hank's shirt, enabling Renaldo to see the divot at the base of Hank's throat, how the sweat gathered there. He noted Hank's large, capable hands, how gently he handled his reins, the length of his thigh muscle as he moved his body with his mount.

Renaldo couldn't look away, didn't want to. What he wanted was to trace his fingertips along the arch of bone behind Hank's ear, which was presently secreted away by the shadow of his wide-brimmed hat, wanted to scratch at Hank's nape where his hair curled in tiny spirals, looking soft to the touch. He wanted to lay his own hand at the base of Hank's spine, feel the muscles shifting against his palm, stroke both hands up the wide expanse of Hank's back, touch the scars he knew were there, cover them with his body and show Hank that while they were a part of him, a part of what made him, they didn't define him.

Hank's kindness, his sharp eye on their surroundings, his wariness that made Renaldo feel as if he was being protected and not that Hank was inherently fearful, the physical things that made Hank a man—the breadth of his shoulders, the lean muscles in his strong arms, his deep voice, the hard line of his jaw, the round curve of his backside—all of those things were what defined him, made him the man whom Renaldo was coming to better understand, to care for. It was what made Hank undeniably attractive in every way.

And there it was, baldly stated and the truth. Renaldo was attracted to Hank, every bit as much as Eduardo was to Hortencia, his father to his mother. When Patricia had offered herself to him that strange night in August, he couldn't imagine anything less appealing, mostly because she was still in his brother's embrace. But the thought of pressing Hank against that same wall, taking Hank's hands and lacing their fingers together, holding them high overhead to feel the hot, solid press of their chests as they came together…

He adjusted himself in the saddle, shaking his head. He knew his brothers had those thoughts about women, had joked and teased one another, but it had always been foreign to him since he was so much younger. Calandaría had snapped at them whenever she caught them at it, and the memory of her chiding her brothers for being so base sobered him.

What would she think of him, knowing that her brother was fantasizing about lying with another man? Would she forgive him for wanting to act on those fantasies after being alone for weeks on end in the company of a man he found utterly fascinating?

"I could go for some of your mama's cooking right about now," Hank said, breaking into Renaldo's thoughts.

"She'd love to have another mouth to feed," Renaldo replied, spurring Paloma on to ride beside Hank once more, shaking off all thoughts of his twin's potential disapproval. "She misses being surrounded by her family, all of her brothers and sisters, their children. She told us often enough as we grew up."

Hank smiled softly, raking his fingers through the copper and white hairs of Cloud's mane. Cloud shook her head, snorting, so Hank said, "Sorry, but you have prickers in there, missy."

Cloud nodded her head, nickering softly; Hank went back to running his fingers through the rough hairs again, finally patting her neck and saying, "*Ashagoteh.*"

"What is that?" Renaldo asked.

"Means thank you," Hank replied.

"How is it again?"

Hank said carefully, "Aw-sh-eh goh-the." Renaldo repeated it a few times until Hank nodded in approval as a slow but sweet smile spread across his handsome features.

It was silly how he lit up from simple praise from this man. Ridiculous for him to hope that it meant something more than what it was. He chided himself for not being more embarrassed, but he couldn't seem to bring himself to care.

"How long did it take you to learn Apache? Or... is it Jicarilla?" he asked.

Hank laughed, "That was Apache, and I learned it pretty quickly. Same with the Kiowa. They wouldn't use any English around me. They knew plenty, but they were testing me. I couldn't eat unless I could say what they were eating."

"That's terrible!" Renaldo exclaimed.

"Nah," Hank said, chuckling. "I was thirteen, hungry, and they wanted to teach me. No better way, really. Makes for excellent motivation, a young boy's growling belly."

"How long until you were finally able to eat?"

Hank twisted in his saddle to look at Renaldo head on. "About an hour or two."

"Oh." Renaldo laughed. "I was imagining days on end."

Hank shook his head. "I hadn't eaten in a few days when they found me, mind you, so I was eager to pick it up. It helped that the women felt sorry for me and made a point of speaking slowly, raising their eyebrows and gesturing toward whatever they were feeding their family. Made it pretty easy, actually. So I learned all the food names first," he said. "They filled me up as fat as a tick those first few days. Then I spent some time figuring out who everyone was and what their names meant. By the time I was really getting good, I moved on to the Apache and had to start all over again. There aren't too many common words between the two languages."

Renaldo gawped at him. "So… how many languages do you speak?"

"Comfortably?" Hank asked. At Renaldo's nod, he took his hat off and scratched his head. "'Bout four. Need to spend more time with you to pick up Spanish proper-like," he said with a grin.

Astonished yet pleased by the thought of Hank wanting to learn something from *him*, Renaldo replied, "*Con mucho gusto.*"

Hank looked at him as though he was parsing each word, then grinned. "*Bien.* And ... how's it go? *Tengo hambre.*"

Renaldo laughed, the sound bright and joyous, reflecting how he felt. "How can you be hungry? We just ate an hour ago."

Hank had that crooked grin of his as he fussed with the hackamore in his hand. "Guess I want to learn quickly."

They rode companionably, stealing looks at one another and chuckling when caught, something that sent Renaldo's pulse racing each time. After a few moments, Renaldo asked, "*¿Como te llamas?*" then pressed a hand to his chest and said, "*Me llamo* Renaldo."

"*Me llamo* Henry."

Renaldo shook his head and clucked his tongue. "No, no. *Te llamas* Hank," he answered, biting the inside of his cheek. "*Soy* Renaldo Valle Santos. *¿Y tu?*"

Hank rolled his eyes, but played along. "*Soy* Henry 'Hank'—" he rolled his eyes once more, but the edges were crinkled with laughter —"Burnett."

"*Muy bien, muy bien.*"

"You're gonna be an ornery teacher, huh?" Hank said, leaning his weight onto his pommel.

"Me?" Renaldo asked, all innocence. "You think I, the youngest Valle Santos child, who had each one of my four siblings treat me like I was an incompetent baby, would ever lord over the ability to teach someone something they didn't know?"

"That's exactly what I think," Hank said.

Laughing, Renaldo replied, "*Muy perceptivo.*"

"Now, if you're just gonna make it easy on me," Hank said, shaking his head, "it'll hardly be any work at all, learning how to properly speak to you."

"I think you do just fine speaking to me," Renaldo said before he could worry that it sounded too bold, that it would give away the thoughts he'd had, the feelings he wished he could act on.

Hank made a noise of assent. "I think the both of us finally figured that one out."

Paloma darted ahead, and the hairs on the back of Renaldo's neck stood on end, aware of Hank's gaze raking over him as he passed.

It was a good feeling.

THEY SPENT THEIR AFTERNOON BANTERING back and forth, Renaldo teaching Hank some of the basics of the Spanish alphabet, trying not to laugh at Hank's first attempts to roll his *r*'s.

"Loosen your tongue," Renaldo said, guiding Paloma around a large sage bush. "Watch, like this." He jutted out his chin, parted his lips, and trilled his tongue in an exaggerated way so Hank could see.

Hank's eyes widened, his gaze locked on Renaldo's mouth. "Like this?" he asked, copying what Renaldo had done, making Renaldo fully aware of the sharp, white edge of Hank's teeth, the fullness of his bottom lip, the lush wetness inside his mouth...

Renaldo tore his gaze away, his cheeks hot, and he nodded, saying, "Just like that."

After a moment, Hank said, "I like how Spanish feels to say, if that makes sense? Rolls off the tongue. Fills up your mouth."

Something hot and liquid pooled low in Renaldo's gut at that. Perhaps... perhaps Renaldo wasn't the only one feeling something illicit growing between them.

Emboldened, he said carefully, "Say, *anaranjada.*"

Hank repeated it, not quite pronouncing the last syllable properly.

"Hmmm, no, you need to make the 'd' almost a 'th.' Push your tongue up against the back of your teeth. Watch," Renaldo stated, pointing at his mouth once more. "*Anaranjada.*"

Hank gave the barest pull on his hackamore, bringing Cloud to a complete stop. Renaldo followed suit. Hank looked down at his hands, nodding to himself, and then looked up under his lashes. There was nothing innocent in that gaze, and the realization of that slammed through Renaldo like a gunshot.

Hank said slowly, "*Anaranjada,*" and said it perfectly, his lips and mouth moving in a way that made Renaldo want to kiss him, want to feel the flick of Hank's tongue against his own as he spoke.

They looked at one another. Renaldo was charged with energy, hot and still and anxious like the air before a lightning strike.

"What's it mean?" Hank asked, his voice a husky whisper. All Renaldo could focus on was how Hank's tongue dipped out to moisten his full bottom lip, wondering just what his mouth would taste like. Salt? A hint of tobacco? The strong coffee he brewed every morning? Would it be strange to want Hank to sink his teeth into the fullness of Renaldo's lip, taste *him*?

Hank's throat worked as he swallowed thickly, momentarily breaking Renaldo from his dirty thoughts. "Well?" he asked.

Barely finding the breath to reply, he processed the question Hank had asked him and huffed a breath. "Orange."

"Orange?" Hank asked.

Renaldo nodded. "It's the word for the color orange."

"Well… damn. Didn't think a color could have such a… huh." Hank lightly tapped his heels to Cloud's sides and they all were moving forward again. He cleared his throat and said, "I guess you see what I mean, then. Feels good to roll it around in your mouth."

"*Sí,*" Renaldo replied, heart racing as he watched how the sharp planes of Hank's back moved under his clothes, how his shirt and union suit stuck to his skin where his suspenders crossed across the expanse of his back, how sweat made the material translucent, allowing the darkness of his skin to show through the fine material. "Although," Renaldo said, "I hadn't considered it before just now."

"Figured," Hank muttered. Renaldo wasn't sure what that meant.

"We'll make camp soon," Hank said some moments later.

That sent a thrill through him. Perhaps tonight they could talk more, could learn more about each other. Renaldo's thirst to know everything about this beguiling man was becoming an insatiable need. Most of all, he wondered how Hank would react to knowing the things Renaldo was beginning to imagine. Today had given him the idea that perhaps Hank wouldn't… be opposed. That sent another jolt of want through him, leaving him aching and hungry for something he didn't quite understand, but hoped that he would soon.

As they crested a small butte, Renaldo could see another stream below, the ground fecund with growth and trees. Up here, they were at the edge of the tablelands, near where the land drove up sharply into the mountains of New Mexico. As they carefully picked their way down the side, the horses managing to avoid the scree and slippery portions with grace, Renaldo could see a solitary figure below. He looked to Hank to see what he made of this, then relaxed at the sight of the huge smile blooming on his companion's face.

"Didn't think he'd—" Hank cut himself off, shaking his head in what looked to be happy disbelief.

"Do you know him?" Renaldo asked.

"Very well," Hank replied, his face splitting with a wide grin. He put his fingers to his mouth and gave three sharp whistles. The man in the distance replied with a high-pitched cry.

Paloma's ears were high and forward, her gait agitated as she attempted to pick up speed, trying to break into a canter and move toward this strange man, but Renaldo held her in check, not ready to trust this stranger, even if he appeared to be a close friend of Hank's.

As they neared the stream, Renaldo could see the man more clearly—he was N'dee, but from which tribe Renaldo couldn't say. The man was setting up a small camp as he and Hank rode near. He was shirtless, his flawless bronze skin on display, a slightly richer color of brown than Renaldo's. He wore only soft-looking leather leggings topped with a breechclout. His hair was black as night, falling in an almost liquid sheen halfway down the length of his bronzed back with two thin, wrapped braids framing his face. He had a strong nose, full lips, high cheekbones and wide-set, amber eyes. There was a smudge of white on his forehead and the tip of his nose. He was utterly striking, and if Calandaría had been close by, she would have gasped and sighed over how handsome the man was.

Hank slipped out of his saddle and rushed to the man, who took Hank into his arms and held him close with a smile wide and joyous. He was a bit shorter than Hank was and rested his cheek against Hank's shoulder. Each pass of the man's hand over Hank's back sent Renaldo's stomach roiling.

It wasn't that Renaldo was *jealous*. He just couldn't imagine Hank being so demonstrative. Hadn't they spent the past few weeks together, just the two of them for company? He didn't think he could recall a time when Hank had touched him. He certainly would remember if Hank had. Actually, he couldn't remember a single time when Hank had said Renaldo's *name*. He'd only called him "Valle" a handful of times. Had he actually imagined that he and Hank were close? His hands itched to reach forward, pull Hank back from this stranger who Hank was *still* holding tightly in an embrace.

He forced himself to admit it: He was jealous.

Eventually the two broke apart, and Hank held the man by his shoulders and gave him a little shake. "Didn't think you'd show yourself, you *fils de pute!*"

Renaldo was alarmed when the man caught Hank around the head, dragging him in a circle while saying something in a language Renaldo didn't understand, but when he climbed down from Paloma, who was twitching and nervous, he could see that Hank was laughing and the man smiling.

They broke apart once more, and Hank pulled his clothes back to rights. "Sorry about that," he said, nodding at Renaldo. "This is my friend. Call him Tsá-cho. Tsá-cho? Renaldo."

Shocked at the sound of his name being spoken, Renaldo blindly held out his hand from years of his mother's training, only to feel foolish when Tsá-cho stared at his hand for an uncomfortable moment. Just when Renaldo was going to pull it back, Tsá-cho took it in one of his own, the grip strong as if he had something to prove, and shook it once, firmly, saying in a flat tone, "Hello."

"Well, I hope you brought your own supper, because me and Renaldo here are on a tight budget, food-wise," Hank said.

Tsá-cho rolled his eyes and pointed over his shoulder where several headless cottontails, hung upside down from a bit of string stretched between two sticks allowing the blood to drain into a shallow ditch Tsá-cho must have made, were waiting to be skinned. "Don't think you're going to get any, either," Tsá-cho replied, his voice slightly nasal and clipped.

"Is that any way to treat an old friend?" Hank asked, and the look Tsá-cho fixed him with sent waves of unease through Renaldo. They had history, those two, and Renaldo couldn't quite figure out if it was *still* history, and what it could have been. What he suspected did nothing to lessen the tightening in Renaldo's chest.

"How do you know this *ish-kay-nay*?" Tsá-cho asked Hank, disregarding Renaldo as if he wasn't there. Feeling increasingly unhappy, Renaldo busied himself with unsaddling Paloma.

Hank shot Renaldo a look before turning back to Tsá-cho and saying quietly, "Don't call him that."

"But he is, isn't he?" Tsá-cho said, not bothering to lower his voice. "You. Boy." He whistled sharply once, and it sent a spike of anger through Renaldo.

He looked up and glowered at this interloper, but he did not answer. Instead of the reaction he expected—irritation, anger, perhaps a physical challenge—Tsá-cho simply grinned and laughed.

"Maybe you're not *ish-kay-nay* for long, then," he said. "You know how to skin *gah-che-lé?*" he asked, pointing to the rabbits.

"You're not sharing, you can do the work yourself," Renaldo snapped, hoisting Paloma's saddle and blanket and carting them to a flat boulder.

"You said it yourself," Hank said to Tsá-cho, chuckling. "You ain't sharing."

Tsá-cho shrugged, pulled a knife from a sheath strapped to his leg and sat down in front of the ditch, where he proceeded to skin the rabbits with deft strokes, removing the hides in one complete piece with the fur turned inside like a sleeve. He then began scraping chunks of fat off the skins, flicking them into the fire he'd built before Renaldo and Hank's arrival. The glistening yellow bits of fat sizzled, giving off a pleasant, succulent aroma.

"Well," Hank drawled, "maybe we can share a *little* something if you can find it in you to do the same."

Tsá-cho grinned. Renaldo noted that they continued to smile at one another for longer than seemed necessary. This was going to be a long night.

WHILE SITTING AGAINST THE BOULDER where his saddle was resting, Renaldo rubbed leather oil into his reata to keep it supple. He wasn't sulking. He just wasn't participating in the ongoing conversation Hank and Tsá-cho were deep in, mostly because he didn't understand a single word they were saying.

He thought he heard bits of French now and then, but mostly they spoke in what was either Apache or Jicarilla.

Whatever they were discussing, Hank seemed to enjoy it. His eyes were bright and his laughter came easily. Tsá-cho didn't behave like any man Renaldo had known, either. He carried himself like a warrior, even while sitting on the ground. His back was strong and his eyes were fierce when he cut his unwavering gaze toward Renaldo on occasion and forced Renaldo to stare back until Hank would say something or ask a question, drawing Tsá-cho back into their private circle of two.

Tsá-cho had no problems being physically demonstrative with Hank, either, laying a hand on Hank's arm or leg, poking a finger in Hank's side, stroking his fingers over Hank's beard and laughing, as if he'd never seen Hank with facial hair before. It was… Hank just *allowed* it, still smiling, laughing, listening raptly as Tsá-cho spoke in a rhythmic cadence. Hank replied in kind.

Maybe later when he wasn't so irritated, Renaldo would remind himself that Hank wasn't touching Tsá-cho back. Even he could see how pitiful he was being, so he focused intently on the leather in his hands, allowed himself a moment to imagine roping Tsá-cho and dragging him away.

When his task was complete, Renaldo was out of things to do. The sun hadn't set, they had finished their early supper, and he didn't feel compelled to volunteer his services in salting or smoking the rabbit hides for Tsá-cho, who continued to stare occasionally at Renaldo, clearly evaluating him. He heard the man say his name to Hank, his voice rising with a question, and noted Hank shaking his head, waving a dismissive hand.

"Leave it," Hank said quietly but firmly to Tsá-cho.

Renaldo stood, dropped his hat and stripped off his vest, and stalked downstream where the hobbled horses were grazing. If nothing else, he could bathe. He felt dusty and grimy, irritable and short-tempered. Maybe the water would cool him off.

"Where you going?" Hank asked.

Renaldo didn't answer, but nodded his head toward the horses, unbuttoning his shirt. He stripped himself of his boots and all of his clothes save his union suit and waded out to where the water was deeper than knee-high. It wasn't much, but dropping to the sandy bottom brought the water's surface to his shoulders. He dipped back to soak his hair, sat up and ran a hand over his face to clear it as the steady movement of the water pushed against him, making his body bob and rock with the current.

Hank was watching him. And not just Hank, but Tsá-cho, too. Hank said something in Tsá-cho's general direction, but didn't wait for an answer. He, too, stripped off his shirt and breeches and waded into the stream, muttering something to the horses as he passed them. He came closer, moving slowly and cautiously, his head tipped to the side, reminding Renaldo once again of a bird of prey, wary, calculating.

"Good idea, and you beat me to suggesting it," Hank said. "Got a little carried away reminiscing back there." He stopped several feet from Renaldo and hunkered down in the water, soaking his clothes and wringing them out. "It'll help us when we get back out there not to stink so much of man. Don't know how much interaction the *mesteños* have had."

"I thought this way you wouldn't be able to tell me that I smell," Renaldo said, intending his tone to be coy, but he sounded bitter and sullen.

Hank sighed, looking off in the distance. After a long, tense moment, Hank said, "He doesn't trust outsiders easily." He meant Tsá-cho.

"Neither do I," Renaldo snapped.

"Oh, I know," Hank said with a brief flash of mirth before he sobered again. "Don't take it personal. It's just… we grew up together. Not too far from here, actually. 'Bout two days' walk, half a day on horseback, in fact."

"Was he a part of your Apache family?" Renaldo asked, looking upstream to where Tsá-cho was stretching the rabbit skins over the low fire, putting green branches of sage over the flames to produce a thick smoke, aromatic even at this distance.

"Family? Not like your family, your brothers and sister, if that's what you mean," Hank said, leaning back on his hands so his feet floated on the water's surface. "Family can mean a few things to them, but we were in the same tribe, I guess you'd say. In more ways than one," he said quietly.

Renaldo turned to look into Hank's eyes, trying to determine if the hidden meaning was what Renaldo suspected. Before he could say anything, perhaps be bold enough to ask Hank once and for all if he, Renaldo, would have been considered a member of that "tribe," Tsá-cho stalked over, stripped out of his deerskin leggings and untied his breechclout, letting it fall to the bank.

He stood still, stretching his arms high overhead, seemingly unbothered by his own nudity. His hairless chest was slight, but the muscles were well-defined as Renaldo had been able to see since they'd met. His legs were almost hairless as well, long and lean, with the muscles so tightly bunched that Renaldo could see the very fibers flex and move under his tawny skin. His cock hung limp between his legs, settled in a thatch of black hair. Face hot at the boldness of it all, Renaldo snapped his gaze up and was caught by Tsá-cho, who smirked at him before making a derisive noise in the back of this throat.

He said something to Hank that Renaldo didn't understand, something that upset Hank. Hank snapped, "*Ça suffit !*" and stood up with his underclothes stuck against his body. Renaldo wasn't the only one who noticed. Tsá-cho nodded and waded into the river, dropping his hand on Hank's forearm, tugging him close as Tsá-cho sank down into the water, drawing Hank back down with him into the river.

Renaldo watched, saw the intensity on Tsá-cho's face as he said something too low for Renaldo to pick up, and turned away. He began scrubbing at the seams of his shirt with sand, focusing on removing any traces of his sweat from his clothes before wringing them out as best as he could. He draped them over an outcropping of sandstone and turned his back to the other two men, taking handfuls of sand to scrub at his skin, using his fingertips to roughly scrub at his scalp. His hair was getting long and unruly. He'd need to cut it soon to keep it neat.

He busied himself with these tasks to keep from listening to the soft voices of conversation where he wasn't invited, where he imagined all manner of personal details were being shared. It had taken him ages to get Hank to open up to him, and he wondered what it was about this brusque newcomer that made him privy to so much.

If he wanted his clothes to be dry by morning, he'd need to stake them near the fire. Well upwind from the rabbit skins. He grabbed them up and tried to avoid looking at where Hank and Tsá-cho were sitting, their thighs pressed against one another,

Tsá-cho turned toward Hank, hand now resting against Hank's chest as they spoke rapidly and in low tones. Renaldo didn't look at Hank, didn't want to see whatever he imagined would be there. They were both undeniably handsome, manly and beautiful with their dark skin tones in harmony, both with broad shoulders and high cheekbones. It hurt to look at them, to imagine how well they would fit together—Renaldo was now sure they had fit together at some time.

He began to wade to dry land. It was a bitter pill to swallow, finally realizing this... quirk of spirit within himself, acknowledging that his longing for Hank was more than just an apprentice with his mentor, far more than that. Just when he felt brave enough to act on those feelings, someone from Hank's past showed up, someone who clearly owned a special place in Hank's memory.

Hank tried to grab Renaldo's arm, but his wet fingertips slid across Renaldo's wrist before it could find purchase. "I know we're being rude," Hank said, and the plaintive quality to his voice made Renaldo stop in his tracks. "Haven't seen one another in a few years, but that's no excuse to cut you out like we've done."

"*Me rindo*," Renaldo said. "I understand."

Hank narrowed his eyes, as if he knew that it wasn't what Renaldo had actually said in Spanish. Not that it mattered. Renaldo had decided to give up, that it would be pointless to... to *pine* over a man he couldn't have. A man he shouldn't want in the first place. And he certainly wasn't going to watch himself be soundly rejected, either.

"I'm going to check the fire, get these dry," Renaldo said, turning and walking away with a sharp nod. He could feel Hank's

139

eyes on him the whole way. Renaldo's face burned as he bent over to tug his boots back on but he was unwilling to look back.

After he had his clothes stretched on some sticks near his fire—he used his boot to push half the embers to a fresh clearing—the other two joined him. Hank turned his back and stripped out of his sopping union suit. Renaldo couldn't help but stare. He was transfixed by Hank's body, by the flexion of muscle in his backside, but he turned back to the fire before Hank caught him.

He didn't care that Tsá-cho had noticed him staring; he was fairly certain Tsá-cho had done the same thing. Tsá-cho was standing near the fire without a stitch on, evidently preferring to dry completely before pulling his clothing back on.

He couldn't take another moment of the tense silence, didn't want to be excluded or allow himself to remain an outsider. He asked, "Will your… *brother* be riding with us until we return to Vista Verde?"

Hank ran a hand over the top of his head roughly. His hair was growing longer, but because it made such tight curls, it looked thick and plush, not unruly as he imagined his own appeared. Hank's beard was only slightly thicker than when they'd left. He looked unsure of himself there in the deepening twilight with the firelight warming his complexion, softening his features so Renaldo could imagine him as a young boy, a teen who had been turned out of his house, passed among strangers, leery of his ever-changing surroundings. How he must prize anything that he'd been able to keep or make on his own!

"No," Hank replied. "He's coming with us to find the *mesteños*," he said, leaning his weight on one leg, putting a minute distance between Tsá-cho and himself. "That's what he came here for, to help with that."

Tsá-cho grunted something that sounded as if he disagreed, but Hank said again, "That's what he's here for, and since he tracked the herd in the first place, he'll get first pick."

"That... seems fair," Renaldo said, looking at the two men and trying to discern what silent conversation they were having with their bodies. Hank's arms were folded stiffly across his chest even as Tsá-cho put his hand to Hank's shoulder.

"It is fair," Tsá-cho said in his nasal, clipped voice. "The gray horse is beautiful. Yours?"

Renaldo glanced at Paloma, standing still with her head down, resting. He folded his arms across his chest, mirroring Hank. "Yes, she is."

Tsá-cho narrowed his eyes. "Are you worried I'll take something away from you?"

He was. But it wasn't Paloma he feared losing. Instead of responding, he turned to Hank, asking, "Is there anything I need to be made aware of to ensure our success when we find the *mesteños*?"

"Let a fellow settle down for the night first, would ya?" Hank asked, then crossed to the stack of bedrolls, grabbed Renaldo's first and tossed the bound roll to him easily. Renaldo caught it and spread it out on the opposite side from where the rabbits and clothes were staked—near enough to feel the warmth should the temperature drop as it might in autumn, but not too close. He left plenty of room to the side for Hank as he usually did; his stomach soured at the realization that it may have been unnecessary given the strange tension among the three of them.

Maybe they would go elsewhere to sleep. Maybe they wanted privacy. Maybe *that* was what had Hank so twitchy.

Surprisingly enough, Hank unrolled his bedding close to Renaldo as he'd done every night for weeks, then stretched out with a sigh. Renaldo followed suit, not quite able to relax.

"Remember what I told you about how you felt when you met Paloma," Hank said. "If you're skittish or agitated, she'll be even more so. You know as well as anyone that your horse feels what you feel. If I say stay put, you stay put. Stallions don't like folks messing with their harems, even if the ladies aren't in heat. We should be getting to them at just the right time, but you never know."

Renaldo did know—his father told a horrible story about a foolish man in San Antonio who didn't know anything about horses and decided he wanted an intact stallion, no matter how many men told him to buy a gelding. The man had boldly walked toward a penned stallion, who was already enraged at being isolated. He got close enough for the horse to bite him viciously right in the neck. The man died almost instantly. Renaldo and Calandaría had grown up hearing that story told again and again, an explanation for why there would be no stallions at Vista Verde. They hired stud services when they needed them.

"You follow my lead," Hank said softly, "and you'll do just fine. It's best to watch and learn the first time, keep you from having any expectations that might trip you up if it all goes catawampus."

Tsá-cho watched them from where he stood, then seemed satisfied as he turned to dress.

"Where will he sleep?" Renaldo asked, nodding at Tsá-cho's retreating back as he walked to a small pile of skins Renaldo hadn't noticed before.

"He'll find a place. Don't worry," Hank said. He didn't cover his face with his hat, but lay with his eyes fixed above, his body tense.

Renaldo, too, lay stiffly by his side, watching the stars overhead. Tsá-cho, adding more green branches to his portion of their fire, began to sing softly to himself. The repetitive cadence was soothing. That, coupled with the long day's ride, enabled Renaldo to fall into a deep sleep.

THEY STAYED AT THE CAMPSITE for another day. Tsá-cho had seen the herd moving their way, which was why he'd come to find Hank. He hadn't warmed up to Renaldo, but then Renaldo hadn't warmed up to *him*.

It wasn't that Tsá-cho was antagonistic. Renaldo wouldn't have stood for it. But it was clear to him that Tsá-cho was proud of the relationship he'd had with Hank and wanted Renaldo to be aware of it. To Hank's credit, he tried to include Renaldo as much as possible.

"Well, this was about, oh, seven, eight years ago," Hank said, leaning back against the saddle where it rested on the ground, picking up small pebbles and tossing them at Tsá-cho where he sat across from him. "A hunting party—soldiers from a fort up in Oklahoma—were looking for N'dee, didn't care which tribe, just wanted to take any and all of them out."

Tsá-cho grunted, drawing something in the ground with his finger as he frowned.

"So me and my friend here," Hank continued, gesturing toward Tsá-cho with a grin, "we crept up on where they were camped out, slipped the hobbles off two of their horses, and climbed aboard. But here's where it got tricky."

Renaldo watched the two of them as Hank told his story of them as young men, roaming across the prairie together for days and weeks at a time. He was desperately unhappy to see how bright and animated Hank had become since Tsá-cho's arrival. Not that he didn't want Hank to be in good spirits. He just wished it wasn't because of someone else.

"So this one here," Hank said, shaking his head at Tsá-cho, who was laughing silently, "gives a big war whoop, which sent the whole battalion—"

Tsá-cho interrupted with something in his native tongue, something that made Hank roll his eyes playfully.

"Well, it felt like we had a whole battalion after us. We had about ten or so soldiers shooting at us, and damn if they didn't hit one of the horses. Killed it right out from under Tsá-cho here."

Renaldo's mouth fell open. "What did you do?"

"Nothing to do but circle back and load him up behind me."

Again Tsá-cho said something Renaldo couldn't understand, but the intent behind the words was obvious: gratitude, and something private between the two men, something personal and very private, leaving Renaldo feeling all the more left out, feeling foolish that he believed he could share something like that with Hank, as well.

"I cut that horse I was riding tight around the poor critter that'd been shot," Hank said, "reached down and pulled up my friend here behind me."

Tsá-cho leaned back on his hands, grinning at Hank, not bothering to note Renaldo's presence.

"We took off hell-bent for leather," Hank continued, "me holding onto the mane like my life depended on it, and him holding onto me. We laid down low on our bellies, hanging on for dear life and whooping like a couple of idiots the whole time. But then two of their bunch apparently could ride *and* shoot, and caught up with us, determined to unload every bullet they carried into us."

"Did you get shot?" Renaldo asked.

"Nah," Hank drawled, waving a dismissive hand. "The bullets would come up the middle, so he'd go that way," he said, pointing left with his thumb, "and I'd lean right. The horse was running so damn fast, his neck was stretched out almost level with the ground. Every bullet that whizzed over his head just egged him on faster."

Tsá-cho spoke then. "I don't want to admit this," he said, cutting his eyes to Renaldo and then back to Hank where his gazed softened once more, "but I have never understood how we did not fall off."

"Pure luck and straight up cussedness," Hank laughed.

"You're a good friend to brave all of those soldiers shooting at you to bring him to safety," Renaldo said. If he didn't already hold Hank in such high regard, this would have certainly told him everything he needed to know about the man and his sense of honor.

Hank shrugged, seeming embarrassed by the praise, but Tsá-cho spoke up, eyes alight with merriment. "If your horse had been shot out from under you, *I* would have kept going."

Hank chuckled, but it sounded hollow to Renaldo's ears. "The *Natages* would have skinned me alive, if I came back without you," he said.

Tsá-cho stood and cupped Hank's chin, saying something soft that Renaldo couldn't understand. Hank looked away and nodded, standing and stretching and walking off. "'Scuse me, gentlemen."

Renaldo watched him walk to a stand of juniper trees and sagebrush, then turned back to find Tsá-cho staring at him, head tilted and eyes narrowed as if Renaldo were a puzzle to be solved. With a sigh, Tsá-cho walked off to the horses, murmured to Cloud and patted her neck; he was clearly finished with Renaldo.

He felt like a child, like an outsider, and he couldn't stand it for much longer. But, he realized with a sickening feeling, he had no idea how long Tsá-cho would be staying with them.

The rest of the afternoon was spent preparing their horses and gear for the next day. Tsá-cho spoke mostly to Hank in his native tongue and only spoke to Renaldo when he had a command or instructions, that is, when he bothered to acknowledge Renaldo's existence at all.

Hank seemed to sense Renaldo's discomfort and tried to draw him into their conversations as much as he could. Tsá-cho would touch Hank's arm, lean against him, roughhouse and wrestle him, laughing and speaking in Apache in what Renaldo knew was his attempt to exclude Renaldo as much as possible.

Tsá-cho was practically saying, "Hands off, he's mine," with all the posturing he was doing. By nightfall, Hank was engrossed by a story Tsá-cho was telling—one Renaldo couldn't follow, of course—so Renaldo decided to turn in.

"*Buenas noches*," he said, turning his back to them, the sound of their laughter and hushed voices grating on his nerves. It took him a long time to fall asleep; his loneliness and isolation were so profound that it was almost a physical ache throughout his body.

HE WOKE WITH A START, sucking a shocked breath through his nostrils as his eyes tried to adjust to the night's darkness. It was very late or possibly very early. The fire was still high, though. Perhaps a burning branch breaking had woken him? And then he heard something else, and he knew it hadn't been a branch but *that*, this other sound was what had woken him: a soft gasp followed by a deeper grunt, quiet whispers.

Blinking the sleep from his eyes, he pushed up on one elbow and saw that Hank wasn't sleeping at his side, even though his bedding was still there. Farther along the ground, almost out of the circle of light the fire created, he could see two people entwined.

Renaldo couldn't feel his hands; his chest was hitching with shallow breaths, his face was hot and his heart pounding as he realized just what he was seeing. The bodies shifted, and he could see by the shape of their silhouettes that Tsá-cho was stretched atop Hank, his long hair pushed to the side, his hands gripping Hank's shoulders, Hank's leg bent at the knee—still clothed, and it was strange how Renaldo was noticing all of these details in sharp relief when everything in him wanted to look away, to go back to sleep, to be blissfully unaware that yes, Hank did harbor those same feelings for men that Renaldo had discovered within himself.

Hank just didn't have them for *him*.

Tsá-cho's abruptness with Renaldo made perfect sense. To him, *Renaldo* was the interloper, the person who didn't belong. It was agony to be trapped here, embarrassed at his own foolishness, his naïveté.

A burning branch broke apart just then, the momentarily bright firelight illuminating how Hank's face was turned toward where Renaldo lay frozen. As Tsá-cho murmured something in Hank's ear and as Hank opened his eyes, a sick, piercing sensation struck deep in Renaldo's chest when his eyes found Renaldo's. To him, it seemed that Hank appeared overtaken with lust, his lush mouth parted, his eyes wide and pupils dilated, their black depths swallowing up the scant light afforded them.

Quickly, Renaldo turned to his side, away from the answer to the question he hadn't been brave enough to ask. He could hear the two men: Hank's voice firm and almost sharp, Tsá-cho quickly responding softly, the sound of a kiss and more of Hank's voice.

Renaldo screwed his eyes shut and wished there was something to drown out the sounds he couldn't bear to hear. He didn't understand, didn't understand what they were saying, how they could lay with one another without a care that he was so close, or what it was about the sharp, brusque Apache that appealed to Hank's more gentle nature. But then, Tsá-cho was only sharp and brusque with *him*. And now Renaldo knew why. He couldn't blame Tsá-cho for his earlier attitude.

Was it their shared childhood? Becoming men at the same time? Perhaps it was their comfort in rough terrain, the ability to live simply that drew them together. Renaldo didn't know. He just knew that he was horribly out of place, feeling more like a little boy than ever before, unaware of the real life of men who made their living out in the wilderness.

Hank and Tsá-cho whispered quietly to one another, and Renaldo couldn't hear any more sounds that resembled love-making, but perhaps they were just waiting for him to fall asleep before taking up their... activities once again? He forced himself to remember stories from his childhood, songs he and his twin would sing when children, anything to distract his mind until he could fall back into a fitful, unhappy sleep.

He dreamed of wandering an empty prairie, void of animal or insect, and whereas usually the prairie was where he felt most at ease, its vastness instead left him feeling as if he was drowning.

CHAPTER NINE

RENALDO WOKE, BLINKING AT THE dawning light while curled into a miserable ball, facing away from his companions. He'd never woken before Hank, but then again, he couldn't recall Hank ever staying up as late as he must have done last night. Eyes screwed tight and heart clenching, he remembered what he'd witnessed the night before, something he clearly wasn't meant to see.

Preparing himself for what he might find—Hank and Tsá-cho wrapped up together in an embrace—he turned himself over and let out the breath he hadn't realized he'd been holding. Hank was on his bedroll near Renaldo's, face turned toward him. He was alone. Tsá-cho was stretched out on his deerskin several feet away, still sleeping.

It probably didn't mean what Renaldo hoped. The most likely answer was that the two men had become embarrassed or possibly even worried about Renaldo's reaction and had separated before turning in. Maybe Hank hoped Renaldo would chalk it up to a dream.

As much as he wished it had been some horrible dream, it wasn't, and Renaldo couldn't forget.

Striding off toward a clump of sagebrush to relieve himself, he shook his head, sighing and feeling ridiculous. He told himself that it was for the best that he hadn't acted on his feelings for Hank, hadn't given in to his base desires. His father had sent him out here to learn a skill, not fall in love.

Renaldo draped an arm over his face. Love? Oh, how Calandaría would laugh at him, tease him for having such a romantic heart, just like their father and Francisco. Walking back to put his bedroll to rights, he thought about what his feelings truly were. Renaldo *admired* Hank. Respected him. Enjoyed his company. He was not in love.

He pulled his now-dry clothes from where he'd hung them and dressed quickly, crossing to where Paloma and Abuelita were grazing. He ran his hand down each of their sides in turn. The warm solidness of their bodies was a familiar comfort. Paloma turned from where she'd been nibbling blades of gamma grass to lip at the open button placket on Renaldo's shirt. He smiled at her, pushing her face away.

"If I let you eat my clothes, you'll get sick, and then where will you be, hmmm?" he said, scratching under her chin the way she liked. She made a soft noise of appreciation, and then turned back to graze. Abuelita turned her gentle gaze to him, ears twitching forward, one leg pawing in the air before returning to stand perfectly still.

"Did you think I would forget you?" Renaldo said, stroking the backs of his fingers along her face, using both hands to rub behind her ears. She closed her eyes and dropped the heavy, solid weight of her head onto his shoulder, making him laugh as he kept up his ministrations. "How could I ever think I was lonely with *mis dulce damas* by my side?"

"*Are* you lonely?" a voice asked.

Renaldo turned his head, his hands buried in Abuelita's mane, and saw Tsá-cho standing there, yawning and scratching his chest.

"*Estoy bien,*" Renaldo replied with a shrug.

Tsá-cho regarded him and then nodded at Abuelita. "You're good with them."

"I grew up with horses," Renaldo replied, perhaps a little too sharply, but he didn't care for the tone of surprise in Tsá-cho's voice. Hank, however, overheard their exchange and laughed, the familiar low rumble of it making the hairs on Renaldo's arms stand on end.

Tsá-cho smirked, and then looked off into the middle distance.

"*¿Hablas Español?*" Renaldo asked.

Tsá-cho tilted his head, confused.

"Do you speak Spanish?" Renaldo clarified. "I heard you speak in French yesterday, so I wondered."

"Some Spanish words I know," Tsá-cho replied. "Some French. I don't often find need for either."

"You speak English very well," Renaldo said, turning to Abuelita to smooth her mane back to rights. She stepped back as he moved his shoulder forward, guiding her farther away from Tsá-cho and toward their camp.

Tsá-cho laughed, a derisive snort, and said, "And so do you."

"*Era obligatorio aprender Ingles en la escuela,*" Renaldo responded, an ugly flash of pleasure at being able to speak without Tsá-cho understanding him for a change.

Instead of being frustrated, Tsá-cho simply stared back, holding Renaldo transfixed by the intensity of the man's gaze, until Tsá-cho nodded and turned away without another word.

Hank, still in his union suit, was hunkered down at the fire, poking it back to life and resting the speckled blue coffee pot over two flat stones. Watching him perform the same tasks as he'd done since he and Renaldo had first left Vista Verde should have been a comfort. Instead, it was strange to see things continuing as normal when everything inside Renaldo felt as though it had been turned upside down.

But today was an important day, and Renaldo had a job to do. A job he must learn how to do, and well enough not to need any more training with Hank, not now. There in the harshness of daylight, standing not a foot away from fresh horse chips, his earlier hopes of being neighbors with Hank, of an extended potential relationship, seemed foolish, the thoughts of a child. He inhaled deeply, drawing in the scent of sage and distant pine, and yes, horse shit, and told himself to let his silly fantasy go. He turned away when he saw Tsá-cho approach Hank, speaking in tones too quiet for Renaldo to hear.

They prepared a simple breakfast, since their stores were quite low, but Renaldo didn't see any worry on Hank's face as he put their few remaining supplies back in their saddlebags, so he trusted him to ensure they didn't starve. When they were all focused on their plates, Renaldo noted that Hank seemed tense. His normally taciturn morning manner seemed exaggerated today; he barely gave them as much as a one-word response. Tsá-cho seemed upset. He snorted sharply at Hank and turned away when Hank apparently didn't reply the way Tsá-cho had expected.

153

As Renaldo saddled Paloma, Hank touched Renaldo's arm. "Give me a moment. Need to clear this out." He tapped his temple. Renaldo nodded, watching as Hank wandered off alone, hands on his hips.

With Paloma's saddle in place and cinched tight, Renaldo looked for Hank, finding him several yards upstream, head hanging low and shoulders down. Tsá-cho, nearest to Renaldo, was squatting next to the moving water, muttering something under his breath with his hands in the stream before he pulled them out, looked to the sky and sighed. Hank returned to saddle Lady. Before they left their camp, he pulled on a stiff leather jacket from his saddlebag. Tsá-cho hopped onto Cloud's back easily, sitting bareback with his hands on his thighs, waiting.

A hawk cried overhead. Tsá-cho watched it soar along the butte's edge, diving to catch its breakfast, and smiled. "*It-sá,*" he said, nodding his chin at Hank.

Hank looked sad, his body not straight and proud in the saddle as it usually was. He said, "Tsá-cho," and touched his chest, just over his heart.

Paloma snorted, prancing in a tight circle. Renaldo let out his breath and patted her neck. "I'm sorry, *cariño,*" he murmured.

Tsá-cho sighed, looking off in the distance, and then got Cloud moving. Hank turned to Renaldo with a cautious smile. "Ready?"

"*Sí,*" Renaldo replied, gently squeezing Paloma's sides to follow the others as they left their camp.

They headed northwest with the rising sun almost directly behind them, until Renaldo could see a small mesa in the distance.

Tsá-cho rode alongside Renaldo, silent for a long while. Finally, he said, "*It-sá.* You know this word?"

Renaldo glanced at him, nodding. "Hawk. We say, *halcón.*"

Tsá-cho shrugged. He touched the center of his chest and said, "Tsá-cho."

"Yes, I know," Renaldo snorted.

"Do you know what *that* word means?" Tsá-cho asked, a dry, irritable look on his face.

"Your name, I thought?"

"No," he replied, shaking his hair over his shoulder. "It is the name *It-sá* gave me. It means 'eagle.'"

With his intense, sharp gaze, it seemed a perfect name for the Apache.

"Hawk, eagle. These are names of strength. Courage. They are names for men who act, who fight," Tsá-cho said, eyes forward. "I do not know what 'Renaldo' means." Renaldo's name sounded stilted, flat in Tsá-cho's accent. It sounded weak.

"I know what you're trying to do," Renaldo said, his teeth grinding together. "I will not be insulted by you, *Águilito.*"

"What is that word?" Tsá-cho asked, eyes narrowed, dangerous.

"It is the name I am giving you." And with that, Renaldo spurred Paloma on, riding just ahead and far to the side of Hank, needing space from both him and "little eagle." There was no reason for Tsá-cho to flaunt his relationship with Hank. Renaldo was fully aware of what they were to each other. He was ready to be finished with this entire venture.

By mid-morning, they were close enough to the mesas to see a good fifteen or so *mesteños* moving about at its base. Tsá-cho and Hank came to an immediate stop. Hank held his hand up, and then said softly, "What's happened here?"

Renaldo came astride Hank to his right where he could better see the animals. A group of about ten or so were racing in circles; one dark chestnut mare led the group farther away from where Renaldo and the others stood with a dun-colored stallion hot on her heels. Another group of four horses—two in varying shades of buckskin, a chestnut and another tobiano—stood in a nervous group around a large white horse, which was twisting on its side and making pained noises as it tried and failed to get back to its feet.

Tsá-cho said something in his native tongue that had Hank nodding. "Looks that way," Hank replied.

Renaldo—doing his best to keep Paloma calm as she snorted and fidgeted under him, her ears twitching back and forth as she took in everything—examined the horse on the ground as much as was possible from their vantage point. Deep red ran down its legs and neck in gory bouts and splashes.

"Dominance?" he asked, directing his question to Hank, who nodded.

"They don't always go to the death, don't usually need to, but looks like this one came close." Hank pulled forward. Lady slowly approached the skittish group with her head down. Abuelita quivered at Renaldo's side. She wanted to go to the other horses, one of which was a mother with a twitching foal at her side.

Not every male horse fought for breeding rights, but when they did, it was an awful thing. Their bodies coursing with adrenaline and testosterone, mad with lust and rage, they lashed out at each other, biting viciously at whatever vulnerable place they could reach, bucking and kicking one another brutally in a display of dominance, attempting to assert their control over the herd.

The group that had run off circled back around, the horses moving in tandem not unlike a flock of birds until they were close enough to see without being close enough for Renaldo or Tsá-cho to touch, alert and all eyes on Hank as the men slowly made their way to the fallen horse. His screams of pain were simply awful to hear. Before they got too close, one of the mares standing over the fallen animal bared her teeth, whinnying high and sharply at them. Hank brought Lady to a stop and dismounted, blindly tossing her reins to Renaldo. Hank kept his hands to his side and walked closer, stopping before he got within kicking or biting distance of any of the agitated mares. The larger group with the victor kept their watch from yards off, curious, but so far not showing aggression to the smaller group.

Hank got as close to the wounded animal as he could, stood perfectly still and didn't say a word for several moments. Finally, he turned on his heels and walked just as carefully back to Renaldo and Tsá-cho.

He sighed and spat on the ground. "Two legs broken. Couple of bad bites to his neck, too, bleeding steady."

Renaldo's stomach turned over. There was no recovery from a broken leg, much less from two. If a horse couldn't stand, it couldn't live.

Tsá-cho, glancing at Renaldo briefly, asked Hank, "Use it as a distraction?"

Renaldo made a face at that, gratified to see that Hank seemed displeased by that notion as well.

"Surely we will put it out of its misery," Renaldo said, trying to keep Paloma still; her tail flicked harshly and her steps were agitated. She wanted to leave the terrible scene, and he couldn't blame her. But they couldn't just leave. Renaldo couldn't, at least.

Tsá-cho looked at Hank, ignoring Renaldo completely. That was it. His temper flared hot and fierce. He swung his leg over Paloma, dropped to the ground and tossed Lady's and Paloma's leads to Hank.

"Everyone, every creature deserves dignity in the end." Hank seemed startled by the emotion in Renaldo's voice, but he was so angry he didn't care.

This poor beast had taken care of its family, had protected them against threats, had increased their herd, and now he lay on the ground in agony, dying slowly and most assuredly in a painful way, and they were thinking of using that as a *ploy*?

He grabbed his knife from a leather pouch on Paloma's saddle and stretched his neck from side to side, bracing himself for what he knew must be done.

"Take this," Hank said, slipping out of his jacket. "In case he tries to bite you."

Renaldo pulled it on, unable to revel in the body heat trapped in the material as the felled animal writhed and cried out in pain once more. He turned toward the pitiful tableau, walking slowly and carefully as Hank had done.

"*Pobrecitas,*" he murmured, watching as the mother startled, the colt at her side trembled, both of them going completely still yet remaining wary and alert. As he came closer, he caught the rolling and bloodshot eye of the panic-stricken stallion. Something in his chest snapped, his heart breaking as he felt the horse recognize what was to come.

"Shhh," Renaldo said softly, his hands at his side as he came closer. The stallion stared back at him, his breathing labored and eyes bulging. Renaldo sank to his knees near its head. The stallion could bite him, could easily tear a chunk of exposed flesh from anywhere vulnerable, but it didn't. Renaldo felt a hot itch sting his eyes as he reached out a hand, laid it on the horse's neck, shushed and soothed him.

"*Lo siento mucho,*" he whispered, his voice cracking. "I'm so sorry."

The stallion sank back into the ground with a grunt. Renaldo took in the horse's body, its powerful muscles, the sickening twist to its back leg—the hock bone shattered, most likely—the clean break at its knee.

"You did well," he whispered, stroking the horse's neck; it was sweaty, hot to the point of being feverish. The stallion closed his eyes, breathing harshly. It was all so terrible, so foolish, so *stupid*. The stallion had done what nature had intended, had been a part of something, had cared for his herd, and all it took was one fight with the younger male to end its life brutally, horrifically.

Well, it hadn't quite ended it. With the present wounds, it would take an hour, maybe even longer for the animal to bleed out, in agonizing pain the entire time. Renaldo couldn't let it suffer like that.

Renaldo blinked away the moisture stuck on his lashes, wiped his hand on his pants and adjusted the grip on his knife. "*Vaya con dios,*" he said, using both hands on the knife to apply enough force as he drew it low across the animal's neck, making sure he caught both sets of its carotid and jugular veins, blinking away droplets of blood as he did so. The horse kicked its back legs once, almost in reflex, and sighed, eyes locked on Renaldo.

Renaldo laid a hand on the animal's side, felt it take a few shuddering breaths and then … nothing. He hung his head, said a little prayer, and then stood, looking down at what had been a magnificent creature. Its flanks were smeared with blood and dirt and it had several bite marks on its rump and chest in addition to the ragged ones on its neck. The three mares whinnied, stretched their necks, smelled the body, walked around it as if they had completely forgotten that Renaldo was there.

"It was the right thing to do," Hank said, suddenly at Renaldo's side.

Nodding, Renaldo shrugged off Hank's jacket, then used the back of his wrist and sleeve to rub at his eyes. Hank's hand settled low on Renaldo's back, warm and shocking in its suddenness yet still soothing. Renaldo could feel every point of Hank's fingers against his skin like a brand, exhilarating and nerve-wracking all at once. He wasn't in the right frame of mind to appreciate the touch; he was too aware of how meaningless that touch was now.

"Terrible thing," Hank said, and when Renaldo looked sideways at him, he realized Hank was talking to the remaining horses.

"What should we do?" Renaldo asked, his voice low so as to keep from spooking the horses, which were still standing vigil over their friend, making quiet noises to one another.

"Grieve with them for a moment." Hank's thumb worked back and forth along Renaldo's back, who sank into the comfort. "Then we'll see who all wants to come with us."

Renaldo didn't know what that meant, exactly, but he nodded.

"Seems like he was a fine fellow," Hank said, and again, it seemed to be addressed to the mares.

Something startled the other group, still standing several yards off, and many of the mares ran away, their tails high, only to circle back when their new stallion chased them back into place.

Hank watched the other group; his hand spasmed on Renaldo's back before he pulled it away. The heat from his hand immediately cooled, leaving Renaldo keenly aware of its absence.

"If you're ready, as my friend says," Hank said, once again speaking to the mares in a quiet tone and nodding at Renaldo, "*vamanos.*"

And with that, Hank turned away and walked slowly but surely back to Lady and the others. Renaldo stood still, torn between watching Hank walk off and the mares and colt.

"Well? You coming?" Hank said over his shoulder to Renaldo.

Renaldo nodded, and with a heavy sigh, turned his back and headed back to Paloma, who was nickering with her ears forward, waiting for him. He could hear movement behind him, but he continued walking without further acknowledgement. When he swung into his saddle, he was shocked to see all three mares and the skittish colt heading toward them, the tobiano mare in front swishing her ears back and forth as she watched for any threat.

She must have sensed something. She laid her ears back flat and broke apart from the small group, circling back toward the others where the victorious stallion was charging toward her. She reared back and pawed at him, driving him back momentarily.

"He's going to lose a chunk of skin because he wants more than he needs," Hank said. "For some creatures, enough is just never enough."

The three men watched as the mare and stallion went back and forth. A sense of dread flooded Renaldo that the beautiful tobiano would meet the same fate that the older stallion had. Tsá-cho was practically vibrating next to where Hank stood until suddenly, he took off running, heading directly for the group of ten or so mares milling about, waiting for their new mate to return.

Tsá-cho took a running leap, landing on a pretty paint's back, grabbing her mane with both hands and giving a series of high yips. The horse reared back on her legs, higher and higher until Renaldo was sure both horse and rider would flip over, hurting, if not killing, both of them, and still Tsá-cho kept his seat, his forearms taut, his thighs clinging to the mare's sides, straining to hold on, a wild and fierce look of determination on his face.

The horse fell forward, bucking and kicking, with Tsá-cho remaining firmly seated, his body supple and strong, moving fluidly with the great muscles in the horse's back and neck, his hands buried in her mane to help maintain his balance. Renaldo watched as Tsá-cho dipped forward and to the side as the mare stretched out her neck, trying to shake him off. Tsá-cho cried out, his voice almost playful and most certainly elated, and then finished with a piercing cry. The mare took off like a shot across the prairie, running along the base of the mesa, with Tsá-cho moving his body in tandem as they raced away.

The herd's new stallion screamed, deciding that was a more pressing issue than the tobiano mare, and raced after them. Most of the females he'd won over followed him, tails and heads high. The two who remained circled in confusion, their ears and bodies on alert. The tobiano from the first group, the one who had stood up for the dead stallion, whinnied, snorting and stamping the ground. She turned her back and trotted toward Hank and the other horses.

Renaldo heard a familiar high-pitched cry and turned to see Paloma, her eyes wild as she tried to get her head, pulling on her reins, her back legs almost buckling behind her.

"Let her know it's okay," Hank said to Renaldo, climbing onto Cloud's unsaddled back, his hands on his thighs, not unlike Tsá-cho. He was perfectly calm and still, as was Cloud, patiently waiting as one of the new horses approached, sniffing Cloud and Hank's pant leg, murmuring to one another.

"*Palomacita*," Renaldo called out, whistling once. "The danger has passed, *cariño*." He held his palm out to her, shushing and whispering praise until she stamped forward, lipping at his hand, her tail flicking back and forth, most likely disturbed by flecks of blood Renaldo could feel drying on his face. "I know, I know," he replied. "You don't like this change of events. You're not the only one," he muttered.

Hank tossed him a look over his shoulder, and then walked Cloud to Abuelita. "Come on, Grandma," he said, running the backs of his fingers down the side of her face, as Renaldo had done that very morning. "Let's introduce you to some friends you can fuss over."

With nothing more than the pressure from his knees, Hank guided Cloud toward the new group. Abuelita followed eagerly. As they approached, one of the mares stretched out her neck, baring her teeth and making angry noises.

"No one's gonna make you do anything you don't want, ma'am," Hank said softly, hands on his thighs as Cloud backed up a few paces, and then stood patiently, waiting for instruction.

The mare snorted and feinted forward, ears up and eyes wild, but Cloud didn't respond with fear or aggression, and neither did Hank. They patiently waited for the new horses to realize he and Renaldo weren't a threat.

After several minutes of nothing more than standing still, watching and waiting, Hank said, "Well. Let's go." He took a handful of Cloud's mane, and turned her away, guiding her to slowly walk back to where their group had come from. Tsá-cho was nowhere to be seen, nor were the horses that had taken off after him.

"Should we wait for… your… friend?" Renaldo asked, not needing to use the reins as Paloma seemed perfectly content to follow wherever Hank was headed.

"He'll most likely come back here later today for the meat," Hank said, his eyes hardening.

"The meat?" Renaldo asked.

"A horse is a source of medicine as well as food," Hank said. "It would be wasteful to ignore it."

Renaldo got the impression from the tense line of Hank's shoulders that Hank didn't quite agree, which was a relief. Horses, while technically livestock, had never been seen that way at Vista Verde. Horses were revered, treasured. They were companions and treated as such. To eat one… It just wasn't his custom, nor his family's, but he could respect the idea of not letting anything go to waste.

"Now what?" Renaldo asked.

Turning to him, Hank raised an eyebrow, and then looked ahead. "Now we head home."

"This was it?" Renaldo asked.

"Not what you expected?" Hank asked, scoffing.

"No," Renaldo replied, fingering his supple reata tied to the saddle. "There was no coercion. I didn't have to use my lasso." He twisted in his saddle to look behind them where the three mares and the colt placidly plodded along behind them. The two lone horses from the larger group did not join them.

"I believe I told you when we first met," Hank said, "that it's never a good idea to force it. Either they want to come with you, or they'll fight you the whole way, not ever really trusting you."

As they walked on, Renaldo's mind whirled. It made sense, the more he thought on it, that Hank, whose life began from a coerced union, would reject participating in anything resembling that. He thought about Francisco and Patricia, realizing in that moment that they would never be happy together.

About an hour into their return to their camp, they heard pounding hooves. Hank said, "Just keep your eyes forward."

Renaldo couldn't ignore the sound, though. He glanced back and saw the two mares from the larger group, one with a starburst between her eyes, the other a red dun, racing toward them, ears and tails up, not showing any signs of aggression that he could see. Taking his cues from Hank, Renaldo snapped his gaze forward, keeping his body loose and his mind calm. Paloma's ears twitched back and forth, gauging from him what she should do about this new situation, so Renaldo patted and stroked her neck, praising her bravery and lightly nudging her on with his heels. She nickered and kept moving forward.

"Five plus a colt is a pretty good haul," Hank said, reaching for his tobacco pouch. "Any more would just be greedy."

Renaldo watched as he rolled a smoke, casual as could be, and turned, marveling over the small herd they'd acquired by doing nothing that Renaldo had assumed the job would entail.

165

"See," Hank drawled, "when you approach life thinking you know what to expect, that's about when life knocks you for a good one. You end up with nothing but disappointment."

"I'm not disappointed," Renaldo said, thinking.

"No?"

"No, not at all. In fact," he replied, taking a deep breath. "As long as what I had to do before isn't a normal occurrence— "

"It isn't, not at all."

"Then I'm not disappointed. I'm surprised, certainly." Renaldo ran his fingertips through Paloma's mane, thinking of how putting down that stallion had been the first act of violence he'd ever committed against a horse. He hoped it was the last, but knew that was most likely naïve of him, given the line of work he planned to take on. His whole family revered horses, yes, but they only served as a part of the beginning of the horse's life, the birth and upbringing, the early years of training to be ready for sale. The end of their stories had never been the responsibility of Vista Verde.

Why, even the poor beast old Tom Garrison had dragged back from the high plains had been rehabilitated instead of euthanized.

"Is that a good thing?" Hank asked casually, crossing his arms over his pommel as they plodded onward.

"I… yes," Renaldo said. "I'm pleased that we didn't have to use force," he said, remembering the state of the poor animal dragged to their ranch all those years ago. "Pleased with the respect shown them, the choice they're allowed to make. Surprised it worked, but—"

He rubbed his hand roughly over his face, trying to find the right way to articulate what he meant by all of this.

"But I'm also not surprised," he continued. "I know that you can't gain a horse's respect through violence."

Hank hummed his agreement.

"I just hadn't thought of treating them like equals."

After a moment, Hank said quietly, "Well, I guess you figured out my secret, didn't you?"

Renaldo gave him the briefest of smiles. He'd learned more than that one, unfortunately.

"I am very happy, very *grateful* to learn a better way. So thank you for that."

"*De nada,*" Hank said with a sad sort of grin.

"Although," Renaldo said, "I must admit that it makes me uncomfortable not knowing where things are going, what to expect each time."

Hank snorted. "I've had that feeling a time or two. You get over it," he said.

Renaldo cleared his throat. "Tsá-cho," he said. "He's an incredible rider. I've seen people stay astride bucking green-brokes, but nothing like that."

The corner of Hank's mouth tugged up at one corner; his eyes filled with mirth. "Well," he drawled. "He grew up with horses, too."

CHAPTER TEN

THEY RODE IN SILENCE BACK to their previous camp. Renaldo couldn't decide if Hank was being quiet because he didn't want to startle the horses or because Tsá-cho had left. He also didn't know if or when Tsá-cho would return. The new horses followed them easily, used to being in a large group and most likely finding comfort with them after the events of the day.

After they arrived and dismounted, Hank made a noise of surprise. Where they'd had their bedrolls the night before was a deerskin wrapped around something. Hank opened the impromptu package and grunted. Renaldo peered over Paloma's back from where he was unbuckling her saddle and saw several freshly-killed rabbits, a mound of fuchsia prickly pears, another of screwbeans, tiny red berries that Renaldo was unfamiliar with, nuts and seeds. They found a small pouch filled with salt.

"Who?" Renaldo asked, shocked.

"Tsá-cho," Hank said, a sad smile on his face. "It's his way of apologizing."

"Apologizing?"

"Mostly for how he treated you, among other things. He knew he was being rude, but him." Hank shook his head, setting the leather pouch aside and scooping up one of the cottontails. "He doesn't always care how he treats outsiders."

"I noticed," Renaldo muttered.

"He has good reason not to trust folk who aren't N'dee," Hank cautioned. "Just because you're running with me isn't good enough for him. He knows we only met a few weeks ago. It takes a long time for him, and I don't blame him for it."

Renaldo dropped Paloma's saddle on the same boulder as before, leaning heavily against it on his forearms. "Do you?" he asked, picking at the edge of the horse blanket.

"Hmmm?" Hank asked, his attention on skinning the cotton-tail, using the same technique as Tsá-cho had, leaving the inside-out sleeve of fur on the ground.

Renaldo chewed his lip, and then asked, "Do you trust me?"

Hank paused and then grabbed up the next rabbit for skinning. "I do."

The steady, aching pressure Renaldo had been carrying around in his chest since yesterday eased some at that admission. It didn't ease completely; he was still miserable about the night before as well as from the tragic events of the day. But it was something.

"Get a fire going for these, would you kindly?" Hank asked, gesturing to the rabbits.

It was quick work to pick up kindling from the dried shrubs and mesquite trees along the stream's banks and stoke a new fire. He didn't build up a large blaze—they were limited on kindling close-by. They'd use what they had and move on in the morning. They'd leave nothing but the ashes from their fire as the only sign they'd been there, nothing left to tell any newcomers who they'd been or what they'd done.

That sorted, he saw to his two girls. "Should we hobble them?" he asked Hank, nodding at the new group from where he was crouched at Abuelita's feet.

"Not the first night," Hank replied. "We'll let them get used to us before doing anything that might spook them. And besides," he said, stretching the meat over the fire on green branches, "they'll see how well our ladies handle it, won't be so quick to distrust us when it's their turn."

Renaldo nodded, finishing his task, wishing a huge gulf hadn't opened between Hank and him.

It didn't feel right between them, not anymore. The ease, the relaxed joviality he'd spent weeks building with Hank seemed to be gone completely. Hank was guarded and watchful as they settled in, as if he expected Renaldo to be the one who spooked, not the wild horses.

After washing the stallion's blood from his face and hands, Renaldo refilled their canteens from the stream, settled by the fire and passed one to Hank, who nodded in thanks before taking a long drink. Renaldo watched his throat work before turning away.

He didn't know how to solve this, how to make them comfortable with one another once more. Aside from the ache over not being the man Hank would choose to be with, he was filled with mortification, for mooning over someone who wasn't interested.

"Should... should we save one for Tsá-cho when he returns?" Renaldo avoided Hank's eyes as he reached for another of the roasted rabbits.

When Hank didn't respond, Renaldo turned to look and saw Hank with his head tilted and a confused look on his face.

"He ain't coming back," Hank replied, eyebrows together. "That's part of what I meant by this being an apology," he said, motioning toward the food they were eating.

Oh. That must be why Hank looked so out of sorts.

"Do you get to see one another often?" Renaldo asked.

"Hadn't seen him in a couple of years," Hank answered, "and don't think I'll be seeing him again for a long time." He cleared his throat, poking at the fire just enough to send a smattering of sparks skyward.

"If I wasn't here, perhaps you two could have spent more time together. For that I'm sorry." His voice sounded stiff to his own ears, but he couldn't help it.

"Why?" Hank asked. "Why would you be sorry?"

"Because he matters to you," Renaldo said, unsure as to why Hank looked so taken aback.

"Well, yes, and there aren't many I do care about, but—" He exhaled sharply, stood and crossed to their bedrolls. "I thought… thought you might not—"

"Might not what?" Renaldo asked, taking his bedroll from Hank.

"Approve, I suppose." He rolled out his bedding, and then stood quietly, his eyes downcast and a hand on his hip. "Figured you might have gotten the wrong idea about a few things, actually."

Renaldo smiled, but it felt plastered on, false. "You don't need to pretend with me," he said. "I understand perfectly."

"No," Hank drawled, "I don't think that you do."

171

"I didn't sleep enough last night," Renaldo said, cutting off the conversation before he was made to suffer through Hank's feelings for the man he couldn't have, either. Perhaps one day they could laugh about having that in common, but not tonight. "So I'm going to turn in. *Buenas noches.*"

Hank didn't respond, as Renaldo turned away to wash his face in the stream before it was too dark to navigate beyond their campfire's circle of light. The cool water was soothing to his heated face, but he didn't know what he could do to settle his mind, ease his loneliness.

ONCE AGAIN, RENALDO WOKE WITH a start, his face jerking as something soft and ticklish moved over him. The soft, low sounds of a curious horse washed over him—as well as the horse's breath. He blinked. One of the new horses—the tobiano—was sniffing him and his things curiously, making her way around where he lay. He pushed up on his elbows as she circled him, stepping right between his bedding and Hank's, ignoring Hank completely.

Evidently satisfied, she jumped over him and joined one of the other mares a few yards away, standing watch.

"Guess you made an impression," Hank said, his voice muffled by his hat.

"I guess so."

"Ladies," Hank said, pulling his hat off his face and twisting around to where they stood. "The man said he was tired, so if you'd kindly?"

They snorted and walked back to the river where the buckskin mother and her colt waited.

"There. Not that you need it," Hank said, his voice light and teasing, "but now you can get your beauty sleep."

With that he covered his face once more and fell back asleep immediately. Renaldo, however, did not.

THE NEXT MORNING WAS QUIET. Hank shot Renaldo pensive looks as they ate and gathered up their belongings, striking their camp. Renaldo didn't say anything when he realized that the less he spoke, the more inquisitive the new horses became, much to Abuelita's delight and Paloma's consternation. When Paloma bared her teeth at the colt, who startled and fell in place behind his mother, Hank took her lead and put her on the outside of Cloud, ponied off Lady.

"Hell, if they want to get to know you, let's let 'em," Hank said, pulling ahead and leaving Renaldo several paces back with the new herd.

After a half hour, all six horses were walking side by side with Renaldo and Abuelita.

"They accept you as one of their own," Hank said, twisting around in his saddle. "When it comes time to gentle them into leads, I think it'll be best to have you do it. Don't you?"

Renaldo surveyed the new animals. The tobiano appeared to be their leader, but didn't appear to mind deferring to Abuelita when she made corrections to their path. He held out a hand to the buckskin, who smelled it all over before making a noise of approval.

"Yeah, yeah," Hank said, grinning. "You're likable as all get out. Don't be a showoff."

If only, Renaldo thought.

THEY ARRIVED AT THEIR CAMP late in the afternoon. Now that October had arrived, the sun was setting earlier, the days were growing noticeably shorter. The days were still warm, but the nighttime temperatures were dropping. They took extra care to build up a store of wood. While Renaldo got the new horses familiarized with his scent, walking among them, running his hand over their quivering bodies while shushing them, Hank went to look for food.

"Now," Hank said, holding out one hand, the other behind his back. "N'dee won't eat these, not any I know, but they're good eating as long as you don't believe they're unclean evil spirits." And with that, he pulled his other hand from behind his back; the long, fat line of a dead snake hung from it.

"I can't say that I've ever had that," Renaldo said. "How on earth did you get it?"

Hank wiped his knife on his kerchief, dropping it to the ground. "Well," he said, grunting as he began pulling the skin off in one long tube, "dumb luck, actually." He grinned up at Renaldo. "I poked a stick after a prairie dog; it jumped down a hole thinking it was its home, but this fella had already moved in. While it was busy with the prairie dog, I got him."

The snake was easily four feet long, without its head. Hank tossed the skin aside, flipped the snake the other way around, looking for something near its tail. When he found it, he said, "You see that vent?" He pointed at an opening in the musculature. "Slip the tip of your knife in there, and—"

With a flick of the wrist, he drew the blade swiftly up the length of the snake; the innards spilled out to the ground. He took a long stick from their wood pile and pierced the snake meat onto one end, wrapping it around and around. He used some salt from their stores to season it.

"Then you just roast it up. It's all meat, after you clean 'em," Hank said, stacking a few rocks on either side of the campfire and resting the stick on them to keep the meat just above the flames.

Since Hank had gotten their dinner, so to speak, Renaldo took it upon himself to clean up the innards, dropping them far away from their camp and where the horses were grazing, then kicking dirt and sand over the pool of blood. Anything to keep busy, to keep from being alone with nothing to do but think.

They ate in relative silence, Renaldo praising and thanking Hank for the food.

"Tsá-cho and his people," Hank said, then stopped, looking worried. "The Mescalero, most of the other Apache tribes, won't eat snake. They're missing out."

Renaldo nodded, resting on his elbows to watch the clouds pass over the moon.

"Used to be you'd never stop asking questions, and now," Hank sighed, "it's like pulling teeth."

"I'm sorry," Renaldo said, shrugging. "I don't have much to say today."

After a moment, Hank burst out with, "Is it so terrible, then?"

Renaldo blinked up at him, shocked to see such emotion on Hank's usually calm face. "I said that I liked the food?"

Hank gawped at him. "I don't mean the damn food. I meant what I am." He ran his hand over his head. "I'm guessing that's why you won't talk to me, because you're disgusted. I thought you—doesn't matter what I thought," he mumbled to himself.

"What did you think?" Renaldo asked, his stomach in knots. "That I wouldn't mind? That it wouldn't bother me see you both—" He couldn't finish his sentence.

Hank tilted his head, studying Renaldo, and then asked, "Explain to me what you believe you saw."

Renaldo scoffed, his face burning. "I think it's pretty clear."

Rolling his eyes, Hank drawled, "Let's pretend it wasn't." He shifted closer. If Renaldo wanted, he could reach out and grab a fist full of Hank's shirt. "I want to hear from you what you believe you saw last night."

Renaldo swallowed thickly, worrying the inside of his cheek with his teeth. "I… I saw you two together. Lying together." Hank's eyes were shuttered, but he nodded. "And if I hadn't woken up, you two would have—"

"No," Hank said. "That's not what happened."

"*No me mientas.* Don't lie to me, Hank," Renaldo spat. "There clearly are feelings between you two. And it's clear that my presence ruined your… reunion."

Hank laughed, but it was humorless. "There *were* feelings between us, years ago. That's the truth," he said. "But that was years ago. At least on my end of things."

Renaldo, his chest heaving, sat and waited.

"You remember what I told you about *nde'isdzan?*"

The word sounded familiar, the one he hadn't understood.

At his nod, Hank said, "The Kiowa have a word for it, but it's not meant as a compliment. It's why they didn't mind letting me go to the Apache. It's *ee-haw-gyah,* or sometimes *ma-ye-tin.* It means 'woman heart' in English, but they say it when a boy isn't a proper boy."

His eyes bored into Renaldo's.

"The Mescalero, though, they call it *nde'isdzan.* It's something good, something good for the tribe, a person who can walk both sides of the fence, so to speak."

"That's why you felt like you belonged," Renaldo said, understanding. "And Tsá-cho—"

"Is, too." Hank drew figures in the sand at his knee. "You can imagine what a relief that was for me, young boy, strangers figuring out what I was before I even knew it was a thing to know. And then to find people who didn't make me feel ashamed about it, like I was broken or something."

Renaldo sat up, their knees almost touching.

"He was a comfort to me," Hank continued. "I was for him, as well. But once we became men—fully grown and adults in their eyes, I mean—we had it explained to us that what we'd shared as young men couldn't come with us into this next stage of living. It's greedy," he said, shaking his head. "A *nde'isdzan* is special, a spiritual advisor. It's an honor to be with one, a gift. They aren't meant to be tied down to one person."

"So—" Renaldo cleared his throat. "You had to leave? But did you wish you could stay?"

Hank shook his head.

"Then what did I see last night, if it wasn't a reunion between lovers?"

Hank didn't reply. He studied Renaldo's face for a long time. "So it doesn't bother you, me being the way I am, does it?"

"No."

177

"And that's because…?"

Hank seemed to be waiting for his reply, but Renaldo wasn't quite ready to say that out loud. Instead, he asked, "*¿Qué fue eso anoche?* What did I actually see last night, then?"

"When I left to make my own way," Hank said, poking at the fire, "that was that between us. Not only because it had to be because of tradition, but because I didn't want to see him coming out of someone's wickiup some morning. But friends? Friends I could do."

Renaldo nodded, waiting.

"He got a taste of what I'd experienced years ago when he saw you," Hank said, shooting Renaldo a cautious glance. "Got ideas about us. When you went to bed all in a huff—"

Renaldo made an angry noise, but Hank only grinned.

"You did, and you know you did." He knocked his knee against Renaldo's in a familiar gesture. "We moved away, not wanting to wake you. He wanted to talk, see if we, oh, I don't know," he said, heaving in a deep breath. "See if I was still interested in him that way."

"Are you?"

"Nope."

Renaldo fixed him with a disbelieving look. "It certainly looked like you still were."

"We were talking late, as I said, stretched out like when we were just boys. We had good memories, and I guess reminding him of some of them gave him the idea to see if he could make new ones."

Renaldo shook his head, tossing bits of dried grass into the fire.

"Why doesn't it bother you knowing I'm the way I am?" Hank asked again.

Shaking his head, Renaldo muttered, "It doesn't matter why."

"What if it did?" Hank asked. "What if it mattered to me? Mattered a lot?"

Renaldo could see the ever-present watchfulness in Hank's face as well as something else.

"You know, when I first saw you back at your ranch," Hank said, his hands on his knees, so close to Renaldo's that Renaldo thought he could feel the heat from them, "I thought you were one good-looking man. But then you opened your mouth." He laughed softly.

"And I watched you with your sister, your brothers, could see how much you cared for them, how much you all cared for each other, and it made me a little lonesome, truth be told."

Renaldo watched the backs of Hank's fingers twitch closer, thinking back on the shock of meeting him.

"What you all have out there, well, it's like a dream." Hank drew the barest edge of his knuckle against the hard edge of Renaldo's knee.

Barely able to breathe, Renaldo, said, "It feels that way to me, too."

"I thought so," Hank whispered, before continuing. "You have that big, loving family, and they were good to me, your mother welcoming me inside like it was nothing." Two fingers now circled and stroked against Renaldo's leg. "And I don't know what changed, what made you think you had to be embarrassed by them, but—"

179

"I know," Renaldo said, eyes following the up and down strokes of Hank's fingers against him, "I know I ruined it, and it took me a while to figure out how to repair the damage I'd done."

"I didn't make it easy on you," Hank said, grinning. He brought his hand back to his lap. Renaldo wanted to grab it back and hold it in place. "But we figured things out, I'd thought? Made it good? Between us, that is?"

"I thought we had, too," Renaldo said softly.

"You woke up just when Tsá-cho was making a last effort to woo me."

"How far did his effort go?" Renaldo asked.

"Just what you saw. Didn't want any of it," Hank said. "Not from him."

"No?" Renaldo asked, his pulse picking up from the intense look on Hank's face, the implication in his words.

Hank shook his head. "Why doesn't it bother you that I'm the way I am, Renaldo Valle Santos?" he asked softly, enunciating each syllable carefully, perfectly.

Renaldo took a deep breath for courage. "Because I'm the same way."

A slow, sweet smile spread across Hank's face just as a log fell apart in the fire, making the flames burn brighter momentarily. "You made your peace with it, you think?" Hank asked.

The firelight danced over Hank's skin, showing his cheek-bones, the fullness of his lips in sharp relief. Renaldo was transfixed by the way Hank's mouth was slightly parted, by the dark hair of his short beard, wondering how that would feel against his own face. He looked into Hank's eyes and said, "Yes."

"Then you won't mind terribly if I do this?" Hank asked, leaning forward, eyes on Renaldo's as he closed the distance between them. He cupped Renaldo's cheek with his large hand, and as he stroked his thumb softly over the ridge bone, Renaldo's eyes closed at the sensation.

His breath caught when he felt the heat of Hank's breath over his face; he opened his eyes to see Hank right before him, so close he could barely see Hank's eyes. "*Te quiero besar,*" he murmured, drawing the tip of his nose along Hank's, both sighing at the touch.

"What's it mean?" Hank whispered.

"This." Renaldo brought their mouths together, just a press of lips at first, his heart racing, until he felt Hank's thumb on the point of his chin, just the barest amount of pressure.

Almost lightheaded with the sheer intensity of his desire, Renaldo opened his mouth just as Hank directed him, tilting his head so that he could work their mouths together more closely. The quiet rasp of Hank's beard against Renaldo's upper lip and cheek was exhilarating. Renaldo could feel the tip of Hank's tongue where it licked at his lower lip, and gave back everything Hank was giving him, their mouths slick against one another, their quiet moans and gasps swallowed by each other as they kissed and kissed.

Hank pulled back, bringing their foreheads together as he panted. "Been wanting to do that for a while, now."

Renaldo didn't want to stop, didn't want the kissing to end, the touching, this discovery of what could be between two people. He pushed to his knees, leaning forward once more, but Hank shook his head. At the soft noise of dislike Renaldo couldn't help, Hank chuckled.

"I just mean not like that. Come here." He shifted onto his bedroll, lying back. He held out a hand, which Renaldo took.

This time, this night it was *him* draped across Hank's solid chest, it was him silhouetted by the fire as he gazed down, the private smile on Hank's face was for *him* and him alone. He gave in to his earlier thoughts about what this could be like, the two of them together so intimately, and drew his fingertips along the solid muscle of Hank's chest, trailing over the round muscle of his shoulder, along the biceps definition he could discern through Hank's shirt, to end at Hank's hand, lacing their fingers together and drawing them along the edge of his mouth.

He could feel Hank's chest heaving underneath him; he felt as if he was coming undone, as well. Pressing their joined hands high above Hank's head brought all of his weight down onto Hank's body, where he could feel every hard, solid inch of him.

Hank lifted his head to bring their mouths almost together and said, "*Te quiero besar,*" with a grin.

"You're a fast learner," Renaldo said, pressing kisses under Hank's jaw line, drawing his lips along the tendon in Hank's neck that had so fascinated him for weeks. "*Cuello,*" he murmured, kissing a trail upwards, "*oreja,*" he said, over-emphasizing the rolled 'r' as he nibbled softly on Hank's ear lobe. "This is *mejilla,*" he said as he trailed back along Hank's cheek, "and this," he whispered, drawing his parted lips back and forth over Hank's mouth before whispering against them, "*Es tu boca.*"

Hank groaned softly, letting his legs fall open to better accommodate Renaldo's body. He tugged his hands free, burying them in Renaldo's hair to hold him close as they kissed again. A hunger rose in Renaldo that had his whole body thrumming, his breath quickening. The sensation of Hank's fingers holding his head in place, his wet lips, his tongue, the long, solid line of his body pressed so intimately against his own–Renaldo would go mad if it ever stopped.

Hank shifted under him to get his mouth on Renaldo's neck. The ticklish sensation of Hank's beard left Renaldo breathless and giddy, barely able to sigh out sweet words of encouragement as Hank bent one knee, holding Renaldo over him, rocking his hips up.

The unimaginably pleasurable friction of their bodies rocking against each other had Renaldo shaking with desire, gasping with desperation against Hank's neck.

"Will you let me show you?" Hank asked, brushing Renaldo's hair off his forehead.

Renaldo dipped to capture Hank's mouth in another bruising kiss. "Show me? Yes, anything, just—" He rocked his hips again, grinding them down against Hank's, licking at the seam of Hank's mouth to make him open up to him once more.

Everything flipped. He was now looking up at a grinning Hank.

"You said I could," he chuckled.

"*Sí, mi querido*, but no, come back to me," he said as Hank pushed off him. Hank, however, began unbuttoning his shirt.

"*Mi querido*, huh? I like that." He dropped his shirt to the side, untied his trousers to kick them off and then crawled back over Renaldo's body, resting his weight to the side. "What else could we call each other, hmmm?" he asked, untying the laces to Renaldo's trousers as well.

"*Corazon*," Renaldo sighed, drawing the backs of his fingers along Hank's cheek. Hank tugged Renaldo's shirt up and out of his trousers, straddling his body to work the buttons loose on his shirt. Hank helped Renaldo out of it, then unbuttoned Renaldo's union suit, running the flat of his hand over Renaldo's chest to push it off Renaldo's shoulders. The air was cold, and he could feel his nipples pebbling in the open air, but Hank kissed each of them, flicked the sensitive tips with his tongue.

"What else?" Hank asked, following his mouth with the rough pad of his thumb.

"*Cariño,*" he gasped when, with the barest of touches, Hank's fingers traced the outline of Renaldo's hardening cock. He was grateful that his clothing dampened the sensation so he didn't spend then and there.

Hank sat up and pulled Renaldo's trousers off. The pale color of their remaining clothing was in shocking contrast to their skins, to the darkness of the night all around them. Hank tugged a blanket from the other bedroll, draped it over his shoulders as he laid back down, nestling himself between Renaldo's legs and sighing when Renaldo cupped his face, pulling him down for a languid kiss.

Slowly they revealed more of each other's skin, kissing and touching one another almost reverently. Weeks of pent-up desire left Renaldo almost shaking with need, yet he was desperate to take his time, to savor this discovery of how the pleasures of the flesh could make his heart aching and full.

As Hank rubbed the scruff of his beard over the sensitive skin of Renaldo's neck, he arched up, needing relief from the way every brush of their cocks against each other made the hot pulse of his heartbeat throb between his legs.

"*Desde que te conocí no hago nada más que pensar en ti,*" he said, sighing against Hank's temple as the other man scratched his fingers through the line of hair leading down to where he was most in need of touch. "Since I met you I've—" He gasped when Hank's hand slipped through the opening of his underthings, circling his aching cock and pulling it out. "I—I've done nothing else but think of you."

Hank looked deeply into his eyes, pupils blown and eyelids heavy, the thick, curling fringe of his eyelashes softening his features. "Say that again." He stroked his hand up and down.

Renaldo did, arching his back and driving his hips up in counterpoint to Hank's ministrations. "*Y tu también. Déjame tocas,*" he said, "Let me touch you, too."

Hank dropped his head to Renaldo's shoulder; a small groan escaped him. He brought Renaldo's hand down where he could cup and stroke Hank, all of his senses centered on the heavy feel of Hank's cock against his palm, the petal softness of the skin stretched over the solid weight, the moan Hank couldn't hold back when Renaldo dragged the pad of his thumb over the slit, catching the beads of moisture pooling there.

The angle was wrong, not what he was used to as he took care of himself in private, those moments when he could slip away from his classmates, from his family, hiding behind the barn to relieve the tension, but now, with Hank gasping against his neck, thrusting his hips forward and driving himself through Renaldo's fist, it felt right. Something locked into place, the missing piece that had up until this moment kept him from fully connecting with the world, from standing on his own and feeling complete.

"Just... just like that," Hank gasped, undulating his hips and trembling when Renaldo swept his thumb over the head once more.

He didn't care that Hank's hand had gone lax on himself. To see Hank, so taciturn and stoic, polite and distant with most people, to see him coming undone, shaking, gasping Renaldo's name as Renaldo gave him pleasure was like no power he'd ever imagined.

He sped his hand up, sensed Hank's release nearing and whispered against Hank's ear, "I want to taste every inch of you," grinning into his skin when Hank shuddered. "I want to do this to you in daylight, I want to watch your face, see how you look with my hand on you, *amorcito.*"

Hank caught Renaldo's mouth in a bruising kiss, his whole body shaking. Renaldo could feel his release, pulsing hot and wet over Renaldo's fist, dripping onto his belly. Hank trembled once more, hissing when Renaldo squeezed him low, twisting his hand as he milked the last drops from Hank's spent cock. Hank dropped to his side, still wrapped around Renaldo's body, gasping and catching his breath.

Renaldo pressed tender kisses all along Hank's hairline, whispering praise and sweet names into Hank's temple. After a moment, he brought his hand to his lips, dipping his tongue out tentatively to taste. Hank groaned, saying, "You can't do that to a man so soon after he's lost a cockstand," making Renaldo laugh.

He shifted to his side to look into Hank's eyes. "I told you I wanted to taste every inch of you."

"I've never met your like," Hank said, running his hands through Renaldo's hair. Renaldo closed his eyes and pressed into Hank's touch.

"That's a good thing, isn't it?" Renaldo asked, idly dragging his fingers through the cooling mess on his belly.

"The very best thing," Hank murmured, kissing Renaldo as he once more took Renaldo in hand, stroking lightly as his tongue worked in Renaldo's mouth. "A most wonderful thing, *cariño.*"

Was it possible for a person to feel this happy? Renaldo's whole body responded to Hank's touch, to him whispering back the words and phrases he'd learned, *"corazon"* and *"querido"* never sounding sweeter than when spoken by Hank's lips as he kissed and touched and stroked Renaldo, quickly bringing him to release.

They continued to trade kisses as Renaldo's body, his spirit came back down to the ground. *"Tocarte… besarte es como ver las estrellas,"* he sighed, kissing the inside of Hank's wrist before holding it to his chest.

Hank raised an eyebrow, so Renaldo grinned, feeling slow and drunk, euphoric. "To touch you, to *kiss* you is like seeing stars."

Hank rumbled a pleased noise, his thumb stroking back and forth across Renaldo's bare chest. "Didn't know you'd be a poet. Sure are pretty words for a man like me."

Renaldo held Hank's hand firmly, saying around a yawn, "A man like you deserves pretty words."

Hank grew still, enough so that Renaldo cracked one eye open. The low firelight flickered shadows across Hank's face; his expression was indiscernible.

"¿Por que, mi querido?"

Hank shook his head slowly, dropping to his back. Renaldo pushed to his side, worried he'd said something wrong.

"Just… I've never known the likes of a man like you," Hank said again, smiling softly.

Renaldo kissed Hank's shoulder, turning to his stomach so he could draw patterns on Hank's forearm. Stifling a yawn, he quietly said, "Maybe you should keep me, then."

The fire crackled, the horses softly whickered to one another, and Hank whispered, "Maybe I will."

CHAPTER ELEVEN

THE NEXT MORNING, RENALDO WOKE to something tickling his arm. When he opened his eyes, he found Hank, on his back and grinning. It wasn't Hank touching him, though, but the buckskin colt, his black ears up, knobby tan legs splayed as he bent to smell the inside of Renaldo's elbow.

"Think he likes you," Hank murmured, covering his face with his hat. Renaldo could still see the smirk on his face, though.

"*Buenas dias, chiquitito,*" Renaldo said, holding his hand out for the colt to sniff, laughing when it darted off only to run back to the men, quiver with energy, and bound over to his mother, who was watching near the water's edge.

"I'll get the coffee, you get the food?" Hank asked, lifting his hat and turning in question to Renaldo.

Renaldo pushed up on one elbow, drawing the flat of his hand down the length of Hank's exposed chest, elated that he was able to do this now. He quickly dropped a kiss at its center, right where Hank had a narrow patch of black curls. He smiled against Hank's skin, enjoying the dichotomy of silken skin and scratchy hair against his lips.

"I'll check the ladies," Renaldo said, kissing him once more before standing and stretching. Sleeping on the ground night after night left him stiff and sore, but the company made it worth it, he thought, as Hank hooked an ankle around Renaldo's to keep him from walking off. "Now who's the lazy one?" he asked, as Hank dropped his hat back over his face to hide his laugh.

It was a comfortable rhythm they knew well, breaking camp, packing up, checking the horses' legs and hooves before saddling them. It was a big day for Paloma, too. Today she would be on a lead, riding amongst the newcomers. Renaldo found her standing with the tobiano, a good sign that she was accepting the new animals into their herd.

As they continued on their long trek back to Vista Verde, the morning sun shone in their faces, bright and warm. Renaldo recognized various aspects of the landscape on the return trip, a strangely shaped rock outcropping here, the odd bunch of agave there, and wondered how he'd ever imagined it to be featureless.

Even with the addition of more animals in their care, the day was the same as before: comfortable stretches of silence, the steady clop of hoof on the baked caliche soil, the soothing rock of the saddle. But now there were new and wonderful additions to the day's ride. Now he could ride alongside Hank and, instead of wondering if he could ask about his life, if his curiosity would be rude or invasive, Renaldo knew that it would be welcomed.

Far better were the times when Hank came up behind Renaldo, nudging the side of Renaldo's knee with his own, or when Renaldo would tug on Hank's shirtsleeve, leaning to the side to ask for a kiss, elated when Hank complied, awkward though they were on moving animals.

They were in the center of their own private world. The horses seemed to pick up the lightened mood. Their steps grew more lively, their nickering and chatter more animated. Paloma clearly wanted to be in the middle of all of these warm and affectionate feelings, often coming between the two men on their mounts, demanding attention.

"So spoiled," Renaldo laughed, pushing her nose from his neck.

"Mmm," Hank grunted, eyes forward but the edges crinkled with mirth. "I can see why she'd be fond of that particular spot."

Renaldo laughed, delighted to have Hank teasing him, reminding him of the night before, of Hank's rough cheek against the tender skin under his jaw, Hank's lips kissing away the sting, their bodies aligned so perfectly.

There was a playfulness between them now, both of them having stripped away all caution. Hank whistled a cowboy song under his breath while casually lassoing Renaldo, chuckled when Renaldo pulled it off, only for Hank to reel it back in and do it all over again. Later, Renaldo managed to grab Hank's hat, galloped ahead and laughed when he could hear Hank's lasso whistle through the air once more.

When they made camp, Hank pulled out a sturdy-looking pair of iron scissors and sat near the water's edge on a large rock with a metal canteen in his lap.

Renaldo, unbuttoning his shirt so that he could wash it, asked, "What are you doing?"

Hank looked over at him, did a double-take and laughed. "Cutting this down," he answered scratching through his beard.

Renaldo frowned. Not having much himself, he quite enjoyed the sensation of Hank's scratchy beard and said so.

"If you could see the mess I made of you just there," he said, gesturing at his own neck, "you'd agree with me."

"Is it that bad, then?" Renaldo took the canteen from Hank's lap, trying to get a clear picture of himself, although the metal was scratched and warped. "Here, you won't be able to see anything in this." He dropped the canteen and stood before Hank with his hand out.

Hank raised an eyebrow, but Renaldo continued to hold his hand out. "Don't you trust me?"

"You can't pull that card every time," Hank laughed, handing over the scissors.

"*Claro que no*," Renaldo agreed, all innocence. He cupped Hank's face, turning it this way and that. Hank's beard was just long enough to curl over the tips of Renaldo's fingers as he raked them through the stiff, coiled hairs. Hank's eyes slipped shut; his chest rumbled with a pleased noise.

"Yes?" Renaldo rested the scissors on Hank's knee so he could scratch Hank's cheeks with both hands, earning himself a low moan that went straight to his blood.

Hank leaned into Renaldo's hands, smiling happily.

"You're as bad as Paloma." Renaldo scratched under Hank's chin.

"Told you I could see why she was so fond of you," he murmured, dropping the scissors onto the ground next to his boot.

Renaldo bent for a soft kiss. A playful hum rumbled in the back of his throat when Hank caught him at the nape of his neck to keep him in place, their mouths sliding against each other until Renaldo felt breathless.

"Do you want your beard trimmed or not?" he whispered against Hank's mouth, kissing him once more.

"You gonna do more than this if I say not?" Hank asked, rubbing his chin just behind Renaldo's ear.

Renaldo laughed, shoving at him in a playful way. "*Deja der ser travioso*, and sit still."

Instead of obeying, Hank pulled Renaldo onto his lap. "I don't know what that means, but I think it means I'm getting my whiskers trimmed."

"*Sí*," Renaldo said, standing up. "And then you can have the other. Now," he tugged at Hank's shirt. "Take this off."

"Thought you said none of that business?"

Renaldo rolled his eyes but laughed. "I said you would later. Come on, *hacia arriba*, up."

Hank stripped out of the top of his union suit as well, letting it pool at his waist. He sat back on his hands, jutting his chin out. "Clean 'er up, pal."

Renaldo snorted but tilted Hank's face to the side. The only sound to be heard was the steady *snick* of the scissors. He made quick work of it, and then carefully brushed away the beard trimmings from Hank's shoulders and chest—perhaps too carefully, given the heated look in Hank's eyes.

"Is it later?" Hank rested his hands low on Renaldo's hips, his thumbs rubbing over Renaldo's hipbones.

"No," Renaldo teased. "Clean, fire, eat, tend the horses and *then* it will be later." He tugged Hank to standing and handed him the scissors. "Because once we're able to be together, I won't want to do anything else."

Hank took a deep breath and held it, blowing it out all at once with a laugh. "You heard the man," Hank called out to the horses. "But I think it should go horses, fire, eat, clean and then later." As he said the word "clean," he dragged the back of his hand along the bulge in the front of Renaldo's pants, sending Renaldo's pulse skyrocketing once more as all his blood rushed below.

"*Tu me vuelvas loco,*" Renaldo sighed, catching Hank's hand and giving it a squeeze.

Hank blinked, and then grinned. "Making you crazy?"

"*Sí,*" he replied.

Hank leaned in and kissed just under Renaldo's ear, his shortened beard still scratchy, but in a way that sent shivers down Renaldo's spine. "*Y soy,*" Hank said.

Laughing, Renaldo shook his head and said, "*Y yo.*"

"Not if you keep correcting me." He snatched Renaldo's shirt off the ground and nudged him in the side. "Horses. Fire. I'm on chow after I get these washed up."

As they took care of their tasks, Renaldo couldn't help but search out Hank, smiling and laughing when their eyes met, his heart, his spirit light. Hank was doing it, too, seeking him out. All of the hunger he'd felt for Hank, wanting to know his story, know the sort of man he was, was turning into a different kind of hunger. He wanted to feel Hank's skin, taste his lips, twine their bodies together and never be apart.

Every touch Hank dropped to Renaldo's arm or shoulder as he passed, every heated glance, every low rumble of his voice as he teased Renaldo only added to Renaldo's need. The heat pulsing through his veins with every beat of his heart was close to burning him up, consuming him. Hank wasn't immune to whatever this growing desperation between them was, either. He seemed unable to keep his hands to himself: caressing Renaldo's nape as he walked past, delicately running his fingers through Renaldo's hair, giving him little touches and heated glances as they finished settling the camp. They took turns to eat, hobble their horses and check the newcomers for signs of distress. Finding none, they took their metal dishes and cups to the stream to rinse them off.

Hank took the plate and cup from Renaldo's hand and placed them on the ground before leading Renaldo by his wrist upstream to where a shallow pool had formed near a swirling eddy. They didn't speak as they fully undressed; their clothes were jumbled together in a pile. The water was cold enough that Hank hissed a little as he stepped in. There wasn't quite enough room for two men in the little stream, and the rocks under their bare feet were slimy from algae, but they figured out how to maneuver in the tight space.

Renaldo turned Hank to face away from him, then drew Hank back into his arms. He dropped little kisses along the nape of Hank's neck, bit playfully at the joining of neck and shoulder, held the skin in his teeth and smiled when Hank shivered.

"*Lobo*," Hank murmured, holding Renaldo's hands over his chest as Renaldo drew the tip of his nose along his hairline.

"A wolf? Me?" Renaldo asked, freeing a hand to cup and pour water over Hank's back. All of his skin, both the smooth and the damaged, were beautiful to Renaldo, and he kissed both equally, smiling as Hank shivered. "Hmmm, do the wolf and the hawk fit together, you think?"

Hank didn't answer, so Renaldo slipped his hands down to his strong arms, drawing him back against Renaldo's chest once more. He hooked his chin over Hank's shoulder and asked, "Did I say something wrong, *querido*?"

"I like that one best, I think," Hank replied. "*Querido*. One of those 'use your whole mouth' words."

"Mmm, I'm learning how much you enjoy using your mouth," he teased.

Hank chuckled. "What's that one from… *anaranjada?*"

"*Sí,*" Renaldo answered, leaning in close to nuzzle and then whisper in Hank's ear, making his voice husky and needy. "*Orange.*" He bit Hank's ear playfully as the other man laughed. "So very sensual."

Hank's laughter died down; he turned in Renaldo's embrace to face him, smiling soft and sweet as he pulled Renaldo into his lap so they could fit together in the little pool. "I like that you can make me laugh."

Renaldo grinned, feeling both bashful and proud under Hank's intense gaze. He felt as if Hank could see everything inside him, how he'd been muted, faded, not quite his full self until this trip, until this man had come into his life.

"You see, eagles and hawks," Hank said, running his fingers through Renaldo's thick hair, "they don't usually work together. They're at odds, you understand, being similar creatures."

Renaldo wrapped his arms around Hank's waist, holding him there with him. Tsá-cho—eagle, a name that meant courage— had been Hank's first love. Renaldo knew that he had Hank with him now, but feared that after this business was done, Hank would take flight again.

"Aren't we similar?" Renaldo asked, stroking his thumbs along the lower curve of Hank's spine. "This way we're coming together, what we're feeling?"

"*Sí, querido,*" Hank said, clearly pleased with himself for the use of the endearment. Renaldo was, too. "We are the same there," Hank said, dipping down in the water to catch Renaldo's lips in a tender kiss, aching in its sweetness.

195

When they finally pulled apart, Renaldo asked, "Then…?"

Hank sighed, dropping his forehead to Renaldo's shoulder, who began rubbing Hank's neck, working some of the stiffness out. After a moment, Hank sat back up and said, "A wolf has a pack, a family." He cupped Renaldo's cheek. "They grow up knowing how to work together, how to play, to protect, to love. An eagle leaves its nest. A wolf adds to his pack."

Renaldo swallowed, his breathing shallow, waiting for Hank to continue.

"And hawks…"

"Are you trying to tell me that you're going to be leaving?"

"What?" Hank gripped Renaldo's forearms, pulling him closer. "No, course not. I'm trying to tell you why it wasn't difficult for me to choose *you*, not Tsá-cho." As Renaldo sighed, relaxing in Hank's hold, Hank laughed. "Not all of us have the ability to woo with pretty talk like others do, *Señor* Valle."

"You want pretty talk, eh?"

"What I want," Hank said, slipping his hands between their bodies, "is for us to hurry up and get to the later."

Renaldo sighed, his eyes closing as Hank stroked him under the water's surface. "*Quiero que seas mío*," he said, his voice hoarse, his throat dry as Hank nipped and kissed at Renaldo's neck, his hand lazily dragging up and down Renaldo's cock.

"Mmm, don't even care what it means," Hank said, giving the other side of Renaldo's neck equal treatment as Renaldo sighed, sinking further into his embrace.

"Not even if it means that I'm deciding to live a life of celibacy from this moment on?" Renaldo touched Hank in a similar fashion: just enough to tease and titillate, but not enough to bring either of them to climax.

"Doesn't seem like you're making good on that vow," Hank replied, grinding his hips up in a slow roll to make his point.

"Hank?" Renaldo asked, pulling away to take Hank's hands off him.

"Hmmm?"

"It's later."

HANK SAID HE COULD SEE the wisdom in having everything finished for the evening as they fell to their combined bedrolls, entwined in one another's arms as they kissed and gently rocked together.

"*Es verdad*. It's true: I'm very intelligent," Renaldo agreed.

Hank lightly bit his side, holding firm as Renaldo squirmed, laughing in his arms. "Bet I know loads more than you."

"Mmm," Renaldo agreed, dragging his instep along Hank's shin, delighting in how the crinkled hairs of their legs rubbed against each other. "I bet you do, as well. Aren't I here to learn from you? Isn't that the point of this adventure?"

He meant it in a teasing, light way, but Hank had gone stiff in his arms.

"*¿Cariño?* What is it?"

Hank pushed his weight to one elbow, his free hand resting on Renaldo's chest as he looked down, eyes serious, forehead creased. Renaldo reached up to smooth it, and then stroked the pad of his thumb over Hank's cheek as he waited.

"You know there's older men out there who take advantage of young boys, just kids, really, trying to be cowboys and outlaws."

"Yes," Renaldo said, not sure how this had anything to do with the two of them.

"Some of those kids set out with hopes of finding men like that, knowing they're inverts and hoping to find a place they can be themselves."

Renaldo hadn't heard the term "invert" before, but he could guess what it meant.

"Some folks just want the fun. Like Silvestre." Hank pulled away from Renaldo's touch but didn't move his body from where he was.

Renaldo had searched his face as he'd spoken, trying to discern what Hank meant, and when he mentioned Renaldo's brother, he understood completely. "No, no, *querido.*" He cupped Hank's cheek once more. Hank didn't pull away.

"I don't want this to be nothing but a dalliance, a passing fancy, if that is what has you worried." At Hank's minute nod, Renaldo grinned, pulled him down for a languid kiss. "I thought I'd made myself clear."

"Probably said it in a way so I couldn't make head or tails of it," Hank replied, nudging Renaldo's legs apart and settling between them, kissing a trail down to Renaldo's chest, mouthing at it.

"*Perdóname, corazon.*" Renaldo sighed at the delicious friction the hair low on Hank's belly made against his own stiffening erection, mindlessly rocking up against it to chase that feeling. He used both hands under Hank's arms to hoist him up from where he'd been kissing and sucking on Renaldo's nipples; Renaldo was close to bursting from a flood of sensations.

"Let me teach you something." Hank kissed and stroked along Renaldo's belly, pausing as he raked his fingertips through the hair that led from Renaldo's navel to the thatch of hair surrounding his cock. "Will you?" he asked, looking up at Renaldo.

Renaldo pushed to his elbows, staring down the length of his own chest and belly to where Hank's mouth was so close to where Renaldo ached with need. He ran his fingers over Hank's head, traced his fingertips over the delicate curl of Hank's earlobe, and nodded. When Hank buried his nose right at the base of Renaldo's cock and then drew his lips up the length, Renaldo fell back onto the blankets, gasping and trembling when Hank engulfed him with his mouth. The wet heat, combined with the play of Hank's tongue along the shaft, pulling off and suckling tightly over the head, only to do it all over again, left Renaldo breathless, feeling untethered from his body.

He'd never imagined anything feeling so wonderful, never understood just how two people could express their feelings for each other without speaking. As Hank used his mouth, he touched Renaldo all over, stroking the tops of his thighs and the tender skin just inside where they met his groin, his thumbs stroking over Renaldo's hipbones, his fingers dragging down Renaldo's chest, his mouth sliding and twisting, up and down again and again until Renaldo thought he would shake apart.

He gripped Hank's head with both of his hands, focusing on the texture of Hank's hair, the hard bone of his skull, anything but the obscene, wet noise of Hank's mouth, his own desperate moans as he drew closer and closer to climax.

Hank must have sensed him growing tense, as he pulled off with a lewd noise, kissing the sensitive bit of skin inside Renaldo's hip. "Are you close?"

"*Dios mio, amorcito.*" Renaldo draped his arm over his face, panting. "Yes, I'm… I'm sorry."

"Don't be sorry," Hank chucked. "I want you to. Remember you mentioned how you wanted to taste me? Well," he said, running the flat of his tongue from root to tip, "I do, too."

"You want me—" Renaldo fell back once more. "*Ay, mi amor. Nunca me he sentido así.*"

Hank held Renaldo in his hand, circling and stroking his cock, and kissed the head, flicking at it with his tongue in a way that had Renaldo arching off the ground. "What's that mean?"

Renaldo draped a leg over Hank's shoulder, holding him in place, keeping him there as Hank slipped his mouth down, down, all the way and back again, Hank's hand covering what his mouth didn't as he suckled the head of Renaldo's cock. He was shaking all over, so close to release, but managed to gasp, "Never. I've never felt like this before."

Hank hummed, and Renaldo could feel the vibration from his core all the way up his spine, his hair standing on end as his body arched off the ground, gasping and jerking as he pulsed over and over in Hank's mouth, Hank swallowing around Renaldo as he did. His eyes stung with unshed tears; the muscles in his thighs were trembling; he could barely *breathe*. He hissed, overly sensitive as Hank pulled off, kissing his way up Renaldo's body.

He was transfixed by how puffy Hank's lips were, lightheaded when he realized *why*. Just as the night before, he felt drunk, exhausted, every part of his body pleasantly spent and used, but he could feel where Hank was still hard and needy, moisture from the tip of his cock leaving a tacky spot on Renaldo's thigh. He reached down, but Hank pushed it aside, turning Renaldo over with a kiss at the top of Renaldo's spine.

"I just need this," he said, draping himself over Renaldo's back.

Renaldo tried to see over his shoulder, unsure of what Hank was going to do, but Hank shushed him, kissing his shoulder blade, his nape, nuzzling his face in Renaldo's hair.

"Open your legs a little," he murmured, fumbling between his legs until Renaldo could feel the hard line of Hank's cock as it dragged between his thighs. "Squeeze them tight, just like—"

Hank gasped, dropping his forehead to Renaldo's back. He dragged the head of his cock over the sensitive skin behind Renaldo's testicles and between the globes of his ass as Hank squeezed them together, his hips undulating, grinding back and forth as he sought his own release. Renaldo pushed back, rocking in tandem against Hank, reaching back to hold Hank's head, keep him close. The heat pouring off Hank's body was a comfort that kept him grounded.

"*Mi querido, ay, mi amor.* You feel so good," Renaldo sighed, never having realized how sensitive his body was, how he had nerves lighting up all along his spine as the fat head of Hank's cock pressed so intimately against his body before sliding back and forth again and again.

Hank paused, lacing their hands together and tucking them firmly under Renaldo's chest. He laid his cheek against the nape of Renaldo's neck and murmured something too soft for Renaldo to hear. They worked together, Renaldo squeezing his muscles as Hank thrust over and over, pistoning his hips in a steady fashion until he trembled, sucking in a harsh breath and thrusting a few more times until they became uneven, his hips shuddering as he spent himself between Renaldo's thighs.

He dropped his weight onto Renaldo's back, caught his breath, and it was wonderful: being held, being kissed, being loved. He meant what he'd said to Hank: He'd never felt like this before, and he never wanted it to end.

They cleaned up quickly, wrapping themselves in their shared bedding and trading soft kisses and tender words until they were breathing deep, pressed together from nose to knees as sleep took them.

THE NEXT MORNING WHEN RENALDO woke, it was to Hank nosing at his side, dragging his teeth lightly over his ribcage and higher. Renaldo massaged Hank's skull with his fingertips, sighing when Hank pushed Renaldo's arms over his head, nibbling and kissing his biceps.

"*Anoche soñé contigo*," Renaldo said softly, arching up into Hank's touch, "Last night I dreamed of you."

He could feel Hank's smile against his skin.

"*Y esta manana no me quiero despertar*," he added, cupping Hank's cheek and drawing him in for a chaste kiss. "And I didn't want to wake up. Mmm, maybe I haven't."

"You did," Hank said, kissing him again. "You want to go back to sleep?" He rubbed his chin over Renaldo's neck in a familiar gesture.

"Possibly." Renaldo stretched like a cat, wrapping his legs around Hank's waist. "I could get used to mornings beginning this way."

Hank didn't respond beyond a smile. Finally, he stood, stretching and twisting his body until his back cracked; he sighed in relief, then shook out his legs. Renaldo wanted to sit up and bite the round curve of Hank's backside, but didn't get the chance. Hank quickly stepped into his clothes, foregoing putting on his shirt or pulling up his union suit.

As he stoked the fire's embers back to life and began making their coffee, Renaldo indulged himself, watching the play of muscles under Hank's skin, smiling to himself because he knew now how they felt under his hands.

"Better stop gawping at me and get to work, pal, if you want any of this," Hank said, motioning with the coffee pot.

"Fine, fine," Renaldo answered, getting up and dressed himself. "But *pal*?"

"I'm sorry," Hank said, getting the pot settled over the fire and pulling out their frying pan. "Not as nice-sounding as your love names?"

A thrill raced through Renaldo at that word from Hank's mouth. Hank must have noticed, as a slow smile spread across his features.

"*Mi querido*, I know you like that one. Me, too. Let's see," Hank said, dropping some fatback into the skillet where it sizzled, the smell tantalizing "*Corazon*, that one's just…" He shrugged. "I like *mi amor*."

He had his back turned as he said that. Renaldo could see the tense line of his shoulders, as if he was bracing himself for Renaldo to think differently in the light of day. On the contrary, for Renaldo, hearing bald admissions of feelings without the cover of night had his spirit soaring. The light of day revealed all truths, his mother had always said, and he believed it.

Renaldo came up behind him, his hands working at the stiff muscles in Hank's back. "I prefer it, too."

Hank grinned down at the frying pan.

It was a long day on the trail, without much of a breeze, but since they were well into October, the sun wasn't as brutal as when they'd set out. The horses had fallen quickly into the men's rhythm, and were now used to the sudden movement of picking up a saddle and settling it over Lady or Paloma, Abuelita or Cloud, to the noise of buckles and packs shifting, to the scent of humans or their fire.

The colt was especially friendly, trotting happily along behind each of the mares, with Abuelita taking a special interest, her ever-watchful gaze on him as he bounced along, staying close to his mother as if Abuelita wanted to protect her, too. Used to a large, social herd, the colt's mother tolerated it. It was a good sign, their easy acceptance of one another.

"Makes it easy to train 'em up when they pay close attention to one another like they're doing," Hank said nodding at where Paloma was deferring to the wild tobiano as the new horse pushed in front.

"Will you help train them?" Renaldo asked, smiling as he thought about the two of them breaking the horses to wear saddle blankets first, warming them up to the idea of more weight on their backs to prepare them for saddles, and eventually riders.

"That's not what your *padre* hired me for," Hank said, eyes forward.

And with that, reality came crashing down. This lovely fantasy he'd been living, this safe existence with a man with whom he was sure he was falling in love, this life he was picturing of waking every morning together, sharing their days and their nights, it all disappeared like water vapor.

Within a few short weeks, they would return to Vista Verde. To the home where his parents had sent one of their children away for his sexual proclivities. What would they think of Renaldo? Of Hank, whom his father held in such high regard?

"I know," Hank said quietly.

"This cannot be it." The ache in Renaldo's chest was almost unbearable as he realized how foolish he'd been. "I can't let you *go*."

Hank didn't say anything, but Renaldo could see him grit his teeth, staring off in the middle distance. Finally, Hank asked, "You think you might leave? Join me out on the range? Maybe not all the time, but—"

His immediate thought was to agree and wholeheartedly. Wasn't that what he wanted? To be with Hank, to have their mornings and evenings together, for always? But he thought of his sister and brothers, of his mother and father, of the land they'd tamed, turned into something verdant and lush, a *home*.

"I figured as much," Hank said softly, nodding to himself.

"No," Renaldo said, his voice rising in a sort of panic. "No, you don't understand."

"I do, though," Hank said, and his voice was forgiving, no anger or frustration. "I'd want that place, too. You have something most people fight their whole lives for, and many never get it."

Renaldo's mind raced, trying to solve this horrible problem. "But earlier you said that you might settle down in Del Rio?"

Hank chewed on the inside of his cheek, mindlessly stroking Lady's mane. Finally, he said, "I don't know if they'll sell me any land, me being who I am. They wouldn't back East. I'd like to, you know, but maybe it's all just a fairy tale I've built up in my head." He turned to face Renaldo, a sad smile on his face as he said, "There's a reason I don't have my own place yet, you know."

"Then you'll buy some from my father," Renaldo said, indignant. "He wouldn't refuse you. He'd be honored to have you as a neighbor. Hank, he *reveres* you."

Hank hung his head, smiling. "That's—well, you're father's a good man. I appreciate it."

"Please," Renaldo begged softly. "Please don't just leave."

"But how could we—" Hank cut himself off, ripping off his hat and scrubbing his hand over his head. "Let me think on it."

Renaldo nodded. "Of course, *mi querido*."

Hank shook his head, his jaw working. "I don't know how to make it work," he said, "but I'll do my damnedest to try. I don't know how your people will feel about someone like me, and I don't like the thought of lying to them, not when they opened their home to me. Your mother *fed* me, kissed my cheek. I couldn't lie to her, not about you, about that."

"But they *love* you, they adore—"

"That was when I was just *Señor* Burnett, the *mesteñero* who's helping your father build his empire. It's a far sight different to be the invert who's frigging his son."

Renaldo balked at the harsh tone of Hank's voice, but he understood Hank's frustration; it matched his own.

He had absolutely no idea how to make this work. But he had to try. He *had* to. He'd find a way to make his family understand.

CHAPTER TWELVE

THE DAYS BLED INTO ONE another; a flavor of desperation soured what had once been so sweet. Some nights were spent wrapped together, learning how to satisfy one another with hands and mouth alike, Renaldo's heart aching with how much he longed for this to be his future, to have every night end with them in each other's arms. Other nights they spent lying side by side telling each other stories from their pasts. Hank's voice was soft and quiet in the starry dark of the prairie, the pleasant, deep vibrations of it managing to fill every crack and cranny in Renaldo, all the lonely corners of his soul that had been waiting for someone like Hank to come into his life.

After saying that very thing to Hank late in the evening when their voices were nothing but whispers into each other's skin, Hank had laughed, running his hand down Renaldo's bare arm. "I don't know what books you read growing up, or just if it's your way," he said, kissing Renaldo at each corner of his mouth, "but I sure like how you make me feel when you say those kind of things."

As lovely as those moments were, as much as Renaldo wanted to pour every ounce of feeling into this man for whom he was growing to care so deeply, the fear of what would happen upon their return still hung over their head. And they still had their work to do. Renaldo was grateful he had more to do day in and day out than worry about his parents learning their youngest son's darkest secret.

Hank decided after a week that it was time to get the new mares used to being handled. After making camp, he took out a long coil of rope and one of the light blankets from their bedrolls.

"Ma'am, you think you might let me show you this?" he asked the wild tobiano mare, holding out the bit of rope for her to investigate. He gave her his hand, stroking her nose and scratching her jaw, and then draped the rope over her back: nothing more than that, to allow her to be used to being touched, to feel weight where she never had before.

Her whole body jolted, alert and suspicious, but when nothing more happened, she relaxed. When she did, Hank removed the rope and held it out to her for investigation once more.

"Just a little rope, see?" he said. "You gonna let me try that again?" He waited for her to relax. They went back and forth like that time and again, the other new mares watching raptly as their leader allowed Hank to drape the rope over her neck and back, running his hand down her back and flank as the coiled rope remained draped over her, talking in low tones and explaining what he was doing.

"If you come with us, we'll see to it that you get fed better than you even knew a body could eat," Hank said, patting her neck. "Wait 'till you get a taste of Gordo and alfalfa. Won't have to stand out in the rain, neither. No coyotes nipping at you. Sounds like a pretty good situation to me, but you think on it."

Renaldo thought about how intimately Hank knew the hard life of living wild, always hiding from predators, those who could harm him, constantly on the move simply to feed himself.

Hank made a loose loop and slowly worked it over the tobiano's head and neck, letting it dangle freely. "Not gonna do more'n that, you have my word." She endured this, eying Hank as if to make sure he would stick to his promise. When he pulled it off, she snorted, nodding her head, and allowed him to rub her face and neck, patiently standing still for the sake of attention.

When the other horses saw that there was nothing to be afraid of, Renaldo approached the buckskin mare and repeated Hank's actions, delighted when she showed no signs of resistance. Her foal came over, curious and willing to let Renaldo touch him in any way, a pet on his nose, a hand along his back, scratching between his ears until the colt's entire body shivered with delight.

The foal was growing up to see how it could be to be cared for, hand-raised and treasured, and he would be far easier to train than the older horses. He would be a perfect candidate to be trained for a spade bit, a five-year process, just as Paloma had been trained.

"Gettin' pretty good at this horse thing, *Señor* Valle," Hank said, grinning down at the ground as he wrapped his stiff lasso over and around his arm.

"*Gracias,*" Renaldo said, rolling his eyes.

"Oh, *de nada.*"

209

OCTOBER WAS DRAWING TO A close, and even though they were losing more and more elevation every day as they traveled south, the temperatures were dropping, especially at night. Even the horses would congregate near the campfire at night instead of remaining hobbled off in the distance. Hank said they were already getting spoiled, but Renaldo took it as a sign of the animals' intelligence.

There was an urgency when they came together now, a need to catalog every look and sound, map every inch of skin. Perhaps this would be the last time they could be together, or at least the last for a long time. Esteban wouldn't need to acquire more horses from Hank for at least a year, after all, and no one else in Del Rio needed unbroke mustangs.

One such night, they were together, their gasps and moans lost on the wide prairie where there was nothing to create an echo, nothing to trap the sounds of their lovemaking, nothing to keep it there with them, private and only theirs. Renaldo's hips were lined up so perfectly, moving himself in a slow grind against Hank below him, Hank's hands gripping Renaldo's backside, guiding his movements.

Renaldo shuddered, moaning low and brokenly when Hank slipped a finger between the cleft of his ass, stroking in a tight circle over his entrance. He couldn't help but push back into it, needing more. Never had he known how sensitive his body was just there, how much pleasure could be found.

"Yeah?" Hank asked, his eyes heavy-lidded and his voice throaty as he stroked more firmly. "I just need… *querido*, do you trust me?"

"Now—*ah!*—now who is playing that card?" Renaldo gasped as Hank pressed more insistently, sucking high on Renaldo's neck. "And yes, *mi amor*, I trust you."

Hank twisted under him, stretching for one of the saddlebags nearby but not near enough. Renaldo rolled off of him to allow him to do whatever it was; when Hank came back, he showed Renaldo the tin canister of leather oil. A thrill raced through him. He grew excited and nervous as he began to understand where this was headed, but he was willing to trust Hank, always.

"Just relax. Let me take care of you," Hank said. He caught Renaldo's mouth in a deep kiss, licking his way inside when Renaldo felt Hank's hand shift between his legs, his finger, now slick, circling once more.

He gasped, but Hank swallowed it down, his tongue stroking along Renaldo's to match his finger's movements. It was a strange sensation, but not unpleasant. The longer he stroked and caressed Renaldo, the more his muscles relaxed, allowing Hank deeper. When Hank began to rub a second finger along the delicate skin behind Renaldo's cock and balls, his index finger now fully inside Renaldo's body and stroking within, Renaldo couldn't help but splay his legs wider. He wanted Hank to have all the room he needed to continue making Renaldo's body thrum like a string stretched tight, yet also wanted to wrap his legs around Hank's body, bring him close, inside, wanted every inch of their bodies to join together.

Hank broke away, his eyes almost completely black, swallowed up by his blown pupils as he looked down at where his second finger was breaching Renaldo, dragging the pads of his fingers deep inside Renaldo's body, circling as if he was searching for something. "You like that?"

Renaldo buried his hands in his own hair, arching and grinding his body down against that pressure. "*Ay, que rico.*" As Hank stroked along his sensitive rim with a third finger, two already buried as deeply as they could go, his whole body jolted. Hank had stroked over something inside of him, had applied just the right sort of pressure that had Renaldo shaking as if he was about to climax. "*Se siente tan bueno, querido.* So good—" He could *cry* from how good it felt, almost overwhelmed by a need to come. "*¡Seguir adelante*; don't stop!"

With his free hand, Hank draped one of Renaldo's legs over his elbow, opening Renaldo even more, driving all three fingers inside, but he didn't stroke over that spot that had Renaldo seeing stars just before. Renaldo whined, rocking down to find it himself, but Hank chuckled darkly and removed his hand, pouring a little more of the warm-leather smelling oil into his palm and stroking himself slowly, deliberately, watching Renaldo's face as he took in the sight.

"*Amado, metémela,*" Renaldo said, his voice sounding rough and raw, but he *needed* Hank inside of him, his body now aching and empty. He hooked a hand behind Hank's neck, pulling Hank down to kiss him, to be covered, to be filled, *anything* other than this sharp, lonely ache where he'd once been full, but Hank shushed him, rubbing the head of his cock where Renaldo was ready, waiting for him.

They both groaned as Hank surged forward. Renaldo's body lit up from the tips of his toes to his scalp, where every hair prickled as places he didn't know could feel pleasure were electrified by the hot, solid bar of Hank's cock filling him, bringing the two of them closer than he thought it would be possible, every thrust of Hank's hips sharp and pointed, rolling his hips and grinding against Renaldo's body as if he could go farther inside, as if he needed to get even closer, as well.

Hank bracketed Renaldo's head with his arms, kissing and sucking at Renaldo's neck, breathing hot, moist air over Renaldo's skin as his hips continued their relentless drive, pulling back just enough to catch on Renaldo's rim, only to drive back forward, his hips pressed tight against Renaldo's ass. Renaldo arched up, trying to make even their bellies touch, to get friction on his own cock as his release continued to be just out of reach.

Hank rooted his knees more firmly between Renaldo's legs, preventing what Renaldo was trying to accomplish, and shushed him, whispering in his ear, "Touch yourself; let me see you."

He was so close, almost mindless with how badly he needed release, so he licked his lips, nodding, and circled his hand around himself; the sweat between their bodies there under their blankets was enough to slick his palm. It was almost too much stimulation: Hank's face buried in Renaldo's neck where he repeated something too softly for Renaldo to understand, the friction of their bodies working together, the comfort of Hank's hand nestled at Renaldo's lower back, how it held his body up and open in such a way that every thrust had Hank sliding over that most perfect spot deep inside him. The way he could feel the flared head of Hank's cock almost catching on his rim before driving back in with a noise that should be obscene but only drove him closer and closer to the edge.

"*Ay, que rico,*" Renaldo gasped, "*Te quiero, amado.*" He threw his head back, speeding his hand up to match Hank's rhythm and grunted as his toes curled, as his body rocked against his lover's, as everything in the universe centered in that feeling of completion rolling over him, of Hank holding him tight and cursing under his breath, his hips stuttering as he found his own release shortly after.

Renaldo's arms fell to his sides, his whole body sagged pleasurably under Hank's weight, unbothered by the mess between their bodies, not when Hank was drawing his lips up the length of Renaldo's neck, kissing his way to his mouth for a slow, deep kiss.

"Did you mean it?" Hank asked, tracing his fingers along Renaldo's cheek.

"Everything," Renaldo said, turning his face to kiss Hank's palm. "Which part in particular?"

Hank laughed, a strange sensation as he softened inside Renaldo's body, but Renaldo didn't want to move just yet.

"The '*te quiero.*'"

Renaldo took Hank's face in both of his hands, locking eyes. "Especially that part. *Con todo mi corazón.*"

Dragging the tip of his nose along the side of Renaldo's, he sighed, "*Y yo.*"

"Pleased" wasn't strong enough to express how that made Renaldo feel. The easy humor between them, the passion, the times when they were calm, when they worked side by side, all of that was wonderful, more wonderful than he knew his life could be. But knowing Hank loved him, too...

"I will not lose you," Renaldo said, the fierceness in his voice making Hank's eyes open wide before he kissed Renaldo once more.

It was uncomfortable to separate; the air was cold, and his body was aching, but Hank took care of cleaning them both before sliding back in beside Renaldo with the blankets pulled up high as they laid side-by-side, staring up at the night sky.

"I'm getting tired of walking away from people I love," Hank said quietly, the resignation in his voice making Renaldo's stomach sour.

"You won't have to this time. We'll find a way, *querido*."

Hank found his hand and held it. "Most of my life, especially those early years, I didn't mean much of anything to anyone. My mama loved me, don't get me wrong," he said, "but she wasn't allowed by circumstance to really be a mother to me once I had to leave the house. And then I had to leave for good almost ten years later. Been passed around ever since, until I'd had enough of it.

"I loved Tsá-cho," he continued. Renaldo bristled at his side, acrid jealousy burning the back of his throat; for him, there would only ever be Hank. "I did, and I'm not ashamed of it. He was the first person who liked me for me, and not just for what I could do for him. But in the end, he was ready to start his new life, and I didn't like how easy it was for him to give me up."

"If it hadn't been easy for him?" Renaldo asked carefully, almost afraid of the answer. It certainly seemed that Tsá-cho had wanted Hank back.

"But it was easy," Hank said gently. "It was, and I figured out some time ago that it was for the best. His people don't let two *nde'isdzan* be together anyway—it's greedy. The gift he has is meant to be shared. But he *does* have an eagle's spirit, after all, and he didn't belong with me, nor I with him."

He squeezed Renaldo's hand. "Now I'm here with you, and … well, I don't have a way with words like you do," he said, his voice light, "but I know that you made me feel something no one ever has."

"And what is that, *cariño*?" He turned to his side, placing the palm of his hand over Hank's heart as if he could protect it, keep it safe.

"Like I belong to you." Hank let out a shuddering breath. "Like you wouldn't just let me go."

"I wouldn't," Renaldo said, "won't. We'll figure out some way. Even if we have to pretend that we are only friends when we get back to Vista Verde—"

"No," Hank said, vehement.

"But, if it—"

"I've never lied a day in my life," Hank said, his jaw tight and voice shaking with frustration, "and I sure as hell ain't gonna start by lying to your father, a man who treated me like his equal from the moment I met him. Fine way to repay a man's respect and regard by lying to him, and about his own son, too. I won't do it. We'll have to think of something else."

Renaldo stared at him, mouth working but no sound coming out. Finally, he said, "Of course I won't force you to do anything you feel so strongly about, *amor*."

Hank sighed, but nodded. "We have to do this honorably. What I feel for you—what I want to have with you can't be had by skulking about, being dishonest or lying and hiding from your family."

Renaldo kissed his shoulder, and then fell to his back, one arm tucked behind his head as he looked up at the stars, wishing they had an answer for him. "I've never lied to my parents, and I don't want to, either. But what if they won't accept this?" He honestly couldn't imagine telling his parents he wanted to spend the rest of his life with a man, even though he did, and couldn't begin to know what their reaction would be when they heard it.

"Then we'll deal with the consequences, I suppose," Hank replied.

That sounded a lot like an eventual farewell to Renaldo.

Hank drifted off almost immediately, still holding Renaldo's hand in his, but Renaldo found he couldn't sleep. He couldn't stop imagining scenarios of his parents or his siblings discovering them. He could picture both their anger and their disappointment. What would Calandaría think of them, knowing how she'd reacted to Patricia and Silvestre? He tried to recall their conversations before he and Hank left.

"*Never forget that no one knows you like I do.*"

She'd been so intent on making sure he knew how much she loved him, that no matter what, she would always love him. No matter what.

She had made comments that Renaldo hadn't wanted to look too closely at, not quite understanding what he was feeling himself, but now he understood that it was attraction toward Hank.

And she'd recognized it. "*No matter what, you are a part of me, cariño, and I will always accept and love you.*"

He covered his face with the crook of his arm; a painful wave of homesickness washed over him, drowning him with its suddenness. He forced himself to breathe deeply until he got himself under control, not wanting to wake Hank with something as ridiculous as Renaldo missing his sister.

He shook his head, though, because now he knew that Hank wouldn't think it was ridiculous. No, Hank would be reminded of that ache he'd carried around for years himself, the loss of two sisters and his mother.

Hank had no one.

He had Renaldo, to be sure, but whether they could actually *be* together was still so uncertain. Hank had mentioned with longing weeks ago that he'd love to have land of his own, a ranch to call home, enough to live on, and nothing more. That was everything Renaldo wanted, as well as someone to share it with: Hank.

What Hank dreamed of having one day was what Renaldo's family had already built and was now expanding to make room for him and his brothers, possibly even a husband of Calandaría's, if he wanted to join the family business. Of this Renaldo had no doubt; the stories his mother and father shared of sprawling family estates, how they longed to have that once more, were fresh in his mind.

If they could come to accept the love Renaldo had for Hank, or if they didn't accept it, but perhaps tolerated it, turned a blind eye, would they allow them to stay on the family's land? His mother wanted so badly to have grandchildren, cousins, the sprawling family she so hoped for all gathered around the great table in their home. She'd always been amused and satisfied by large, noisy groups of loved ones.

And what of Eduardo? His wife, Hortencia? Francisco? He believed Francisco would understand, would know that one loves whom they love. If he was being honest with himself, he didn't care about Patricia's thoughts beyond worrying about her telling tales to her own family.

But no, she wouldn't. Not with what the Valle family knew about her. Not that they would hold it over her head or ever say a word against their own family or shame her in any way. Yet, Renaldo believed Patricia would honor the secrets at Vista Verde, if only out of a sense of self-preservation.

Hank snored softly under his hat, mindlessly shifting in his sleep to be closer to Renaldo's body heat. Amused, Renaldo turned to his side, pressing all along Hank's body and suppressing the urge to laugh when Hank rumbled a pleased noise in his sleep.

What Hank had been born into was a perverted form of what a household should be, what a *family* should be. Circumstances were obviously beyond his and his mother's control, circumstances that had denied him what he'd always longed for, what he'd traveled all over the country in search of: a place to belong.

Renaldo nuzzled just under Hank's ear, kissing the lone freckle at Hank's pulse point. They may not be allowed to stay at Vista Verde, but they belonged together and would stay that way. Somewhere.

"DO WE HAVE ENOUGH PROVISIONS to stay here for an extra day?" Renaldo asked, pulling the saddle off Abuelita as they got to their camp for the night. Abuelita shook her head and neck, and then trotted over to the buckskin mother and her colt.

Hank, his arm draped over the pack on Lady's back, scratched under his chin. "Here? Yeah, we could do that."

They were getting close to Del Rio, camped in the tablelands where several streams and creeks cut through the caliche. As a result, there were nearby trees, plenty of grass for the horses to graze, and food enough for Hank and Renaldo if they set out a few snares.

Renaldo wanted to delay his return home, wanted enough time to think things through, decide how best to approach this very unusual situation with his family. Hank had been right: They must be honest about this, must honor the feelings they shared without sullying them with a lie or by deceit. And Renaldo wouldn't do anything to tarnish the name Hank had built for himself. It was all Hank had: his name and what it stood for.

He also realized that he actually had a way to appeal to his father, and it was right there with them.

"Pass me the bosal and *mecate*?" Renaldo asked, patting the tobiano's neck.

"You think she's ready?" Hank asked. There wasn't any judgment in it, no sign that Hank didn't trust Renaldo, just a genuine question, as though he saw Renaldo as an equal, not his apprentice.

Renaldo stroked his hand up the tobiano's nose, looking into her fathomless amber eyes. "*Chiquitita*, are you ready to choose?"

She snorted, pushing her head up against Renaldo's hand for more affection.

"I think we have our answer," he said, rubbing her face once more. He could hear Hank's noise of agreement behind him as he gathered up the gear.

Renaldo held out the curved, wrapped rawhide for her to smell and become acquainted with. He set it over her nose, checking to see if the weight was distributed correctly. Too arched and it wouldn't touch her face properly. Ill-fitted and it would be a nuisance or even hurt the delicate bones of her sinus passages.

The horse flicked her ears forward and back, nodding out of reach after a moment.

"Yes, I know, very strange," Renaldo said in a quiet, low voice. He buckled on an addition to it. "Shall we try again?"

The horse stamped her foot but continued to patiently wait as Renaldo once again slipped the hackamore over the top of her nose, but this time he added the *mecate*, the special reins, to the bosal in order to help her adjust to the different weight distributions he would apply to guide her. He put it on, left it, and then removed it to show that it wasn't permanent, consistently praising her each time, repeating this over and over. Eventually she tolerated Renaldo simply showing it to her and then quickly slipping it over her nose without giving her any more warning than he would for Abuelita or Paloma.

He held the *mecates* in his hands and stepped forward. She followed, and he continued walking, giving the gentlest of pulls with a crook of his finger, moving in the direction he wished to go, letting her become used to the direction being associated with the slight pressure on her face. It should never be harsh, should never be rough. To train on a spade bit, the horse's mouth and face were to be respected, the reins used as the most delicate of instruments. Force or aggression was the antithesis of proper horse training. Hank had shown him that this was true from the very beginning, not just when it was time to prepare the horse for its future work as the Valle men did.

After making a serpentine path around their camp, guiding her with the tiniest of tugs from his fingertips, Renaldo deemed it a success. "*Estoy orgulloso de ti*," he said, praising her while removing the gear from her head. She shook her head and backed up a few paces but didn't walk off as he half-expected her to do.

"Think it's time you two picked out a name," Hank said, coming up behind Renaldo and setting his hand low on Renaldo's back, his thumb working back and forth. "What do you think?"

Renaldo began coiling up the reins when the horse came closer, smelling the items in his hand, probably catching her own scent on them now. "What do you think?" he asked the mare. "*Jefecita*? Little boss?" She lipped and tugged at the rein, curious, and Renaldo laughed. "No, *La Reina*. That is who you are." He turned to Hank and said, "The Queen. But also—" He nodded as she continued to mouth at the leather.

"I like that. It works in English and Spanish. Something for you and for me," Hank said. Renaldo patted her on the rump, watching as she trotted off to join the others.

The more they desensitized the newcomers, exposed them to all of the new aspects of what would be expected of them, the easier it would be for them to adjust to ranch life as a harmonious, united herd. A family.

Darkness was swiftly approaching, so Renaldo and Hank settled in for the night. Even though they were getting closer to the Rio Grande where winters were mild, the nights were still cool after the sun set. They shivered in the night air as they dressed in their warmer, long-sleeved union suits and climbed into their combined bedroll eagerly.

"Tomorrow," Renaldo said, throwing an arm over Hank's chest and humming his approval when Hank pulled the blanket up to cover him, "we'll talk to *Mamacita*, the buckskin, and see what she thinks about becoming a proper *caballo*."

"Maybe you let me name that one," Hank teased.

"Of course, *mi amor*," Renaldo said, barely stifling a yawn against Hank's shoulder. "Something for you and for me, no?"

Hank didn't say anything for a moment, then tightened his arm around Renaldo and murmured into his hair, "*Sí.*"

IT WAS THE FIRST WEEK in November; they were less than half a day's ride from Vista Verde.

The buckskin mare had been named Cecelia, and although Hank hadn't explicitly stated why he'd chosen that name, Renaldo had the impression that it had been his mother's. It was Hank giving his mother another chance, giving her the freedom to be the mother she could have been had circumstances been different. Cecelia was attentive and tender with her colt, both playful and loving.

Renaldo had held him the night Hank named her, respecting both Hank's privacy and how difficult it was for him to share such personal information. When Hank was ready, he would talk. And Renaldo would be there to listen.

By this time, Cecelia as well as *La Reina* now allowed riders on their backs. Renaldo used the hackamore with a *mecate* and *fiador* that Hank normally used with his two horses, but Lady and Cloud were so comfortable with Hank astride them that he could ride bareback.

It was all a part of Renaldo's plan to have as many of the wild *mesteños* past the first stages of training as possible to prove how successful this trip had been, prove how well Renaldo and Hank worked together.

And how beneficial it could be if they were allowed to stay together.

The sun was obliterated by clouds for most of the morning. As they followed along the base of a rambling line of buttes, the air carrying the almost-turpentine scent of juniper and Ponderosa pine, they came to Rio del Diablo, Devil's River, near the place they'd crossed when they'd first left all those months ago. This was the family's secret, the place where a freshwater spring, a mineral spring and a ten-foot rushing waterfall pouring off the Devil's river all met, making a wide creek with the most delicious water his mother called *riquísimo*. The family guarded it fiercely; even Hank had first believed this to be the infamous sulfuric, almost poisonous spring of Vista Verde.

Renaldo and his brothers often came here to swim and enjoy themselves; it was Renaldo's favorite place on earth, and a place the whole family was determined to keep secret. It was where they claimed sulfuric fumes spoiled the water, making the whole place inhabitable.

"Follow me," he said, grinning over his shoulder at Hank as he led across a twisting path through hills and patches of scraggly trees, finally leading the group around a squat, crumbling butte. As soon as they turned south, the vista opened up before them. The land was covered in flora; sycamores and great pin oaks dwarfed the smaller understory trees and shrubbery they'd grown so used to; much of it was still green in the temperate climate. But what was so special was the water before them. It wasn't a sickly green from algae; it wasn't clear or blue to match the mood of the sky. No, it was turquoise, bright and shining and dazzling.

Paloma seemed to sense where they were headed; her steps were lively as she cantered forward with the whole procession following. The closer they got, the louder the steady rumble of the falls where they cut through the red sandstone and white limestone mesas, the various elevations weaving along the exposed walls in a beautiful contrast of colors. They followed the sound until they came to a shimmering pool where the water was jade-bright and almost effervescent from the steady pounding of the waterfall combining with a mineral spring.

They dismounted quickly, dallying the reins over the horns to allow the horses to graze freely.

"It will be cold, *querido*," Renaldo said, tugging his shirt off over his head, unable to control his grin when faced with a place that he so strongly associated with his brothers, a place they would come all by themselves, diving into the water, leaping from the rocks and challenging one another to make the biggest splash possible. All petty bickering, arguments or bruised egos would dissolve once they came to this place. Even Eduardo, ten years older than Renaldo, hadn't been immune to its charms.

"But it's worth it," he said, dropping his trousers and tugging off his boots.

Hank hadn't removed anything.

"What is it?" Renaldo asked, pulling his union suit off and kicking it onto the pile of clothes. "Don't you want to come in?"

"Maybe I want to see you test those waters for yourself, first," Hank replied, backing toward the horses as if he believed Renaldo would grab him up and force him in. "Shallow stream heated up by the sun is one thing... that's another entirely," he said, nodding at the water.

Renaldo rolled his eyes. "You'll see." He backed away, watching Hank where he stood next to Reina, wary. Renaldo turned, climbed up onto a worn flat of limestone and gave out a loud cry, ran a few feet and jumped into the water where he knew it was deepest. It *was* cold, cold enough to make his breath catch, his lungs burn, but he knew from experience that if he swam in place, his body would heat up comfortably.

He popped to the surface with a gasp, splashing at Hank. "You see? I'm alive and well."

Hank scowled at him, but begrudgingly unbuttoned his shirt and pulled off his suspenders. "If my heart gives out in there, I'm going to come back as a ghost and haunt you."

"*Mi amor*, I would just be grateful to continue having your company dead or alive." Renaldo laughed, floating on his back before growing cold and diving into the water again. Hank didn't jump in, but slowly walked into the water, shivering and cussing the whole time, trying to keep his balance on the slippery rock.

"You must get in all at once!" Renaldo said, treading water and laughing as Hank hissed, stopping when the water reached his thighs. "*Eres tan patético,*" he laughed.

"I'll thank you to leave me to doing this in my own way," Hank huffed. "Gol-dammit," he muttered. He took a deep breath and ducked down all at once until the water hit his chin.

Renaldo was glad no women were around, given the stream of obscenities that poured from Hank's mouth as he sputtered and shivered, side-stepping awkwardly until he was deep enough to float at the surface.

"There, *queriño*," Renaldo soothed, swimming to Hank and pulling him in his arms. "You'll feel better soon." He kissed

Hank's temple, hiding his amusement. "So stubborn. It's so much easier if you just get in all at once."

"D-don't know how deep it is," Hank said, his bottom lip quivering as he shivered and shook in Renaldo's embrace. "D-don't know what the b-bottom's made of, neither. I d-didn't come all this way to break my n-neck."

Wrapping his legs around Hank's waist, Renaldo rubbed his hands up and down Hank's arms until he stopped trembling. He floated away, moving his own legs and arms to keep the blood flowing. "Eduardo found this place after we moved here. In the summer, a great flood of bats come out of a cave at sunset, thousands upon thousands of them."

"Bats?"

"*Sí, amante,*" Renaldo laughed. "They are harmless, but they're in such great numbers that they block the sky as they exit. Eduardo saw them while riding home and told us all about it. Calandaría would have nothing to do with them."

"I always told you your sister was smart, didn't I?" Hank said.

"You did, yes," Renaldo agreed. "But my other brothers and I wanted to see them. As long as we finished our chores and Eduardo accompanied us, my mother would allow us to come out here on summer nights to watch them take flight."

"I bet this place is much better when it's warmer," Hank mused, looking around. The limestone walls the falls spilled over were steep, any dry cracks were covered in sagebrush, and further down the river, the green, lush river bottoms could be seen peeking around the edge of the red mesa that formed the wall which enclosed the freshwater creek. Beyond that was home.

But would it still be? And would it be home for both of them?

"Might as well clean up before we get back. Maybe it'll make it harder to get run out on a rail if I'm shined up like a new penny," Hank said just before he took a deep breath and ducked under the water.

Renaldo swam to one of the lesser falls, content to let the chilly water wash over him, ridding him of trail dust and camp smoke—the physical traces of their long journey, gone in an instant. They climbed out and stretched along the red rock to let the sun to dry them, each quiet and lost in his own thoughts. *Would he be allowed to stay? Would Hank?* The idea he had of home—the safety and security it represented, his family's effusive love for one another—was so fixed in his mind that he didn't want anything to change.

Yet he knew that it must. He had, after all.

They were quiet as they dressed and mounted their horses one last time. Now dressed in his well-worn trousers and shirt, his vest unbuttoned for comfort, Renaldo thought about how disheveled he must look in comparison to how he'd left home. His hair, thick and unruly and presently curling damp over his shirt's collar, had been left to grow wild. Hank murmured more than once that he liked the way it looked when it brushed the back of Renaldo's neck and ears. The skin on his face and forearms was darker from having been in the sun for days on end.

Also changed was the ease in which he sat on his mount, no longer stiff and worried that Paloma wouldn't obey her training, that Hank would think him new to the whole business of horse work, that he must prove himself to the legendary *Señor* Burnett to please both Hank and his father.

As they rode home, he thought back to something Calandaría had said the night before he left, that she believed Silvestre's actions would have a ripple effect for all of them, that it would change everything for the family and nothing would be the same.

He eyed Hank, sitting tall and strong in his saddle, determined, and to anyone who wasn't intimately familiar with the man, looking completely at ease. But now Renaldo knew better. Hank's gaze never settled, as if he was always on the lookout for a threat; the line of his thigh was tense as if he was prepared to turn Lady around and take off: Maybe he wasn't as sure as Renaldo was that they would be welcomed.

Calandaría had been right: Everything was about to change.

CHAPTER THIRTEEN

EVEN THOUGH HIS BODY WAS alight with nerves and his stomach was fluttering, he couldn't help the excitement of finally coming home. He led Hank and the *remuda* along a familiar, well-worn path, one that he and his brothers traveled routinely to bring home the herds of sheep or goats from where they'd grazed. It was wide enough that he and Hank could travel side-by-side, yet Hank hung back, bringing up the rear.

Where the land sloped downward—a gradual drop leading to the wide river that cut through their property—sat his childhood home with the low-slung eaves he could remember watching Estebán and Eduardo nail into place stretching all along its length. He couldn't help the smile blooming across his face, couldn't help how he wanted to urge Paloma to go faster, couldn't help the way the bottom of his stomach fell when he saw an unfamiliar man, broad chested with strong arms visible even from this distance, standing against the post of the front door of the house, smoking a cigarette.

He went stiff in the saddle, looking around the property, trying to find his father, brothers, anyone who could explain who this stranger was, but there was no one. His heart began to race. Had something happened? His father was becoming quite old, perhaps too old to continue working the ranch and—

He whistled sharply, shifting in the saddle, and Paloma responded instantly, lowering her head and charging forward. Even though he only had a knife, he would find out what had happened, would defend whoever was left.

The man looked up at the sound of pounding hooves, no doubt startled by Renaldo's sudden appearance. He waved a hand and dashed inside. Renaldo continued to race toward the house, quickly dismounting and grabbing his knife from the saddlebag. His pulse thrummed in his ears, panic coursed through him. The door opened and Calandaría came racing out.

"¡Ay, Renaldo!" She clapped her hands together and shouted into the house, "Mama, it's Renaldo!" She flew down the steps and across the yard, her face bright and overjoyed, throwing her arms around him and knocking his hat off into the dirt. He stood there, trying to adjust from fearing that his entire family had been slaughtered, their ranch taken over by some hardened strangers, to his sister crying and laughing in his arms.

Tentatively, he put his arms around her. Finding her solid and real, it hit him: He was home. He was home and his twin was safe. He squeezed her, lifted her off her feet and swung her around. After he put her down, she cupped his smiling face and *tsked*.

"You need a shave. These poor whiskers look dreadful, like a dog with the mange," she said, rubbing at the corner of Renaldo's upper lip.

"I've been gone for months, and all you can do is insult me?" he teased.

Burying her face in his chest, she hugged him again.. "Renaldo, everything is different," she whispered. She looked up at him, her lip wobbling and eyes filled with tears.

The fear he had at first seeing that strange man came slamming back into his chest. Keeping his voice low, he asked, "Are you in danger?"

"*¿Cómo?* Why do you … Of course I'm not! Why would I be in danger?" she said, shaking her head. "*Ay, dios mio,* were *you* in danger? Were you attacked? Are you well? Where is *Señor* Burnett?" She checked him all over before glancing around the yard, as if she expected Hank to materialize before her.

"Calandaría!" he snapped, taking her by the shoulders and bending down so they were looking into each other's eyes. "Who was that man? That stranger?"

Her whole face softened, her cheeks turning pink. "That is Tomás."

Renaldo could hear Hank riding past them, headed to one of the empty corrals with the horses, but he could only focus on his sister. His stomach lurched as if he'd missed a step. "Who is Tomás?"

Before she could answer, his mother came streaming outside, handkerchief already dabbing at her face as she cried, "*¡Mijo!* You are alive! *¡Gracias al cielo!*" She crossed herself, and then used his ears to pull his face close to hers and kissed his cheeks and forehead over and over. "Your father said I should not worry, that *Señor* Burnett would keep you safe, but one never knows; it is so *dangerous* in the wild!"

He untangled himself from his mother's enthusiastic embrace, held her in his arms and kissed the top of her head. "Mama, there was no danger at all."

"Where is *Señor* Burnett?" She twisted and turned until she spotted him closing the corral gate's latch. "There you are! Come here right this minute," she scolded.

Hank went completely still, turning to Renaldo before straightening his shoulders and walking steadily toward them. He pulled his hat off, twisted it in his hands and nodded at her. "Ma'am."

With a cry, she flung her hands in the air and pulled him into a hug, then holding his face and giving him the same treatment that she'd given Renaldo. Hank looked stunned but endured it. Renaldo's heart ached as he realized how long it must have been since a mother fussed over Hank.

"I am so grateful to you," she cried, patting Hank on the arm. "So grateful you brought my baby home to me."

"Oh, Mama," Calandaría sighed. "*¡Basta!*"

"Don't speak to your mother like that, young lady," she replied before looping her arm through the crook of Hank's elbow. "You two are skin and bones," she chided. "Renaldo, come fetch me water for coffee. Now, were you ever in any danger? You must be honest with me," she asked Hank, leading him inside while Renaldo stood in the courtyard.

Calandaría grinned and nudged him with her elbow. "Aren't you glad to be home?"

"I don't know that I can answer that just yet," he replied, following her to the rain barrel. "And you never answered my question: Who is Tomás?"

Calandaría bit her lip, but Renaldo could see the smile she couldn't hide. "*Señor* Aguayo," she answered.

Renaldo held the small bucket they kept nearby as she scooped in the water. "The man who asked Mama's permission to court you?"

She nodded and then closed the lid on the barrel. "He isn't courting me," she answered. With a deep breath, she laid her hand on Renaldo's arm and said, "He's going to marry me."

"*¡Ay, que no!* Really?" Renaldo looked around as if he would find the man standing there with a priest. "Where is he, this man who thinks he will marry you?"

"You're as bad as Francisco," she laughed. "As soon as Tomás saw you and *Señor* Burnett coming, he told us and left through the kitchen to find Papa."

"So he's well? Papa?"

"Why wouldn't he be?" she asked, holding the kitchen door for him. "We are all well, *chiquitito*. Even Silvestre, according to his letters, but," she said glancing around and dropping her voice to barely a whisper, "we try not to talk about him where Mama or Patricia might overhear."

He would demand to know more about that later, but as he walked into the house, he was hit with a wave of homesickness so powerful that his chest tightened. Everything looked the same. It even *smelled* the same, like his mother's cooking and the bunches of yarrow they kept tied by the doors to discourage bugs from coming inside. Like *home*. The great table still gleamed from being waxed each week, and his mother was fussing at the stove, chattering away to Hank who dutifully sat near her, listening intently.

Renaldo could see Hank's polite attentiveness to Renaldo's mother in a new light, now. He could see the hunger in Hank's eyes, the longing, the cautiousness in how he held himself still, not too close or eager, as if he didn't want to get his hopes too high. As if he didn't believe that he would be allowed to stay.

Renaldo poured the water into the coffee pot for her, and when she turned to prepare the coffee, he leaned down, put a hand on Hank's shoulder, thumb working softly just under Hank's shirt collar, and whispered in his ear, "You can tell her no, if you don't want anything."

Hank grinned up at him, covering Renaldo's hand briefly, coughing slightly. Renaldo realized what he was doing, how intimate that would have looked should anyone have caught them, and jerked his hand back as if he'd been burned. His mother turned to him, but before she could speak, he stepped back and said, "Mama, Han—*Señor* Burnett and I will wash up and come right back."

"Yes, you will," she said, her voice bossy and so wonderfully familiar as she bustled about the kitchen gathering food for them.

Renaldo jerked his head toward the kitchen door; Hank followed him after a quick, "Ma'am."

They hadn't thought this through, he realized. He hadn't thought about all of the little ways they hadn't needed to hide their feelings for one another out there, about how they should behave in front of the family, about how much it would hurt if they were turned away.

But before Renaldo could say anything, ask Hank how he wanted to handle this or when, he heard a shout.

"*¡Mijo!*"

They looked toward the field behind the house and could see Estebán riding toward them, waving his hat in the air. Tomás was riding home, as well, on an unfamiliar horse and taking his time about it. Calandaría must have been watching from the door as she came outside to join them. Renaldo watched his

235

sister behave in a way he'd never seen before: smoothing her skirts and bodice, pinching her cheeks to make them pink and rosy, fidgeting and nervous and giddy.

His attention was redirected to his father as Estebán dismounted slowly, a reminder that he was getting on in years. He pulled Renaldo into his embrace, rocking from side to side. "It is so good to have you back home, *mijo*. The house isn't the same without you keeping your sister in check."

"Papa!" Calandaría cried.

"*Señor* Burnett!" Estebán cried, throwing his arms wide, taking Hank's hand in both of his and shaking it enthusiastically. "I am so pleased to see you as well!"

"And you, *Señor*," Hank said, taking what looked to Renaldo to be a steadying breath. "You'd be real proud of your son. He's a natural."

"I knew it," Estebán said, his hands on his hips as he smiled at Renaldo. He cut a severe look to Hank and asked, "He didn't give you any trouble, did he?"

Hank coughed. "No, sir. Not one bit."

"Papa," Renaldo said, interrupting to give Hank a moment, and to take a moment for himself. "Would you like to see the *mesteños* we brought back?"

"*¡Oh, sí, sí!* And how many did you bring? Two? Three, perhaps?" he asked, smiling at them. Renaldo's hands were shaking. His father looked so happy, so proud. Now, faced with having to be honest with his parents, with needing them to understand that the life they'd imagined for him would no longer be possible, he was terrified.

He glanced at Hank, who looked just as tense as he did. "Five, Papa."

"Five? This cannot be!" Estebán said, taking Calandaría's arm as they all walked to see the horses. "Your first venture and you bring back so many?" He turned the corner and could see for himself that it was true. "*¡Ay... caray! Mijo*, I am so proud of you! And you, as well, *Señor* Burnett. What a blessing to have met you!"

"Please, call me Henry. I, well," Hank said carefully, chancing a glance at Renaldo, "I got used to being a little less formal over the past few months, I suppose."

"If you wish it, of course! I'm happy to know that you two have become such friends, then!" He turned to the corral and gasped. "And a colt as well as the others? *Mijo... cariño*, I... I am so shocked! This is wonderful!"

"Of course he would be the best at it," Calandaría said, draping her arms atop the wind-worn fencing and smiling as the colt skittishly approached them before bounding back to his mother.

"No, I am not the best," Renaldo said. "I just *learned* from the best."

"Now, *that* is the respect I wish to see for someone of *Señor*, eh—" Estebán caught himself and grinned, correcting himself to say, "of *Henry's* stature."

"That's not all, Papa." Renaldo hopped over the split rail, his hands at his side as he approached *La Reina*. "This is Queen," he said, smiling as he patted her neck. "*La Reina* has learned a few things while we were bringing them all home."

As he demonstrated how the mares were all comfortable with wearing hackamores, and as Estebán exclaimed in wonder, Renaldo and Hank exchanged a look. Renaldo gave Hank a tiny smile. The first step in their plan was working.

"*Hola,*" a new voice said. *La Reina* put her ears back, fussing and pulling against the reins, so Renaldo dropped them quickly to avoid hurting her. She trotted to the far side of the corral, shaking her head.

"*Perdóname,*" the man who Renaldo had seen in front of the ranch house said. "I'm still learning how to be comfortable around the wild ones."

Renaldo saw Calandaría beaming up at the newcomer, a man a few inches shorter than Renaldo, his chest like a barrel, his arms were strong and large, his round cheeks gave him a jolly expression. His hair was carefully combed, and he had a thick mustache that drooped over the corners of his mouth. Renaldo couldn't guess his age just from looking at him, but he was most likely close to Eduardo's age, which would make him thirty or so.

He stuck his broad, work-roughened hand out for Renaldo to shake. "Tomás Aguayo. And you must be Renaldo! I'm very pleased to finally meet you. I've heard so many things about you from your beautiful sister."

Renaldo raised an eyebrow at his sister. "All of them good, I hope," he said, shaking the man's hand. He half-expected the man to squeeze Renaldo's hand in a macho test of strength, but he didn't. It was firm, but gentle.

"Most of it," Tomás laughed, "but I'm beginning to understand that anything involving trouble was probably because of something *Señorita* Valle led you into doing."

Calandaría made a scandalized sound; Renaldo decided he liked this suitor of hers.

Estebán put a hand to Hank's back, bringing him back into the group. He'd begun to skulk off once Tomás joined them. "And *Señor* Aguayo, it is my honor to introduce the famous *mesteñero*, Henry Burnett. As you may remember, my son has been with him these past few months learning all that he can."

Renaldo's face was hot. Yes, he certainly had learned a lot. He was relieved to see that Tomás shook Hank's hand without hesitation. He couldn't forget Hank's fear that he wouldn't be welcomed or seen as equal in their town, and this was a good sign. Just because they weren't Anglos didn't mean both races always got along with each other.

As Tomás and Hank became better acquainted, Renaldo watched his sister, her eyes sparkling, her face glowing. No one in the world captured her attention but this new man. Renaldo could certainly understand that feeling. At least she wasn't saying anything shocking or revealing about *him* at the moment.

"*Señor* Aguayo is a silversmith," Esteban murmured in Renaldo's ear. "He does very well for himself, beautiful craftsmanship, highly sought after works of art."

Renaldo remembered Calandaría speaking about a pair of ornate spurs that had been created for their father.

"You must let me make you something!" Tomás cried, clapping a hand to Hank's shoulder. "It would be an honor to have someone such as yourself wearing one of my humble designs."

"Humble!" Calandaría said with a laugh. "Your work is exquisite. I've never seen such delicacy in metal before."

Hank and Renaldo caught each other's gaze, both barely able to shut down their grins before being caught.

"Your sister, she is very kind, very generous with her praise," Tomás said, blushing beet red and shuffling his feet.

"Take a good look, *mijo*," Esteban said quietly. "That look on your sister's face? That is what love looks like. It is how I look at your mother every day, how Eduardo looks at Hortencia.

239

And one day, you will find a woman who will make you feel just as we do."

The pit of Renaldo's stomach fell out at that.

"Perhaps," he said, glancing at Hank. Hank looked away, shoulders sagging.

"MA'AM," HANK SAID, LEANING AWAY from the table and holding his stomach. "That was some of the best cooking I've ever had in my life, and that's the truth."

Juana Maria fussed at him, waving a dismissive hand. "Oh, it's nothing, just one of Renaldo's favorite dishes to honor his return, *champurrado*," she enunciated, slowly rolling her R's for Hank's benefit.

"Yes," Tomás said, apparently not wanting to be outdone. "You are such a fine cook. What an honor to eat at your table!"

Juana Maria stood, all the men following, and said, "Of course I've taught Calandaría all of my secrets," she tossed over her shoulder, bringing the water pitcher back to the table.

Calandaría groaned, and then caught herself, smiling serenely at the table, cheeks aflame.

"Oh? I do enjoy cooking, myself," Tomás said eagerly. "It was either learn how to make something delicious or eat slop."

Hank began to clear the table, which prompted Tomás to join him. No matter how hard she tried to dissuade them, Juana Maria was forced to sit and allow the guests to clean up. She looked scandalized, but Esteban patted her hand, kissed the back of it and said, "*Mi querido*, let people fuss over you for once."

240

It was a lot to take in after so much silence, all of the chatter and energy, all of the bodies bustling about. It only served to ratchet up the anxiety building within Renaldo, and he knew Hank was trying to control his own anxiety by keeping busy with mundane tasks, as well. But before he could ask his father for a private word, Juana Maria said, "*Mijo*, we have given Silvestre's and your bedroom to *Señor* Aguayo for his visit." She fixed him with a look that meant he wasn't to argue. "Where will you and *Señor* Burnett prefer to sleep?"

They looked at each other. He knew his parents didn't mean the way that he wished, that they had accepted them as a couple by somehow miraculously understanding what had happened between them these past several weeks, but it took him by surprise to hear it said aloud, nonetheless.

Hank was first to speak, "Ma'am, I'm perfectly content with sleeping outdoors. No different than what we've been doing these past few months."

"I will, too," Renaldo said.

"But … Francisco's room is still available. Don't you want to sleep in a proper bed? *Señor* Burnett?" she asked them.

Yes, Renaldo thought, but said, "Don't worry about us, Mama. I've grown used to his snoring."

"I don't snore," Hank said, sounding almost offended.

"You do," Renaldo replied, grinning, pressing his leg against Hank's under the table. "It's very quiet, but—" He went completely still, realizing that he was about to say that Hank's snoring could only be heard from up close. When they slept together. He cleared his throat, hoping no one caught that slip and said, "But it's only once in a while."

Calandaría's previously besotted expression for her intended became sharp and calculating. Her eyes widened slightly, and she let out a small gasp when her gaze settled on Renaldo. She sank back in her chair; her eyebrows knit together.

Renaldo couldn't breathe. If his sister noticed, perhaps the others did as well?

Hank very carefully set his hands on the edge of the table as if he was steeling himself, but Renaldo could see how they trembled.

"*Señor* Valle?" Hank asked, and Renaldo marveled at how even his voice sounded. "I wonder if you and I could have a word in private?"

"If this is about payment, do not worry! I wasn't expecting you two to arrive today, but we can go to the bank in town tomorrow and—"

"No, that's not a problem at all," Hank said, smiling a grin that didn't reach his eyes. "Just need… your opinion on something important."

Estebán seemed unsure and then pushed away from the table. "This is about Renaldo, I believe?"

Hank didn't look away from Renaldo's father, just nodded his head.

"Excellent!" Estebán said, his voice booming. "I was hoping that you would want to take him under your wing professionally. I've always known that he was a natural horseman, and when you and I met, I just knew that the two of you should be in business together some day."

"Papa," Renaldo said, cutting in. "We would like to speak with you in private, please?"

"*Sí, sí,*" he said, walking to the front door.

Calandaría turned to watch her father leave and then caught Renaldo's gaze. He gave the tiniest shake of his head, not wanting her to let on to the others that she understood—and of course she did.

"Mama," she said suddenly. "Let's play a game of cards."

Renaldo shot his twin a grateful smile, knowing how competitive their mother was. It should keep her occupied in case she wondered what was taking the men so long.

It was like walking to his own funeral, following his father and Hank. He gave Hank's hand a quick squeeze where their father wouldn't be able to see, murmuring so only Hank would hear, "Courage, *mi querido*."

Just as quietly, Hank replied, "*Te quiero*." Instead of calming Renaldo's nerves, that amplified them. The moment had arrived, and he found that he wasn't prepared for it in the slightest.

Estebán led them all the way to the barn. It was where the Valle men held all of their important discussions, far enough away that Juana Maria wouldn't hear them cursing or smell their father's pipe.

"Now!" Estebán exclaimed, dropping onto an uprooted stump and grinning. "What is so..." He looked at them; the smile on his face melted into a look of worry. "*¿Mijo, qué pasó?* What has happened?"

"Nothing bad has happened, Papa," Renaldo said. "At least, I don't believe that it is."

"Then why...?"

Hank nodded at Renaldo. "Let me," he said, then turned to Estebán. "*Señor*, I hope you know how much I respect you."

"*Gracias*, Henry," Estebán said, his face all fatherly affection. "And I hope you know the same in return."

243

"Well, we'll see." Hank ran a hand over his head, took a deep breath, and said, "Your son and I decided that because I hold you in such high regard that I wouldn't lie to you; I refused to do so."

"Lie to me? What is this about, Henry?"

"*Señor*, you know that my background is… unusual." At Estebán's nod, Hank continued. "When I was a young man, I learned some truths about myself, and I was fortunate to live with people who accepted that about me, even if most other people wouldn't."

Estebán sat with his forehead furrowed, trying to follow, Renaldo knew.

"And I hope that you can accept that what I feel for your son is the truth at the very least, even if it isn't something that you can understand or… well, I suppose, support."

"What you feel…? *Mijo*, what is this about?" he asked, turning to his son.

Renaldo's stomach was in knots. His eyes burned and his hands were shaking. Hank caught his eye and nodded. He squeezed his hand; it helped keep Renaldo's resolve, even though he felt as if he might shatter. "Papa. I… *Le amo, Papa. Me estoy enamorando de el.*" He turned to Hank and repeated, "I love him. I'm falling in love with him."

Hank kept holding on, his eyes on Estebán as he added, "*Y yo.*"

Renaldo couldn't help the strangled noise he made at that. Hank's grip on his hand was steady and sure, although he could see Hank's breathing was shallow and his jaw tight as he braced himself.

Estebán said nothing, sitting with his mouth open, a strange smile on his face. "This is… no," he said, laughing. "This is a joke! It's good that you didn't say this to your mother, she—"

"It's no joke, Papa, not what I feel, not what we're saying," Renaldo said, unable to keep his eyes from watering. This was it, then. This was when his father no longer looked at him with pride, but with disgust instead. "Papa, I lo—"

"I heard what you said!" Esteban replied, standing, eyes wild as he paced in tight circles, rubbing his chest. "I… Renaldo, it's not unheard of for men to grow close when they are alone." He glanced at Hank, and then continued. "Men have urges, needs that must be met. I must say that if you had to meet those urges, I am grateful that you didn't seek relief the way Silvestre did. I know of… I have heard of men seeking relief in this way; we all have known a man or two who has done this… this sort of thing out in this wild place without women. But that's all this is, *mijo*, something temporary."

The smile he gave them both was grim, as if his teeth were holding back harsher words.

"Papa, it isn't temporary," Renaldo said, unable to help that he was pleading, willing to beg his father to hear him, to *listen* to what he was saying. Hank dropped his hand and shifted away, leaving Renaldo aching, worried Hank would just drift away into the night. "Please listen to me. What I feel isn't—"

"What you feel?" Esteban said. He cupped Renaldo's face, his gaze tender as he said, "How do you know what you feel? You're still just a boy. You—"

"Is Calandaría still just a girl, then? Is she not old enough, wise enough to consent to this marriage you and Mama have arranged for her?"

Esteban said nothing.

"And what of you and Mama? She was younger than I am now when she married you."

"That's different! She—"

"It isn't!" Renaldo raked a hand though his hair tugging it. Hank rested his palm on Renaldo's lower back; it was the only thing keeping him anchored. "It isn't. It is the *same*. This is what we are trying to tell you."

"What," Hank said, swallowing thickly, "what I feel for your son, *Señor*, is honorable." Hank's voice was quiet, but it shook with emotion. "This isn't—he just … he fits me, who I am, who I want to be."

"And what is that?" Esteban said, finally turning to Hank, not appearing closed-off anymore, but simply confused. "What is it that you want to be?"

Hank turned to Renaldo. The corner of his mouth crooked up in that way that always sent Renaldo's heart pounding. He took a deep breath and turned to face Esteban once more. "His."

Esteban stared at them, at a loss for words, it seemed. "*Señor* Burnett," he said, and Renaldo could see Hank stiffening up, bracing himself over the loss of his first name, "you must know how much I admire the work you do. But this … I don't understand what this is. You are, what? You are asking my permission? Like Tomás hinted just before you two arrived that he would be asking for your sister's hand?"

Renaldo and Hank looked at each other. In a way, that was exactly what they were doing, even if they could never have exactly what Renaldo's siblings would.

"But this is fantasy!" Esteban cried out. "You cannot be as a husband and wife are with one another. The Church does not recognize that, and I don't see how you could hide what you claim to feel for one another from outsiders. *Mijo*, it is *dangerous* what you are wanting to do, can you understand that?"

"Of course I know all of this, Papa," Renaldo said. "It is why I came home to my family. I believed that we could be safe here."

Hank's head dropped, the toe of his boot worrying at the ground, resigned. Renaldo wasn't going to give up just yet, though.

"Papa," he begged. "This is who I am."

Estebán appeared lost in thought, rubbing his forehead and staring off into the night. "But… Tomás and Calandaría, *that* is something of which I can make sense. He will provide for her, she will care for him, and they will have a true marriage, a proper partnership between lovers, natural. You—"

"And what of Patricia and Francisco, eh?" Renaldo challenged. "Do you believe she would ever have a child with him? A child who was truly his?" When his father said nothing, he pressed on. "How holy is *that* union? How love-filled and—"

"It is being blessed by God!"

"But Papa," Renaldo pleaded. "We all know that they will both be unhappy. *That* is the relationship that is most unnatural, not what Hank and I share."

Estebán stammered, "N-no, when they have the child and she sees how good he will be, then—"

"Papa, don't you see that what you wish for Francisco is what I already have? Isn't that what you and Mama want for us all? To be as happy as you both are?"

Estebán said nothing for several moments. Hank turned away, his hands on his hips and his shoulders a tight line. Renaldo ran the palm of his hand down Hank's back, reminding Hank that he was here, that even though everything seemed to be falling apart, they would still have each other. And they would. Renaldo was beginning to realize that it might be *all* they had.

"How would you live? You say that you've thought this through," Estebán challenged, "but what is your plan? How could this even be managed?"

"We have thought it through, and thought about how it would be seen from the outside," Renaldo answered, a tiny spark of hope flickering to life inside him. "We will go into business together. It's expected that we will already, is it not?"

He noticed the shock on his father's face at how true that was.

"From now on, when Hank is hired," Renaldo continued, "I'll join him to acquire new *mesteños*. And when I train them, he will be at my side. We've already managed to prove that we work well together. People will see one of us and expect the other. Don't you see that this could work? Who will be judging us? Who will even know but our family here?"

Estebán seemed to be thinking it through, and then his face darkened. He shook his head, sighing.

"Papa," Renaldo said finally, his voice choked with emotion. "If you want me to leave, if this is—"

"*¡Claro que no, mijo!* Of course I don't want you to leave," his father cried, cupping his cheek once more.

"But," Renaldo said, trying to swallow past the burning lump in his throat, "if you ask Hank—Henry. If you tell him to leave, I will go with him. I *must* go with him. We belong to each other, do you understand?"

With a shuddering breath, Hank took a step closer to Renaldo, close enough so their shoulders brushed.

Hank squared his shoulders and faced Estebán straight on, saying, "But, *Señor*, I will leave, if you ask me to. I don't wish to cause any more upset than I already have. I can't help that

I love your son, don't want to help it. But I also don't want to destroy your family because of it."

Estebán didn't move, didn't speak. His breathing hitched once, twice, and then his whole body sagged as he rubbed his face with both hands. "I… *Señor* Burnett, I thank you for your honesty. *Mijo*, I need to think. Perhaps if I talk this over with Eduardo and Francisco in the morning, they can help me make sense of it all."

Renaldo let out a shaky breath. It wasn't an order to leave in the dark of night. It wasn't acceptance, either, but it wasn't the worst response for which he and Hank had braced themselves.

"This is not anything I expected," Estebán said. "*Mi querido*," he said to his son, "All your mother and I want for you is to have what we have: happiness, a home, a family who loves you. Can't you see that?"

"Of course I can. And I can see a way to having that for myself." Renaldo gripped Hank's forearm, keeping him close, *needing* him close, and said to his father, "I love you. I love my home, my family. I… I love him more."

Estebán's eyes widened at that, and he took a step back. He asked, "*Señor* Burnett… *Henry*. Do you feel this way, too? That nothing is more important?"

"I do," Hank replied. "I will leave right now, and I will never set foot on your land if you wish it. But I will always want your son by my side."

Estebán covered his eyes with one of his hands. "Son, I need to think on this. I cannot—" He heaved a great sigh. "From one of my proudest days as a father to one of the most confusing. I—I am an old man and set in my ways, I'm afraid."

Renaldo's heart sank at that.

"But I love you, Renaldo. You are my baby! My…" Estebán turned away, looking across the courtyard, the fields, the gently rolling land beyond. "I don't know what to think. I… *Mijo*, we just got you back. It would break your mother's heart to have you leave again. Please, stay tonight. Both of you," he added, a blank, unreadable look on his face. "But I must be left with my thoughts tonight before we talk further. Allow me some time to try to understand this, *por favor*."

"*¡Sí!* Of course, Papa! I—" He tried to hug his father, grateful that he hadn't been disowned outright, sent away immediately, but Estebán took a step back and shook his head.

"I cannot be swayed by my love for you, *querido*. There is more to consider here than just your feelings for one another." He rubbed a hand roughly over his chest, just over where his heart was. "You two can stay out here tonight. I… we will speak tomorrow."

They watched in silence as Estebán slowly made his way back to the house, shaking his head and muttering under his breath. When he was out of sight, Hank pulled Renaldo into his arms, swaying him gently from side to side. It didn't hide how he was shaking.

"Wasn't as bad as I expected," Hank said, sagging against Renaldo's chest. "Didn't get shot at least."

Renaldo laughed, a bitter, watery sound. "He wouldn't *shoot* us."

"Maybe not you."

Hank buried his face in the crook of Renaldo's neck as Renaldo worked his fingertips over his scalp, massaging it and following it with a kiss. "Francisco will support us, I believe," Renaldo said.

"And if they all don't?" Hank asked, his warm breath moving over Renaldo's skin, bringing goosebumps to it.

"Then we make our own way, *mi amor*."

Only Calandaría had stood by his side in the way that Hank had done tonight. He believed he knew his father, knew how Esteban would react in most situations, but Renaldo knew that this wasn't most situations

His father had been right about one thing: It was dangerous, their love. No longer in their private world out on the plains with no one to answer to but each other, the danger was painfully clear.

But the warmth and security he felt in Hank's arms, the respect and awe they had for one another, the depth of appreciation for the man Hank was... it was worth any danger. Wasn't love worth fighting for? As Hank gripped Renaldo's shirt in both hands, holding him close, trusting Renaldo with his own fate as well, Renaldo knew without question that it *was* worth it.

He wanted to give Hank what he'd searched his whole life for: a family, love, acceptance. If he alone would provide that instead of his whole family embracing Hank, so be it. They would have each other, and it would be enough.

He would make it so.

Hank shuddered a sigh, and then said softly, "*Te quiero.*"

"*Y yo, mi vida*," Renaldo replied, squeezing Hank tighter.

No matter the decision his family made, Hank was his life now. If it was all the fates would allow him to have, then he could be content with that much. He would have to be.

CHAPTER FOURTEEN

HANK—WHO HADN'T SLEPT MUCH THE whole night, if his tossing and turning was any indication—didn't join the family for breakfast the next day. Renaldo begged him, but Hank kept firm. "Unless they accept what we are to one another, it wouldn't be right for me to break bread with them at the family table. Don't think I could eat much of anything right now, anyhow."

Calandaría had raised an eyebrow at Renaldo when he entered the house alone, but a minute shake of his head implored her to leave it until they could talk privately as he took his customary seat next to her. It was a somber affair for all that Tomás and Juana Maria tried to liven it up, between Estebán's thoughtful silence and Renaldo's pensiveness.

"It's true that great caches of silver are still being discovered in New Mexico," Tomás said, "but your lovely daughter, *Señora* Valle, explained how wise it would be to establish a smithy here where so many people pass through from both the east and west."

Calandaría beamed, straightening her plate and cup with great care.

"Did she?" Juana Maria exclaimed, shooting Calandaría a tense smile. "And that wasn't... well, surely you know more about this type of thing than a young girl."

"Oh, she is a very well-educated young woman," Tomás replied. "A credit to you and your husband, of course," he added, nodding at Estebán. "I find that she has a most dazzling mind, quite the head for numbers and business. So refreshing to find when so many young ladies seem only to care about their appearances. How fortunate for you to have a daughter who is both beautiful *and* brilliant!"

Ah. In addition to him being handsome, Renaldo could see why else Calandaría was so smitten with this man. It was as he'd hoped, then. This man their parents wanted her to marry would appreciate her, her intelligence and personality, not just that she was beautiful. He reached under the table to squeeze her hand; some of the worry on his shoulders abated when she squeezed back.

At least she would be cared for and loved, he thought, his chest aching. He would never have this, he and Hank openly sharing their feelings for one another at the breakfast table with his family's approval. But if they were only able to share their love for each other in private, so be it. He wanted to be through with this, to speak with his father and brothers and know what would happen. The uncertainty was leaving him in knots. He couldn't imagine what Hank must be feeling, alone and without Renaldo there to ease his fears.

With Calandaría happily chiming in, Tomás discussed potential plans for their business with Eduardo and Francisco after they arrived for coffee, having had their own breakfasts with their wives. They'd each pulled Renaldo into their embrace, kissing him on both cheeks and ruffling his hair. It was a bittersweet reunion. So much about his family and their land was just as it had always been, yet Renaldo knew that nothing could be the same ever again. Not for him.

The one bright spot of the meal was getting to know his twin's suitor. Renaldo was pleased to see Tomás deferring to Calandaría often, treating her as his equal.

"It is just as *Señorita* Valle explained to me about creating demand," Tomás said. "How did you say it? It was so eloquent from you; I'm afraid I'll be too clumsy in my explanation."

Calandaría raised her eyebrow at her mother, and then said, "What you make is art, *Señor*. And art should be prized! If you double your prices, it will set a precedent for…"

As she spoke, Eduardo and Francisco smiled at each other, nodding and encouraging her where appropriate. The Valle men all treasured her, and it was lovely to see that their sister would be so well-respected by her suitor. Renaldo just wished his suitor—his *love*—would be so well-respected. The unfairness, if indeed that was what he and Hank could expect, was galling.

When the meal was over, Estebán stood and pulled Juana Maria into his arms, kissed her cheek tenderly and rubbed the spot with his thumb. "*Mi tesoro.* Every day of my life with you has been a blessing. I cannot imagine a moment without you."

Juana Maria blushed and slapped playfully at his arm. "*Te amo, mi angel,*" she said softly, holding her cheek out for another kiss. "How lucky I am to be married to such a romantic… oh, it is so wonderful to have my family almost whole once more!" she said. "Renaldo, would you please take this plate to *Señor* Burnett? I worry about how thin you both became!"

He took it from her and kissed her cheek. His heart was heavy as he watched yet another couple freely express their shared love and he dreaded the conversation still to come.

His father said to his wife in a quiet voice, "I need to speak to our sons privately. You can keep Tomás entertained here, yes?"

"Of course." She looked from him to Renaldo and back again. The lighthearted joviality she usually carried in her eyes dimmed. "Papa?"

"Do not worry yourself," he replied, kissing the tip of her nose. He took the plate from Renaldo's hands and gave it back to Juana Maria, saying, "*Un momento, mi amor*," and motioned toward the door for the boys to go out.

As they all quietly walked to the barn, Francisco drifted to his side, slinging an arm over his shoulder. "It is good to see you, *hermanito*."

"You may not feel that way for long," Renaldo muttered, shaking his head at Francisco's questioning look.

"Renaldo! They're beautiful!" Eduardo cried as they passed the corral. Cecilia and her colt walked along the length of fence, keeping up with them. "I cannot believe how calm they are. You have a gift. Or is it just *Señor* Burnett's gift, and we are giving the wrong man praise?" he teased.

"This gift is something I wish to speak to you and Francisco about," Esteban said.

Renaldo, his foot on the lowest rail of the fence, held out his hand for the colt to sniff as his brothers circled around his father and him. The colt nervously approached him, clearly sensing Renaldo's unease.

"Renaldo, do you wish to tell them? Or would you prefer that I did?" Esteban asked, not unkindly.

255

His stomach twisting, he looked between his brothers, seeing their mild confusion, and then caught sight of Hank coming out of the barn, walking straight to him, his hands fisted at his sides and mouth pressed into a grim line. He looked as though he was walking toward his execution.

Eduardo turned and saw him as well, smiled, and opened his mouth, most likely to politely turn him away so the family could speak, when Esteban beat him to it. "*Señor* Burnett, if you would join us, please?"

Eduardo tilted his head, asking, "Are—Renaldo, will you be leaving with him once again? Is that what this is about?"

Francisco wrapped a hand around the base of Renaldo's neck, giving it a friendly squeeze, saying, "*¡Claro que no!* He's only just come home!"

Hank took his place on the other side of Renaldo with his bootheel hooked over the bottom rail and arms crossed tightly against his chest.

Renaldo looked at the group, his heart aching and yet still full of so much love for every man before him, albeit in different ways. Hank was right, though: They must be honest, open. "I need to tell you something about myself. Something I've only realized recently."

Eduardo rolled his eyes and said, "What, are you a horse thief? You stole these horses? That must be why they are so well behaved, eh?" He laughed, clapping a hand to Renaldo's chest, but when no one else joined him, he sobered instantly. "What is it, then?"

"I want to come home, but I want Hank—I want *Señor* Burnett to be allowed to live here, too."

Francisco smiled, looking relieved. "I have no problem with this! Expand our business? Yes, that seems wise. If Renaldo and my father believe you to be a good man, *Señor*," he said to Hank, "then that is enough for me. It would only benefit the family to have you join us! We could expand our lands this way, too." He widened his stance, stroking his chin as he asked, "What will you do, then? Perhaps build a homestead by the southwest corner? It's close enough to town for you to do business, close enough to the main house here that Mama can keep you well fed."

"No, *Paco*," Renaldo said, reverting to his brother's nickname. "I want all of that, too, our business to grow, for Hank—for *Señor* Burnett to be a part of that, but more importantly," he took a deep breath and said, "I want him to live with me."

Francisco said nothing else, but his eyebrows came together as he seemed to process what Renaldo was saying.

"With you?" Eduardo said. "Why do you believe this to be a problem? Because he is a black man? You know we don't care about such things, Renaldo," he chided, smiling at Hank. "*Señor* Burnett, I imagine that traveling as you do, living out on the plains means that you haven't built yourself a home, then? The two of you seem to be very compatible with animals, so I agree with Francisco: It would only be a blessing for Vista Verde to have you here."

"No, you don't understand," Renaldo said, growing frustrated. Hank tentatively put his hand on Renaldo's lower back. Renaldo looked at his brothers, silently imploring them to listen. "I do not wish to marry a woman. Ever. I do not have those feelings for women, not as you two do for your wives. I… I wish to be with Hank, with Henry," he amended, stepping closer so their sides were pressed together, "and I wish that we could be that way here. I want him here with me, always. But we understand that you may not accept that."

"¿*Que?¿ Que dices?*" Eduardo said, looking terribly confused. "What are you … but you are both men!"

Hank caught Renaldo's eye, and then Estebán's. Before speaking, he cleared his throat, worrying his hands together. Getting a nod from Estebán, Hank said, "Which is why we figured you two wouldn't approve. The … the both of us being men part. We wanted to be honest with you. I won't come to you with any deceit; I have too much respect for you all. And if you won't have it, won't have us, then—" He looked to Renaldo to finish the thought.

"Then we will leave," Renaldo finished, sensing more than hearing Hank's pained sigh.

"¡*Tonterías!*" Francisco said, his voice rising in anger. "I won't have you leaving over this."

"But didn't we send Silvestre away for this very thing?" Eduardo asked.

"Not for this, no!" Francisco said. "He lied, he was deceitful and sneaky. He was faithless, and we all know it. Patricia wasn't the only woman he had been with, wasn't the only heart broken. Wasn't the only mother to a child of his."

Renaldo turned to Francisco in shock. "What?"

"Papa?" Francisco said, looking to their father.

With a heavy sigh, Estebán said, "I learned of another child Silvestre fathered. This was before Patricia. He took the young woman to a midwife who… I don't want to speak of what they did, but we acted so severely with Silvestre because he hadn't learned his lesson, how important it was to honor what a man and a woman can share, what the responsibilities of love can be and that you cannot toss a person aside as if they were a momentary plaything."

Renaldo couldn't conceive of tossing Hank aside; the thought was as foreign to him as... well, as how Silvestre approached relationships, love.

"I suppose it's a good thing they won't be able to make a baby," Eduardo said, not looking amused in the slightest. Renaldo turned away from the veil of distaste falling over his eldest brother's face, caught Hank looking down, unhappy, sweat breaking out at his temples. He squeezed Hank's forearm as if to say *I'm here, we have each other, we'll find a way.*

It was Francisco who asked in a gentle voice, "Can you imagine your lives without each other?"

Renaldo and Hank looked to one another. The corner of Hank's mouth was turned up, his eyes filled with both trepidation and hope. "I can't," he said, sliding his palm up and down Renaldo's back before pulling his hands back to himself, as if he just realized how forward, how bold, that was in front of Renaldo's brothers.

Renaldo felt the loss of its warmth keenly. "I know you cannot understand this," he said to his family, motioning toward Hank, "what we feel for each other. And I know this is... nothing expected. But, please," he said, his heart aching, "I want you to realize that just as you care for Hortencia—"

Eduardo's eyes hardened slightly.

"—and as you, *Paco*, care for Patricia, as our parents feel for one another, that is how I feel for this man. I wish to spend the rest of my life with him. And if we cannot do that here because you will not accept us, we will leave this very day."

259

"But how?" Eduardo asked. "How can you look at a man and feel that sort of love? Passion?"

"Eduardo," Renaldo said, "when you began courting Hortencia, the love in your eyes, your impassioned sighs as you described her merits to us, were things of which I couldn't make sense. Don't misunderstand me. I think that she is lovely, and I'm glad that you married her," he said quickly. "I just didn't understand how you could look at a woman and feel passion, and I didn't understand why I couldn't feel that way for any of the girls at school or in town. Never did those feelings come to me, never. Seeing you both so happy, seeing our parents together and growing up knowing how deep their love was for one another, I believed that I wouldn't have that, that something was wrong with me. Perhaps… I often wondered if the fact that I was born a twin, meant *that* would be the only love I would be allowed. I wondered if Calandaría was given all of the passion while I was left with all of the patience."

Francisco smiled at that.

"It was as though you all knew a language I couldn't learn, would never speak."

Eduardo turned away, shaking his head. "I don't know how this can work. We have our women here, will have children." He turned back to them. "We can't allow—just what do you think we should tell them?"

"That they are dear friends and business partners," Francisco said, arms crossed at his chest. "That they are bachelors, married to their love of horses and the land. This is what you were thinking, yes?" he asked, looking at Hank.

Hank nodded, his gaze not quite reaching Renaldo's brother's eyes. "If it was acceptable to you all, of course."

"And if it isn't?" Eduardo said, the challenge in his voice clear.

"Then, I'll bid you farewell, and you'll never see me again."

"And I will go with him," Renaldo added, a note of finality in his voice. As he noticed Hank staring at the Colt revolver hanging at Eduardo's side, a sick chill ran down his spine at what Hank must fear. "If you will not be our family," he said, squeezing Hank's forearm, "we will be each other's."

Renaldo's brothers stared back at him, at a loss for words.

"Papa, what do you think of—of all of this?" Eduardo asked.

Esteban looked very tired. "I think … that I want my family whole."

A kernel of hope began to take root inside Renaldo as his father spoke, looking at each one of his sons, at Hank, before his gaze settled on Renaldo. There was still love in his father's eyes, proof that whatever horrible expectation Hank was braced for—and it made sense that Hank of all people wouldn't expect to be accepted, would expect to be attacked—that it wouldn't happen. His father still loved him, and it had to mean *something*.

"I said to you last night, *mijo*, that I only want you to be happy," Esteban said. "But you know how the world beyond our gates will see you both," he added with a sharp look at both of them. "With that always hanging over your heads, I don't know how you could ever find happiness. But," he sighed, "as you said last night, you love one another. I believe that you do."

"Papa!" Eduardo said, scandalized.

"*Cállate*," Esteban said, a hand out, eyes still on his youngest son. "*Mijo*, I know this was very difficult for you, and for you, Henry," he said, a cautious smile for Hank. "It takes a tremendous amount of courage to stand before a man, asking him what you have today."

He rubbed the top of his belly and watched the horses once more. "There is no denying that together you have managed something I never could have," he said with admiration softening his tone, nodding at the horses. "You both clearly have a gift, a talent, something about both of you that is unique. Maybe it is this love you share, I do not know."

He leaned his weight against the fence, gazing at the mares as Cecelia nickered at her baby, teasing him and playing as the other horses looked on.

"I don't know that I'm ready to… think too hard about what your relationship is," he continued, his face confused, "but I love my sons and my daughter. I love my family, and losing Silvestre has been a hardship for your mother and for me. She is desperate for Tomás to decide to build his smithy here at Vista Verde or to purchase land close by because she cannot bear to lose Calandaría as well.

"I would do anything for your mother. When I die, this land will go to you boys, and I want you to live in continued harmony here. This can only happen if we are open and fair with one another. And that means, *mijo*," he said with a sad smile for Renaldo, "that your brothers should have a say in all of this since it could affect them, just as Silvestre's choices did."

"I want you to be happy," Francisco said quickly, nudging his elbow into Renaldo's side. "If you can be, then I want that for you, *hermanito*."

Eduardo shot Francisco an annoyed look. "It isn't that I want Renaldo to be miserable or to leave us," he said, rubbing his hand over the back of his neck. "He's my brother, too, I just don't…"

He must have noticed Hank eying his sidearm as Eduardo's face went bloodless, his eyes tracking Hank and Renaldo, and then down to his pistol. "I may not understand or even like this," he said, his voice shaking, "but I would never do what I think you—"

Hank glanced at Renaldo, and then nodded his head at Eduardo. "Most men would."

They all went still. It was true, after all. Renaldo, in his naïveté, had forgotten all that Hank had experienced, all that he must have seen. Even though a cold, leaden weight dropped in his gut at that bald statement, his heart swelled with gratitude that Hank was willing to face that possibility for him. Hank was biting the inside of his cheek, still tense. *It-sá*, hawk. Ready to fly at the first sight of danger.

"*Te quiero, mi querido,*" he murmured, just loud enough for Hank to hear.

"So just how do we go about this?" Eduardo asked, looking to their father, his face still unsure. "We have *Señor* Aguayo to think about, too. I wouldn't want to agree to anything that will hurt Calandaría's chances for happiness, and he clearly makes her so."

"You can't think that I would ever want to deny her happiness?" Renaldo asked. "Nor would Hank?"

Hank nodded at his side, his body tight as a stretched wire.

"Since they are not cavorting about indecently," Francisco said, his voice dry to match the droll expression on his face, "then I believe it's safe to say that our brother and *Señor* Burnett can behave with decorum around Calandaría and her intended."

Hank shook his head and his body relaxed somewhat. "Yes, that I can promise."

"He *has* said only four words since his return, maybe even less. He speaks less than even Renaldo does," Eduardo said, humor creeping back into his voice as he pointed his thumb at Hank. "Also, I don't think he's the type who would attempt to serenade Renaldo in the town square."

"I told you I found that romantic when I was eight years old," Francisco hissed. "When will you let me forget it?"

"Never," Eduardo said, fighting back a smile.

Renaldo looked to his father, who appeared resigned, but not necessarily unhappy. Just settled. Hank was practically vibrating at his side. Truthfully, Renaldo also thought he might shake apart if this uncertainty dragged on any longer. "Papa?"

"You will not build a home on the southwest corner of my land," Estebán said in a voice that would tolerate no argument.

Hank nodded, eyes downcast and hands shaking before he shoved them into his trouser's pockets. "Yessir. I had a mind to find my own, anyhow, so I'll just move on—"

"It is too close to where wagon trains pass through," Estebán said. "Too much noise, too much attention."

"Papa, what about the northwest corner?" Eduardo asked, eyes trained on the ground near Hank's feet. "Near *el fuente amargo?*"

Estebán's eyes went round, before softening. He nodded his head, clearly fighting back a smile. "Now, the northwest corner... *sí, sí.* I believe there is a half-labor of land still waiting for purchase near where you boys would watch the *murciélagos* take flight."

Eduardo took a deep breath and looked to Renaldo, saying, "It's no good for farming. The ground is too rocky for irrigation, but it's excellent for raising livestock. Don't you agree, Papa? Renaldo?"

That corner of land was the farthest from Eduardo's homestead, but it was also the land where the family's secret mineral spring was hidden, where Renaldo and Hank had gone swimming just the day before.

Francisco took a deep breath, holding it in, and then letting it out all at once in a rush. "Yes. Good thinking. That would be an *excellent* site for them to build their home, a place no one would go."

Hank was completely still at his side; Renaldo didn't think he'd even breathed since his father cut him off.

"You mean...?" Renaldo asked, barely able to believe it.

"*Te quiero, mijo,*" Esteban said. "I cannot bear to lose any more family." He gripped Francisco's shoulder, squeezing it. "And if this arrangement also happens to ensure my family's security and legacy, then yes, I mean that you two may live here as... as you wish."

"Two bachelors ready to strike it rich," Francisco said, grinning from ear to ear. "*Vaqueros* with the best land at their back door! Outsiders would never suspect anything else than a brilliant business plan."

Renaldo wanted to pull Hank into his arms, wanted to shower him with grateful kisses, but still Eduardo stood with arms folded. Francisco's smile wavered every time he glanced at their older brother, and Esteban's smile, although present, didn't seem to reach his eyes with the same effervescent joy that usually accompanied any momentous occasion.

But they'd agreed to let Hank join their family, and although Renaldo knew that for now, Hank wouldn't get the reception that Tomás would receive, he was still being welcomed.

With a fortifying breath, Hank crossed to Estebán. Renaldo could see him chewing on the inside of his mouth before swallowing visibly, saying, "I won't disappoint you, *Señor*. I want you to know that your son means the world to me, and this gift of... " He paused, eyes down, breathing rapidly. "This gift of your family not shutting the door on me is something I never thought I'd have.

"*Señor* Valle, Eduardo, Francisco... I know this situation is a hell of a shock. I certainly didn't come here in the first place with the idea of finding someone like Renaldo. I can't explain why I'm the way I am, why I think like I do."

And even though he must be terrified, Hank heaved a deep breath, making himself stand tall and proud. Renaldo loved him so fiercely in that moment, he could almost weep from the depth of it.

"I just know that I plan on spending the rest of my life trying to be worthy of him," Hank said. "And of this family, if you'll allow it."

"*Ay, dios mio*," Eduardo said, a hand to his chest. "Don't let my wife hear you speak so, or she'll remind me of what a clod of dirt I am."

"You *are* a clod of dirt," Francisco teased, slinging an arm over Eduardo's shoulder, pulling him away. "We have work to do, instead of wasting the day by teaching you how to be romantic." Before they walked off, Francisco held a hand out to Hank. "I trust Renaldo. Welcome."

Hank didn't say anything as he shook Francisco's hand. Renaldo didn't think Hank was capable of speech—neither was Renaldo; the love and gratitude he felt for his gentle, romantic brother almost choked him. The reminder of Eduardo's distaste as he walked off without another word kept his emotions in check, however.

"I must go inside and calm your mother," Estebán said. "By now she must think you are running away to live in Comancheria, never to return." He tugged Renaldo close, kissed his cheek. "Be respectful of the family," he said, giving him a pointed look that Renaldo understood meant no public displays of affection. "But also be good to each other. I do want you to be happy, *mijo*."

He shook Hank's hand once more, and turned, slowly lumbering back to the house with his rolling gait.

They were alone once more, turning to each other with shock on their faces.

"Did we manage to pull this off?" Hank whispered.

"Did you think we couldn't?"

"I thought I'd wake up to a shotgun in the face or one of your brothers challenging me to a duel, and that's the God's honest truth," Hank laughed, rubbing a hand over his face. "I don't quite believe it, not just yet."

Renaldo laughed as relief bubbled through him. "It's good to know that the faith I had in my family wasn't for nothing." He looked around to make sure they were alone before pulling Hank into his arms, holding him tight, running the flat of his hand over Hank's back where the muscles still jumped and twitched. "*Mi amor*, we will make this work."

"I—" Hank shook his head, his hands clutching at Renaldo's sides. "Is this…? I can't even get a hold of a single thought just this minute. Just hang on to me, would you?"

They held each other, Renaldo's heart thumping away, overjoyed that they would have a chance.

A door banged in the distance, and they jumped apart, quick as lightning. Calandaría ran to them, her face worried. "You're staying, aren't you?" she asked, grabbing Renaldo's hands and squeezing tight. "You're staying? And he… he is staying with you? You aren't being made to leave, are you, *Señor* Burnett?"

"No, ma'am," Hank said, rubbing the top of his head and trying not to smile.

"How did you know?" Renaldo asked her.

"Papa came back, whispered something to Mama, but when she started to say something, he shushed her, and then smiled at the rest of us, behaving as if nothing was different. But you didn't come back," she cried, wrapping her arms around Renaldo's waist and hugging him tight. "And *Señor*—"

"Call him Henry," he said.

"Call me *Hank*," Hank corrected, smiling at Renaldo. Renaldo started to speak, but Hank cut him off, saying, "Figure she's your twin. I guess I can call her friend."

"Of course you can!" Calandaría scoffed. "And you will both love Tomás," she sighed. "He is *wonderful.*"

"If he is good enough for you," Renaldo said, "I will at least give this Tomás a chance. A small one. *Un poquito.*"

She hummed a sweet little noise into Renaldo's chest. When she pulled away, she had a mischievous glint in her eye. She said, "You will give him *all* the chances, or I will never leave you two alone. How will you two kiss if I'm there in the way?"

"Like this," Renaldo replied, pulled Hank closer for a peck on the cheek. With his twin it was different, and Hank would know it one day, as well. Renaldo knew she accepted them, would not be offended. He smiled into Hank's cheek, amused at how stiff he'd gone in the face of Renaldo's sister.

"You call that kissing?" she scoffed. Hank straightened his shirt, clearly flustered. Renaldo couldn't care just then; everything felt as if it was falling into place.

"And what do you know of it?" Renaldo asked, realizing the implication in her words.

"Wouldn't you like to know," she said, smoothing her bodice and turning back to the house. "Kiss him properly. Hank? Don't settle for anything less than his complete devotion to your happiness."

Hank and Renaldo turned to each other, sharing their shock as she walked away.

"Your sister is a pistol."

"She's something," Renaldo sighed, shaking his head.

Hank tucked his fingertips into the waistband of Renaldo's pants, tugging on them. "What do you say we ride back out to this place your *padre's* so hell-bent on sending us and get… re-acquainted? I do believe I need some wide open space to catch my breath, something to make me feel that this isn't some fever dream."

As he watched the corner of Hank's mouth turn up, as that familiar swooping sensation in his belly left him almost light-headed, Renaldo could picture their lives, the simplicity of ranch life, the solitude they could easily enjoy, the joy of having family close by, people with whom to share their lives.

And every day would begin and end with Hank, his beautiful face, his kind eyes, his goodness. His lonely heart would slowly but surely be filled by every member of Renaldo's family, the wrongs of his past not overwritten by the future, but left far behind, crumbling dust in past of the long life he wished for the two of them. He knew this would be their lives; he could *see* it.

"*Sí, mi amor*. We can do that." They both hopped over the fence into the corral, Renaldo feeling light and free, far more free than he'd expected he could ever feel.

What did it matter if they didn't have the freedom to express themselves openly as they had on the prairie when they could have this solidity every day, this security of an established life? And perhaps one day his family wouldn't mind them sharing little touches, sweet words as the others could do.

"As long as I have you by my side, *querido*," Renaldo said, swinging onto Lady bareback as Hank opened the gate to lead her and Cloud out, "I will be satisfied."

Hank chuckled, and then leaped aboard Cloud's back, getting settled. "One of these days, I'm going to say something so pretty, it'll knock your boots off."

Renaldo laughed, squeezing Lady's sides with his knees to get her trotting off toward their potential homesite. He thought of Hank bravely telling his father how he felt, that he loved Renaldo, and saying so in front of Renaldo's brothers, as well. He'd been unsure of what they would say, what they would do to Hank, he who had experienced the true ugliness of men, he who knew better than most that it wasn't always happily ever after, that bad things happened to good people.

He'd stood before men who could have done him harm and said he loved Renaldo. Had stood by Renaldo's side as he'd said the same thing.

Hank loved him, and they would be honest about it, live with people who would allow them to love each other. It was more than he could have hoped for. *Hank* was more than he'd dreamed of ever having.

"You already have, *mi amor*."

EPILOGUE

RENALDO FOUND HANK STRETCHED OUT on their bed, breathing deeply, one of their pillows over his face. Renaldo wasn't fooled, though. "You're not asleep," he said, tugging on Hank's bare foot where it dangled out from under the quilt.

"Could be," Hank muttered.

"So could I, but someone had to repair and refill a trough after *someone else's* very naughty filly kicked it over and dented it."

Hank chuckled, pulling the pillow away and opening his eyes. "She's a real firecracker, ain't she?"

"With everyone but you, *amorcito*," Renaldo replied, smiling down at him. "She's a pain in the neck, if you ask Paloma. That horse of yours was getting awful testy with that new filly following her around all the time. Remind me to turn the little one out with Cecelia and *Puerco* tomorrow."

Puerco was the little buckskin colt, now a sixteen-hand gelding. They named him "pig" because of his insatiable appetite. They had to feed him in his stall; otherwise, he'd nudge the others away from their food. Their business was doing very well—they were slowly but surely building a reputation for raising some of the finest horses for vaqueros and ranchers in all of Texas and beyond. Renaldo had heard a little boy in town whisper after Hank passed that he'd heard Hank could just crook a finger at a wild mustang, and the mustang would follow him all the way home.

That night at home, Renaldo had pressed Hank up against the wall, slowly unbuttoning his shirt while calling him the "Pied Piper of the Llano Estacado." That had turned into a very salacious joke about flutes and lips blowing, ending with both of them sated and sleepy in their bed.

They had their own bed, their own home, their own business and, best of all, they had a family who loved and supported them close by. Hank and Renaldo maintained a professional relationship when in town or when meeting potential buyers, but here, in the privacy of their homestead nestled near the water and miles from everyone, here they could relax. Here he and Hank could be themselves.

Hank wiggled his foot in Renaldo's grip, angling for a foot rub.

"What was it my mother wanted with you after dinner?" Renaldo asked.

A few nights a week, the entire Valle Santos clan—Estebán and Juana Maria, Eduardo, Hortencia and their three-year-old son Pedro, Francisco and his daughter Silvia, Calandaría and Tomás, and Renaldo and Hank—met at the main house for dinner.

This month found the clan missing Calandaría and Tomás, who were traveling to Mexico City for business, so Hortencia, in her sixth month of pregnancy with their second child, had relied heavily on Hank and Renaldo to keep Pedro entertained. Little Silvia, five years old, was always incredibly well-behaved for her papa, content with sitting in his lap or primly in a chair next to her *abuela*, her dark brown curls cascading down her straight back, her chin up, and her tiny hands neatly folded in her lap. Juana Maria had finally gotten her wish for a young lady who wanted to be dainty and ladylike. It was a wonder Silvia wasn't spoiled rotten.

But then, she had no mother, and as Juana Maria explained, grandmothers couldn't spoil rotten, only love dearly.

Patricia, after giving birth, had received news that Silvestre had run away from the monastery. He had evidently been sending letters not only to his father and brothers, but to Antonia, Patricia's mother. Patricia, miserable with the life that had been forced upon her, had left in the night. No one spoke of her to Silvia, no one but Francisco, and it was always with love. It made the rest of the family too sad to see how Francisco still loved her.

Francisco, however, poured his love into his little girl, and when she would hold his face in her tiny hands and kiss his cheek, right over his birthmark, she called it her "kissing spot." Those were the times when Francisco never looked lonely.

Tonight, Juana Maria had asked Hank to stay behind to speak with her.

"Well? What did she say?" Renaldo asked, rubbing the arch of Hank's foot, grinning at the lascivious moan he let out.

"Ren... just there." Hank sighed deeply, and then laughed. "I don't know why we ever bother keeping things from her. She had me reaching for pots, bringing her this and that, keeping me occupied like she does to disarm a body." Renaldo nodded, and Hank continued. "Then just as casual as you please, she told me about a brother of hers who had... a special friend, too."

Renaldo gripped Hank's foot, shocked. "What?"

"Mmm-hmm," Hank said, rubbing his chest. "She said that she'd been thinking about him over the past few years, that *we* made her think about him. Turns out he and his friend went on trips together, and often, that they were both especially into learning. Real academics, those two, always off learning things in private where they wouldn't be disturbed."

"I bet," Renaldo snorted.

Hank's gaze softened, however, when he added, "And she put her hand on my face, that way she does with you? And she told me that she'd never seen her brother happier than when he was headed off to rendezvous with his friend. And because *he* was happy, so was she."

"I..." Renaldo sank onto the edge of the bed. "What did you say?"

"What *could* I say? I mumbled something about how nice for him, and she said, yes, it was, and then said how lovely it was to see *you* so happy. And, well." Hank ran his hand over his mouth, and Renaldo could see that it was shaking. "She said it was lovely to see me so happy, too."

"*Cariño*," Renaldo sighed, his heart aching with happiness. No one knew better than he just how desperately Hank wanted a mother, how he followed after Juana Maria and did anything she asked, smiling for hours after she bestowed praise or a touch upon him, something she did often.

"Didn't I tell you that they would eventually understand what it is between us?" Renaldo said.

"And didn't *I* tell you that your mama always knew?"

Renaldo laughed. "True, you did."

"You fellas never figured out how smart she is. Where do you think Calandaría gets it? That woman works you all like puppets on a string," Hank said, admiration clear in his voice.

"Says the man who most likely handed her pots she didn't need, only to put them back."

Hank laughed softly, shaking his head. "Well, she hadn't quite made up her mind what she wanted to make for dinner tomorrow."

"Mmm-hmm," Renaldo replied, pulling his shirt over his head. Hank was definitely not asleep now. One arm was bent behind his head as he watched Renaldo undress completely. It was a warm September evening, when they could leave the doors and windows open to catch a night breeze, when they wouldn't have to wear anything at all.

Renaldo grabbed the end of the quilt and slowly pulled it off Hank, revealing his body inch by lovely inch.

Definitely not sleeping, Renaldo thought to himself when he could see how interested Hank was becoming.

"You gonna tease me all night, or come put yourself to use?" Hank said, cupping himself between his legs.

"To use?" Renaldo asked. "Is that what this is?"

Hank nodded, looking up at Renaldo from under his thickly-fringed lashes. "Say, I'm awful tired tonight."

"You don't look tired," Renaldo said, drawing his fingertips up Hank's thigh in little whorls and zigzags.

"Yep, so very tired, *cariño.*" Hank turned over to his stomach, his arms folded under his head. "In fact, I sort of feel like I need you to... take care of things."

Renaldo looked down at his lover's body, the old, faded scars of his past striped across his back. There was a twisted, raw-looking scar on Hank's right hip, too, stark against the deep

275

brown of his skin, obtained after grabbing little Pedro away from angry ram in rut. Its horn had ripped through Hank's shirt, piercing him, but not causing any permanent damage. From that moment on, all of the negative looks from Eduardo ceased. In Eduardo's eyes, Hank should have been elevated to sainthood.

Renaldo kissed the scar, rubbing at the thick muscles of Hank's backside. They didn't do this often, not this way. Hank was occasionally self-conscious about his scars, usually after waking up in the night from dreaming about how he'd gotten them in the first place. But Renaldo had learned over the years just how to prove to Hank that he found him to be undeniably attractive, that there wasn't a single part of Hank's body that he wasn't in love with, didn't admire.

He kissed his way up Hank's spine until he was blanketing Hank's back. He drew the edge of his nose along Hank's nape, along the side of his neck, grinning at the pleased noise Hank couldn't help but make.

"Do you need me to help you sleep, *querido?* Or do you need something more… stimulating?"

Hank arched his back, connecting their bodies in a slow roll. When Renaldo could feel how slick he already was, the image of Hank lying in their bed, preparing himself for Renaldo's return, sent a hot spark through his body where it settled low, pulsing heavy between his legs in time with his heartbeat.

"*Quiero hacerte el amor,*" Renaldo sighed.

"That's… *ah!*" Hank rolled his hips back until Renaldo was lined up perfectly. "That's the plan, *amante.*"

A low growl rumbled from Renaldo's chest. He loved it whenever Hank called him pet names in Spanish, loved the feeling of his strong body pliant underneath, the hot clench of Hank's body, so willing and open to him in every way.

He pinned Hank down at the hips, slowly driving in, both of them moaning and gasping as he did, whispering words of love and encouragement as they built up a rhythm, one fine-tuned over the years yet still surprising. How good, how *wonderful* it felt to be alone together, to be so intimate in their own home each and every night.

It wasn't official, not the way the other members of their family were, but as they rocked and moved together, trading kisses and gasps, Renaldo knew that what they shared was every bit as true, every bit as real and good and *right* as any commitment blessed by God.

His hips began to work up to an ever-faster rhythm, twisting and moving in a way he knew would have Hank reaching his own climax soon, kissing tender name after name into Hank's skin as if he wanted Hank filled in every way with his love, their hands entwined under Hank's body as they rushed inexorably to their climax, crying out each other's names, *que rico, te quiero, te amo.*

They held each other, their breathing labored as they came back to themselves. Hank kept hold of Renaldo's hands trapped under his chest, not letting him up.

Renaldo laughed. "Let me get something to clean up, *querido.*"

Hank groaned happily into his pillow, holding tighter for a moment before letting him go. As Renaldo wet a cloth at the bedside washstand, Hank rolled to his back, stretching and arching like a cat. Renaldo cleaned them both up, murmuring, "Go on to sleep."

Hank sighed. "You're spoiling me. A fella could get used to this..."

"You're not already? Besides, it's good to spoil those whom you love," Renaldo said, rinsing out the cloth and climbing into bed.

Dragging his fingers through Renaldo's hair, Hank said quietly, "*Te amaré para siempre.*"

Their love was forever. Here, close to family who cared for them and where they were building their own lives, in the privacy of their home, in their bed, the scent of their lovemaking wrapped around them, Renaldo could easily believe that was true.

"*Y yo, mi amor,*" Renaldo replied.

THE END

ACKNOWLEDGMENTS

I OWE A HUGE DEBT of gratitude to my best friend for more than twenty years for explaining what I'd gotten wrong about a spade bit and for correcting my Spanish when I wandered off into *usted*. Chrissy taught me how to truly love the desert Southwest. Even better, she let me explore all those great places on Doc's back, the best damn horse who ever lived. I bet there's not an inch of ground we haven't trod from Nevada to Texas, the Grand Canyon to Yellowstone, and one day we'll get back to Zion and hike the way we did every weekend when we were college kids.

DD has been a tremendous voice of encouragement and positivity when I needed it most. Thanks for not only talking horses with me, but also about writing, food, furry bellies, hot men (one in particular) and everything else that gave me a much-needed grin.

Thanks to my girls for putting up with me tearing out my hair while racing towards a deadline while it seemed the world was falling apart around us. Mom loves you, and I'm really glad you know how to drive and make your own dinner. Now stand up straight or you'll get stuck like that.

To Fran, my Titian Goddess and dear friend, you continue to make me feel like I can keep going. When I grow up I want to be just like you.

To Choi, Colleen and Becky, I won the freaking lottery with you guys, and don't I know it. It's been an absolute gift to work with you. And it goes without saying (but I'll say it anyway) that without my wonderful team at IP—Annie, Lex, Candy, Linda and Nicki—this wouldn't exist. Thanks for being patient while is seemed the world was falling apart around me.

And last, even though I don't know if they'll ever see this, a huge thanks to my Uncle Mark and Aunt Gay for sticking me on top of a quarter horse bareback when I was seven years old and only laughing at me a little bit when I wobbled off. Those summers in the mountains were some of the best memories of my childhood, hands down.

ABOUT THE AUTHOR

LAURA STONE IS A BORN and bred Texan, but don't hold that against her. She's a former comedian, actress and Master Gardener, and currently keeps busy as a media blogger, ghostwriter and novelist when not busy raising her three children. They're not fully raised, but then, neither is she.

She lives in Texas as proof that it's not completely populated by hard-line right wingers. And because that's where the good tamales are.

Her first novel, *The Bones of You,* was published by Interlude Press in 2014 and was named a finalist for a *Foreword Reviews* IndieFab Book of the Year Award.

QUESTIONS FOR DISCUSSION

1. Society placed great emphasis on propriety at this time in history. Women's roles were very much defined for them. What made Calandaría bristle so much?

2. Compare what Calandaría wanted for her future to what was expected of her. Was she right to pretend to obey her parents or should she have stood up for her own dreams outright? How would her story have been different if she had?

3. "I have failed you if this is who you have grown to become." Renaldo did not agree with his papa when he said this to Sylvestre. Instead, he says Sylvestre is just a bad apple. Who is correct? What is the reasoning for your answer?

4. "You will learn how to be better stewards of God's creatures" was the way Estebán chose to run his business. How did that differ from other men of the era? How does that differ from businesses today? How would the world be different if more people chose to live their lives in such a manner?

5. Why was Calandaría so certain of Renaldo's sexuality when he wasn't?

6. Seeing Tsá-cho and Hank together solidified for Renaldo that he was attracted to men, specifically to Hank. Would Hank and Renaldo have gotten together without Tsá-cho's presence? Why or why not?

7. How do Renaldo and Tsá-cho differ in their approach to horses? To life?

8. Sylvestre's story sets up a family dynamic that makes Renaldo nervous to share his intimate relationship with Hank. How are the two situations similar? How are they different?

9. Eduardo and Francisco had disparate reactions to Renaldo and Hank's coming out. Whose would you be more like? What did their individual histories have to do with their responses?

10. Each couple in the story got their "happily ever after" in a different way, even Sylvestre and Patricia. Discuss each, and your opinion of the life each couple has chosen for themselves. Which couple does your life most resemble?

11. According to the author's note, Laura Stone did painstaking research to make this book historically accurate. How does it compare with your previous ideas of cowboy culture?

—*AC Holloway*

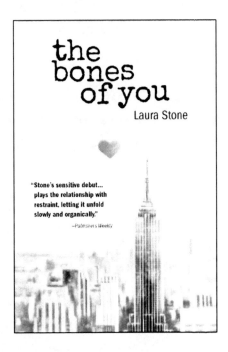

interlude press

One Story Can Change Everything.

interludepress.com

Twitter: @interludepress *** Facebook: Interlude Press
Google+: interludepress *** Pinterest: interludepress
Instagram: InterludePress

CPSIA information can be obtained at www.ICGtesting.com
Printed in the USA
LVOW12s2048200116

471540LV00009B/1171/P